Books by Hortense Calisher

Extreme Magic

HORTENSE CALISHER

Extreme Magic
A Novella and Other Stories

Little, Brown and Company · Boston · Toronto

COPYRIGHT 1953, 1954, © 1956, 1957, 1959, 1964
BY HORTENSE CALISHER; COPYRIGHT © 1963
BY THE CURTIS PUBLISHING COMPANY.

LIBRARY OF CONGRESS CATALOG CARD NO. 64-15045

FIRST EDITION

ACKNOWLEDGMENTS

Some of the stories in this collection have appeared previously
in the following magazines and acknowledgment is gratefully
made for permission to use them here:

"Il Plœ:r Dã Mõ Kœ:r" originally appeared in *The New Yorker*,
1956.

"Two Colonials" originally appeared in *Harper's Bazaar*, 1957.

"A Christmas Carillon" originally appeared in *Harper's Magazine*, 1953.

"The Rabbi's Daughter" is reprinted from *Charm*, 1953.

"Little Did I Know" originally appeared in *The Saturday Evening Post*, 1963.

"Songs My Mother Taught Me" originally appeared in *Harper's
Bazaar*, 1959.

"If You Don't Want To Live I Can't Help You" is reprinted by
permission of *Mademoiselle*, 1954.

"The Gulf Between" originally appeared in *Gentlemen's Quar-
terly*, 1964.

*Published simultaneously in Canada
by Little, Brown & Company (Canada) Limited*

PRINTED IN THE UNITED STATES OF AMERICA

For

Julian Muller

Contents

Contents

Il Plœ:r Dã Mõ Kœ:r

I WAS taught to speak French *with* tears. It was not I who wept, or the other girls in my high-school class, but the poet Verlaine — the one who wrote "Il plœ:r dã mõ kœ:r." Inside forty slack American mouths, he wept phonetically for almost a semester. During this time, we were not taught a word of French grammar or meaning — only the International Phonetic Alphabet, the sounds the symbols stood for, and Verlaine translated into them. We could not even pick up the celebrated pen of our aunt. But by the time Verlaine and our teacher Mlle. Girard had finished with us, we were indeed ready to pick it up, and in the most classically passionate accents this side of the Comédie Française.

Mlle. Girard achieved her feat in this way. On the very first morning, she explained to us that French could never be spoken properly by us Anglo-Saxons unless we learned to reanimate those muscles of the face, throat, *poitrine* that we possessed — even as the French — but did not use. Ours, she said, was a speech almost without lilt, spoken on a dead level of intonation, "like a sobway train."

"Like this," she said, letting her jaw loll idiotically and choosing the most American subject she could find: "Ay wahnt sahm ay-iss cream." French, on the other hand, was a language *passionné* and *spirituel,* of vowels struck without pedal, of "l"s made with a sprightly tongue tip — a sound altogether unlike our "l," which we made with our tongues plopping in our mouths. By her manner, she implied that all sorts of national differences might be assumed from this, although she could not take the time to pursue them.

She placed a wiry thumb and forefinger, gray with chalk dust, on either side of her mouth. "It is these muscles 'ere I shall teach you to use," she said. (If that early we had been trained to think in phonetic symbols, we would have known that what she had actually said was "mœslz.") When she removed her hand, we saw that she had two little, active, wrinkling pouches, one on either side of her mouth. In the ensuing weeks I often wondered whether all French people had them, and we would get them, too. Perhaps only youthful body tone saved us, as, morning after morning, she went among us pinching and poking our lips into grimaces and compelling sudden ventriloquisms from our astonished sinuses.

As a final coup, she taught us the classic "r." "Demoiselles," she said, "this is an *élégance* almost impossible for Americans, but you are a special class — I think you may do it." By this time, I think she had almost convinced herself that she had effected somatic changes in our Anglo-Saxonism. "*C'est produit,*" she said, imparting the knowledge to us in a whisper, "by vibr-rating the uvula!"

During the next week, we sat there, like forty purring Renaults, vibrating our uvulas.

Enfin came Verlaine, with his tears. As a supreme exercise, we were to learn to declaim a poem by one of the famous harmonists of France, and we were to do it entirely by ear. (At this time, we knew the meaning of not one word except *"ici!"* with which, carefully admonished to chirp "œp, not down!" we had been taught to answer the roll.) Years later, when I could *read* French, I came upon the poem in its natural state. To my surprise, it looked like this:

> *Il pleure dans mon coeur*
> *Comme il pleut sur la ville.*
> *Quelle est cette langueur*
> *Qui pénètre mon coeur?*
>
> *O bruit doux de la pluie*
> *Par terre . . .*

And so on. But the way it is engraved on my heart, my ear, and my uvula is something else again. As hour after hour, palm to breast, wrist to brow, we moaned like a bevy of Ulalumes, making the exquisite distinction between *"pleure"* and *"pleut,"* sounding our "r" like cat women, and dropping "l"s liquid as bulbuls, what we saw in our mind's eye was this:

> il plœ:rə dã mõ kœ:r
> kɔm il plø syr la vil
> kɛl ɛ sɛtə lãgœ:r
> ki penɛtrə mõ kœ:r
>
> o bryi du də la plyi
> pɑr te:r . . .

And *so* on.

Late in the term, Mme. Cécile Sorel paid New York a

visit, and Mlle. Girard took us to see her in *La Dame aux Camélias*. Sorel's tea gowns and our own romantic sensibilities helped us to get some of her phthisic story. But what we marvelled at most was that she sounded exactly like us.

L'envoi comes somewhat late — twenty years later — but, like the tragic flaw of the Greeks, what Mlle. G. had planted so irrevocably was bound to show up in a last act somewhere. I went to France.

During the interim, I had resigned myself to the fact that although I had "had" French so intensively — for Mlle. G. had continued to be just as exacting all the way through grammar, *dictée*, and the rest of it — I still did not seem to "have" it. In college, my accent had earned me a brief eminence, but, of course, we did not spend much time *speaking* French, this being regarded as a frivolous addiction, the pursuit of which had best be left to the Berlitz people, or to tacky parlor groups presided over by stranded foreign widows in need of funds. As for vocabulary or idiom, I stood with Racine on my right hand and Rimbaud on my left — a *cordon-bleu* cook who had never been taught how to boil an egg. Across the water, there was presumably a nation, *obscurcie de miasmes humains*, that used its own speech for purposes of asking the way to the bathroom, paying off porters, and going shopping, but for me the language remained the vehicle of de Vigny, Lamartine, and Hugo, and France a murmurous orchestral country where the *cieux* were full of *clarté*, the oceans sunk in *ombres profondes*, and where the most useful verbs were *souffler* and *gémir*.

On my occasional encounters with French visitors, I would apologize, in a few choicely carved phrases that always brought compliments, for being out of practice, after which I retired — into English if *they* had *it*, into the next room if they hadn't. Still, when I sailed, it was with hope — based on the famous accent — that in France I would somehow speak French. If I had only known, it would have been far better to go, as an underprivileged friend of mine did, armed with the one phrase her husband had taught her — "*Au secours!*"

Arriving at my small hotel in Paris, I was met by the owner, M. Lampacher, who addressed me in arrogantly correct English. When we had finished our arrangements in that language, I took the plunge. "*Merci!*" I said. It came out just lovely, the "r" like treacle, the "ci" not down but œp.

"Ah, Madame!" he said. "You speak French."

I gave him the visitors' routine.

"You mock, Madame. You have the accent *absolument pur.*"

The next morning, I left the hotel early for a walk around Paris. I had not been able to understand the boy who brought me breakfast, but no doubt he was from the provinces. Hoping that I would not encounter too many people from the provinces, I set out. I tramped for miles, afloat upon the first beatific daze of tourism. One by one, to sounds as of northern lights popping and sunken cathedrals emerging, all the postcards were coming true, and it was not until I was returning on the bus from Chaillot that, blinking, I listened for the first time that day.

Two women opposite me were talking; from their glances, directed at my plastic rain boots, they were talking about me. I was piqued at their apparent assumption that I would not understand them. A moment later, listening with closed eyes, I was glad that they could not be aware of the very odd way in which I was not understanding them. For what I was hearing went something like this:

"rəgard lamerikɛn se kautʃu sɛkõvnabl sa nɛspa purlɑ̃sɑ̃bl õ pøvwarlesulje"

"a ɛl nəsõpavremɑ̃ ʃik lezamerikɛn ʃakynrəsɑ̃blalotr"

"a wi [Pause] tykonɛ mari la fijœl də mõ dəmi frɛr ɑ̃dre səlwi [or sɛl] avɛk ləbuk tylarɑ̃kõtre ʃemwa alo:r lœdi swa:r ɛl [or il] a fɛt yn foskuʃ"

Hours later, in my room, with the help of the dictionary and Mlle. G.'s training in *dictée*, I pieced together what they had said. It seemed to have been roughly this: "*Regarde, l'Américaine, ses caoutchoucs. C'est convenable, ça, n'est-ce-pas, pour l'ensemble. On peut voir les souliers.*"

"*Ah, elles ne sont pas vraiment chics, les Américaines. Chacune ressemble à l'autre.*"

"*Ah, oui. [Pause] Tu connais Marie, la filleule de mon demi-frère André — celui [or celle] avec le bouc. Tu l'as rencontré chez moi. Alors, lundi soir, elle [or il] a fait une fausse couche!*"

One of them, then, had thought my boots convenient for the ensemble, since one could see the shoes; the other had commented on the lack of real chic among American women, who all resembled one another. Digressing, they had gone on to speak of Marie, the goddaughter of a step-brother, "the one with the *bouc*. You have met him [or her, since one could not tell from the construction] at my house." Either he or Marie had made a false couch, whatever that was.

The latter I could not find in the dictionary at all. *"Bouc"* I at first recalled as *"banc"* — either André or Marie had some kind of bench, then, or pew. I had just about decided that André had a seat in the Chamber of Deputies and had made some kind of political mistake, when it occurred to me that the word had been *"bouc"* — goatee — which almost certainly meant André. What had he done? Or Marie? What the hell did it mean "to make a false couch"?

I sat for the good part of an hour, freely associating — really, now, the goddaughter of a stepbrother! When I could bear it no longer, I rang up an American friend who had lived in Paris for some years, with whom I was to lunch the next day.

"Oh, yes, how are you?" said Ann.

"Dead tired, actually," I said, "and I've had a slight shock. Listen, it seems I can't speak French after all. Will you translate something?"

"Sure."

"What does to *'faire une fausse couche'* mean?"

"Honey!" said Ann.

"What?"

"Where are you, dear?" she said, in a low voice. "At a doctor's?"

"No, for God's sake, I'm at the hotel. What's the matter with you? You're as bad as the dictionary."

"Nothing's the matter with *me*," said Ann. "The phrase just means 'to have a miscarriage,' that's all."

"Ohhh," I said. "Then it was Marie after all. Poor Marie."

"*Are* you all right?"

"Oh, I'm fine," I said. "Just fine. And thanks. I'll see you tomorrow."

I went to bed early, assuring myself that what I had was merely disembarkation jitters (what would the psychologists call it — transliteration syndrome?), which would disappear overnight. Otherwise it was going to be very troublesome having to retire from every conversation to work it out in symbols.

A month went by, and the syndrome had not disappeared. Now and then, it was true, the more familiar nouns and verbs did make their way straight to my brain, bypassing the tangled intermediaries of my ear and the International Phonetic Alphabet. Occasionally, I was able to pick up an unpoetically useful phrase: to buy a brassière you asked for "something to hold up the gorge with"; the French said "Couci-couça" (never *"Comme ci, comme ça"*) and, when they wanted to say "I don't know," turned up their palms and said "Schpuh." But meanwhile, my accent, fed by the lilt of true French, altogether outsoared the shadow of my night. When I did dare the phrases prepared carefully in my room for the eventualities of the day, they fell so superbly that any French vis-à-vis immediately dropped all thought of giving me a handicap and addressed me in the native argot, at the native rate — leaving me struck dumb.

New Year's Eve was my last night in Paris. I had planned to fly to London to start the new year with telephones, parties, the wireless, conversation, in a wild blaze of unrestricted communication. But the airport had informed me that no planes were flying the Channel, or per-

haps anywhere, for the next twenty-four hours, New Year's
Eve being the one night on which the pilots were tradi-
tionally "allowed" to get drunk. At least, it *seemed* to me
that I had been so informed, but perhaps I libel, for by now
my passion for accurately understanding what was said to
me was dead. All my pockets and purses were full of paper
scraps of decoding, set down in vowel-hallucinated corners
while my lips moved grotesquely, and it seemed to me that,
if left alone here any longer, I would end by having composed at random a phonetic variorum for France.

In a small, family-run café around the corner from my
hotel, where I had often eaten alone, I ordered dinner, successive *cafés filtres,* and repeated doses of marc. Tonight,
at the elegiac opening of the new year, it was "allowed" —
for pilots and the warped failures of educational snobbism
— to get drunk. Outside, it was raining, or weeping; in my
heart, it was doing both.

Presently, I was the only customer at any of the zinc
tables. Opposite, in a corner, the *grand-père* of the family
of owners lit a Gauloise and regarded me with the privi-
leged stare of the elderly. He was the only one there who
seemed aware that I existed; for the others I had the invisi-
bility of the foreigner who cannot "speak" — next door to
that of a child, I mused, except for the adult password of
money in the pocket. The old man's daughter, or daughter-
in-law, a dark woman with a gall-bladder complexion and
temperament, had served me obliquely and retired to the
kitchen, from which she emerged now and then to speak
sourly to her husband, a capped man, better-looking than
she, who ignored her, lounging at the bar like a customer. I
should have liked to know whether her sourness was in her

words as well as her manner, and whether his lordliness was something personal between them or only the authority of the French male, but their harsh gutturals, so far from the sugarplum sounds I had been trained to that they did not even dissolve into phonetics, went by me like the crude blue smoke of the Gauloise. A girl of about fourteen — their daughter, I thought — was tending bar and deflecting the remarks of the customers with a petted, precocious insouciance. Now and then, her parents addressed remarks, either to her or to the men at the bar, that seemed to have the sharpness of reprimand, but I could not be sure; to my eye the gaiety of the men toward the young girl had a certain avuncular decorum that made the scene pleasant and tender to watch. In my own country, I loved to listen at bars, where the human scene was often arrested as it is in those genre paintings whose deceptively simple contours must be approached with all one's knowledge of the period, and it saddened me not to be able to savor those nuances here.

I lit a Gauloise, too, with a flourish that the old man, who nodded stiffly, must have taken for a salute. And why not? Pantomime was all that was left to me. Or money. To hell with my perfectionist urge to understand; I must resign myself to being no different from those summer thousands who jammed the ocean every June, to whom Europe was merely a montage of their own sensations, a glamorous old phoenix that rose seasonally, just for them. On impulse, I mimed an invitation to the old man to join me in a marc. On second thought, I signaled for marc for everybody in the house.

"To the new year!" I said, in French, waving my glass at

the old man. Inside my brain, my monitor tapped his worried finger — did *"nouvelle"* come before or after *"année"*
in such cases, and wasn't the accent a little "ice cream"? I
drowned him, in another marc.

Across the room from me, the old man's smile faded in
and out like the Cheshire cat's; I was not at all surprised
when it spoke, in words I seemed to understand, inquiring
politely as to my purpose in Paris. I was here on a scholarship, I replied. I was a writer. (*"Ecrivain? Romancier?"*
asked my monitor faintly.)

"Ah," said the old man. "I am familiar with one of your
writers. Père Le Buc."

"Père Le Buc?" I shook my head sadly. "I regret, but it is
not known to me, the work of the Father Le Buc."

"Pas un homme!" he said. *"Une femme! Une femme
qui s'appelle Père Le Buc!"*

My monitor raised his head for one last time. "Pɛrləbyk!"
he chirped desperately. "Pɛrləbyk!"

I listened. "Oh, my God," I said then. "Of course. That is
how it would be. Pearl Buck!"

"Mais oui," said the old man, beaming and raising his
glass. "Pɛrləbyk!"

At the bar, the loungers, thinking we were exchanging
some toast, raised their own glasses in courteous imitation. "Pɛrləbyk!" they said, politely. "Pɛrləbyk!"

I raised mine. *"Il pleure,"* I began, *"il pleure dans mon
coeur comme il pleut . . ."*

Before the evening was over, I had given them quite a
selection: from Verlaine, from Heredia's "Les Trophées,"
from Baudelaire's poem on a painting by Delacroix, from
de Musset's "R-r-ra-ppelle-toi!" As a final tribute, I gave

them certain stanzas from Hugo's "L'Expiation" — the ones that begin *"Waterloo! Waterloo! Waterloo! Morne plaine!"* And in between, raised or lowered by a new faith that was not all brandy, into an air freed of cuneiform at last — I spoke French.

Making my way home afterward, along the dark stretches of the Rue du Bac, I reflected that to learn a language outside its native habitat you must really believe that the other country exists — in its humdrum, its winter self. Could I remember to stay there now — down in that lower-case world in which stairs creaked, cops yelled, in which women bought brassières and sometimes made the false couch?

The door of my hotel was locked. I rang, and M. Lampacher admitted me. He snapped on the stair light, economically timed to go out again in a matter of seconds, and watched me as I mounted the stairs with the aid of the banister.

"Off bright and early, hmm?" he said sleepily, in French. "Well, good night, Madame. Hope you had a good time here."

I turned, wanting to answer him properly, to answer them all. At that moment, the light went off, perhaps to reinforce forever my faith in the mundanity of France.

"Ah, *ça va, ça va!*" I said strongly, into the dark. "Couci-couça. Schpuh."

Two Colonials

W HEN young Alastair Pines came out from Leeds, England, to teach on an exchange fellowship at Pitt, a small college about a hundred miles from Detroit, Michigan, he was the second foreign teacher ever to be in residence there. Pitt, founded in the Eighteen-sixties by a Presbyterian divine, and still under a synod of that church, had kept its missionary flavor well up to the Second World War. Set in Pittston — a bland village of white and cream-colored houses whose green roofs matched, even in summer, dark lawns compelled by lamasery effort (and perhaps a cautious hint of divine favor) from the dry Michigan plain — the school had kept a surface calm even during the war. It was the centripetal calm of those who, living in the sacred framework of morning, noon and evening service and a perfect round of dedicatory suppers, could not help feeling ever so slightly chosen — of people whose plain living and high thinking was not that of poverty, but of ample funds conserved. Some of the college halls had been built as recently as the Thirties (when labor was so cheap) and the organ (though not baroque to the point of Episcopalianism) was first-rate. Salaries had lagged well behind. Since, however, the non-smoking rule was still in effect on campus, and no teacher was supposed to have wine or spirits in his larder, he was officially helped to escape the extravagances of the age, as well as some of its anxieties. True, the table set by most of the younger faculty was somewhat farinaceous, but this might be less Franciscan than Middle Western, since most of the teachers and students came from that region. A glance at the roster showed a global scattering of names which were American, not international; the Kowalskis and Swobodas were Poles and Czechs from Hamtramck in Detroit, the Ragnhilds and Solveigs from Minnesota, and so on. Alone in the catalogue until the advent of Mr. Pines, the name of Hans Weil — philologist and onetime professor of *Linguistik* at Bonn — represented a Europe not once, twice, or further removed.

With Hans Weil's arrival in 1945, there had also come to Pittston the first of certain changes brought by the war. Like so many other scholars in the days of Hitler, Weil had been passed from hand to libertarian hand like a florin stamped "Freedom" — whisked, in his case, to London, via Holland, in 1939, and from London to Rochester, New York, in 1942, after which he was presumed to be on his own. In 1945, at his own behest, or rather at that of his wife, whose sister and brother-in-law, helped by the Weils to America, now had a flourishing but immovable dry-goods shop in Lansing, he had come to nearby Pitt as provisional candidate for a newly established chair in the humanities, and had remained there ever since. There was small need for philology at Pitt, most of whose students were on their way to being music teachers, social workers or ministers, and Weil, lacking new-world versatility, did not find it easy to "double" in related courses. Nevertheless, he had no fears for his job.

On this fine fall morning of the new term, as Weil walked

across campus at his short, duck-footed pace, the beret that he wore for his baldness emphasizing Raphael curves of cheek which softened the fact that he was almost as old as the century, and — as he would blithely have admitted — as profane, he well knew that his value to Pitt went subtly beyond its being able to mutter behind him that he had recently refused an offer from Yale. Thirty years ago, he was thinking, if by some unlikely chance he had landed at Pittston, he might at least have had to grow a beard, and, under the old tradition that all German professors were a kind of nursery-uncle emissary from the land of sugared postcards and cuckoo clocks, might also have had to submit to being called "Dr. Hans," or "Papa Weil." But as things were, he was not even under any particular necessity of writing those little monographs that sometimes brought him an Eastern offer. For, since the war, the GI Bill, and an engineering endowment from one of the big labor unions in Detroit, although Pitt's lawns were still clear of cigarette butts and its brains still Protestantly clear of fumes, a complexity had entered its air. Through the windows of the music department's practice rooms, once so liturgically pure with Bach and Buxtehude, he could now hear Bartók, Khatchaturian and even Sauter-Finnegan squawking under official sanction. Opposite, in Knox Hall, although there were still two strong classes in scriptural exegesis and one on missions, called "The Protestant Evangel," a visiting divine from Union Theological was treating of Kierkegaard, Niebuhr and Buber in a course called "Quest" — and all four of these classes were embarrassingly near a group of acolytes studying guided missiles, on the grant from the C.I.O.

For "comparative" thinking — the modern disease, the modern burden — had come to Pittston. And as Hans Weil walked down the main street, on his way for a word with Mrs. Mabie, the wife of the art historian in whose house Mr. Pines, the exchange fellow, was to be quartered, he knew that he owed his tenure to it. He had begun by being Pitt's "refugee professor," and, with certain accretions of prestige and affection, he would end that way. He had merely to wear his beret, pay attention in his own classes in Anglo-Saxon, stubbornly drink his forbidden wines at dinner in full sight of whatever of the faculty, and on their insufflated bosoms abide. He was their prideful little exercise in comparative humanity — he had merely to *be*.

A passing car slowed, and the driver, unknown to him, called out, "Lift?"

"Walking, thanks," said Weil, thinking of how often he would have to say this until the new students got used to his intransigence, born of a youth spent with alpenstocks. For here, this near the automotive Rome, driving a car on the shortest haul had nothing to do with economy or abstinence. Even the poorest student might have his second-hand leviathan; Weil himself had his Pontiac at home.

Passing under McFarland's open windows, he waved up at the president's housekeeper, who was airing the living room against a background of teal-dark wall. A good many of the Pittston parlors had taken on this color in the three years since the president's mother had chosen it for hers. And at the curb, McFarland's new two-tone Buick shone in silver-blu beauty, Rhadamanthine sign that by next year or so, other two-tone jobs, less violent in color of course than some that were floating the highways like zooming banana splits, would be chosen by those of the faculty who were "turning theirs in." He would keep his old one as long as he could. Whether from age, or from that creeping anti-Americanism which so often flawed the recipients of American bounty, he had begun to have a horror of turning things in.

And now, just ahead of him, was Mrs. Mabie's. As Mr. Pines, presently riding undreaming through Pennsylvania or Ohio, might well say, once he got to know her — now he was for it. Professor Weil's affectionate remembrance of London and the English went deep, deeper than the language lilt and the old gray streets, down to that sudden rest of the heart when he had stepped off the Dutch plane into a ring of their steady, un-Wagnerian faces. Its compound would already have been working in him, at the good thought of young Pines, had he not been all too sure of what was already working in Mrs. Mabie.

Portia-Lou Mabie, a quondam painter known at her own insistence by her maiden-professional name of Potter (and therefore a constant twinge of explanation in the salons of Pittston and in poor old Mabie-Potter), was an unsuccessful faculty wife who was the more annoying because she gave no sign of knowing it. She was not, however, of that familiar sort, objects of pity, who were always twenty-three sour diapers too late for the Inter-Faith Tea. Dr. Mabie had met and been married by her while he was on a field trip to Mexico City, where — in common with others from St. Louis, Stroudsburg, Orlando — she had been leading the stridulant life of Greenwich Village when it hits the *corrida*. A bony *princesse lointaine* of about thirty-five, who wore her hair in a weak-lemonade waterfall down the small of her back, she was to Weil a confirmation of his private opinion that art historians ought never to come that close to art. She had a talent for endorsing the worthiest convictions in a way that made their very holders wish immediately to disavow them. Openly lamenting that she had been born too late to join the Left Bank expatriates of the Twenties, her shrill disparagements of the crass standardization of life in the United States brought a sudden flush of *amor patriae* to the most disaffected cheek. And ever since the Mabies' recent Fulbright year at Oxford, her conversation, fresh with Anglophiliac sighs and knowing locutions, was likely to become especially matey in the presence of Hans Weil — climaxing on the occasion of the Weils' yearly dinner for the McFarlands, when he had had to explain to the elderly wife of a Kansas divine what Mrs. Mabie had meant when she had left the table with a bright look at Weil, and the remark that she had to go and spend a penny.

Now, on her doorstep, he deplored, for Mr. Pines's sake, the enthusiasm of her offer to house him, but the childless Mabies had two spare bedrooms, and there were not many such in Pittston.

Mrs. Mabie opened the door, chin forward, hair brimming over. "Oh Hans, did you try to ring me? I was out getting in some coal."

"Coal?" He knew the Mabies heated with oil.

"Yes, you know how *they* like a morning fire. And Pattini wouldn't deliver less than half a ton, so I brought some home in the car. Come on in."

"No, no," he said. "I came only to say I cannot go with you to meet him tomorrow; I must go earlier for the language convention in Chicago. So I have here a little note — " He heard his own words, the German juxtaposition, with outrage. He almost never did that any more; the woman acted on him like a solvent, fuddling all his backgrounds together.

She made him come in, and, although he kept out of her sooty clutch the coat his wife, Hertha, had just cleaned for him, he had to follow her up the stairs to see the bedroom.

"Hope he'll like his digs." She flung the door back smartly. "Just finished distempering the walls."

Looking, Weil hoped that Mr. Pines would see nothing more unusual than kindness in the hot-water bottle prominently posed on the turned-down bed, near the radiator, or in the huge, brass scuttle of coal in a steam-heated American room. "Distemper?" he said. He sniffed an odor. "Oh, yes, rubber paint."

"Worst thing about American progress," she said. "Always sure to bring something bloody nasty along with it."

He bent to examine the coal scuttle, thinking that he was not quite enough of an American, although naturalized, to be able to agree with her in comfort. "Didn't know you used this fireplace. Don't you burn wood in the one downstairs?"

Ignoring him, she fingered the hot-water bottle. "Such a naked red, these things look; that's because we only use them for illness. But of course there wouldn't be a cover for it in all of Michigan. I tried the tea cozy on it, but it was no go."

Weil straightened, and took out the note to the expected guest, placing it on the night table, where, next to the neat pile of towels and soap, he saw a worn packet of Players. "Portia-Lou. They are crazy for our cigarettes, you know. And after all, isn't he here to see us as we are?"

She flung out a hand in an impatience that included Pittston, Michigan, the hemisphere. "Don't worry. He will. He will."

"Well —" he said. "'*Wiedersehen,*" and ground his teeth. He no longer said that, except to Hertha.

On his way downstairs, she called after him. "You and Hertha wouldn't have brought over one of those big sponge-things, would you? Isn't that what they use?"

He turned his head. "You mean possibly a loofah?"

"Oh, is *that* what they call them?"

"I wouldn't know. I never saw one in London. But if my reading is correct he would carry his own with him. In something called a sponge-bag." He clapped his beret firmly on his head. "'Bye now."

"Cheerio," said Mrs. Mabie.

Later that night, at about one-thirty, when Weil could not stay asleep, as often happened, he got up noiselessly and went downstairs to forage in the bookshelves and the icebox until Hertha should miss him and come after him. This, the constant nervous rounding-up of what family was left to her — by telephone, by visit, from room to room — was almost all that remained, after all these years, of the effects of the concentration camp. It was why, as long as her sister Elsa and Sigmund had the store in Lansing, as long as she could talk with Elsa every morning, drive over for the biweekly *Kaffeeklatsch,* and exchange Sunday dinners, he would never take up the offers from Princeton or Yale. It was no use telling himself that they might none of them be here now had he not gone ahead to England; he could not forget where she had been while he had been safe from all but the bombs in London, nor would he forget her eyes, so blue under the grizzled hair, when she had said to him, on the morning the letter came from Pittston, "Only that we should be together, Hans! Only that we should all of us be together."

He was reading when she came to the top of the stairs in her nightgown. "Hans! You will catch cold. *Soll ich* cocoa *machen?*"

"*Nein, nein. Ich hab' ein bischen Wein. Und Schmier-käse. Wilst du?*"

She wrinkled her nose, but came and sat at the table, looking over his shoulder. "You are working?"

"No, I just wanted to look something up, and I found it." He chuckled, thinking that he might tell her of his encounter with Mrs. Mabie, but she had little ear or eye for the nuances of their life here, content to display her cuisine at intervals to these supermarket savages, to wonder whether she could get the fruiterer to stock fennel, and to lament with Elsa that there was no little *Conditorei* in East Lansing.

"Here. Let me read you something." He got up and put an afghan around her shoulders. "What they call a stole, *ja? Sehr schön*, matches the eyes."

"*Schmeichelkatz'*. You just want me to let you stay up." But she liked him to read to her.

"Listen." He read out bits of the passage he had hunted up, smiling to himself, in Max Müller. " 'We do not want to know languages; we want to know what language is, how it can form a vehicle or an organ of thought. . . . The classical scholar uses Greek or Latin, the Oriental scholar Hebrew or Sanskrit, to trace the social, moral progress of the human race.'"

He looked up. "You follow? Now listen." He took a sip of wine. "'In *comparative philology* the case is totally different. The jargons of savage tribes, the clicks of the Hottentots, and the vocal modulations of the Indo-Chinese, are as important, nay, for the solutions of some of our problems, more important than the poetry of Homer, or the prose of Cicero.'"

He slapped his thigh, and took another sip of wine.

"'The clicks of the Hottentots.' What you think of that for a title for my little Chicago piece on the Middle West 'r'? Good, hah? In fact, *bloody* good!"

"*Säufer,*" she said. "How much wine did you have? Come to bed."

He was still laughing when she got him to go to bed, and the next morning, looking for something to read on the train, he took Max Müller with him.

Meanwhile, on a Greyhound bus approaching Detroit, Alastair Pines, slumped next to the window he had opened at once on entering, was sleeping off both a night out in New York (paid for with the difference between the cashed-in train ticket sent from Pittston and the bus fare) and the eyestrain of hours of digestive gazing at the country that, unknown to it, he meant to call his own.

The wind, ruffling a blond lock that flopped engagingly over his forehead even when he was awake, passed without a ripple over his well-rigged old Aquascutum, over his skis and duffelbag on the rack above. Travel fitted him like a skin; he voyaged with all the aplomb of his nation, of school holidays spent in Paris, of walking tours on the cheap in Yugoslavia. He was that unobtrusive man to be met everywhere in or out of the sterling area — leaning over the rails of the small steamers that plied the lesser isles of Greece, knees pressed together in the third-class carriage going over Domodossola or through Torremolinos — the Englishman of between twenty and forty, whose berth in life and appearance is also somewhere adequately middle, who, to Americans, travels disarmingly light in baggage and heavy in experience. To his compatriots, he was recognizable in more detail, as that projectile still spinning with leftover impetus down the targetless postwar years, that "type" known to them as "R.A.F."

When he awoke, the bus was nearing downtown Detroit, and he was surprised to see that there were skyscrapers here too, not on a stunning pedestal of bridge and harbor, as in New York, but forming upward like some harder fusion of the smoky, after-barrage air. He leaned forward eagerly, though not romantically; the point about new places, and the duty, was to grip the *fact* of them. New York's air, mica-shot, had the fluid chic of big business; this place had the heavy thunder-shade of industry.

He took out one of their sweets and ate it thoughtfully. With the two strings that he had to his bow, there was no reason why, during the year at Pittston, or after, he should not find some post here that would suit him. He had had three terms reading history at a provincial university, before the war saved him from the likelihood that he would be sent down. After the war, the government had been well pleased to send him to an engineering college, where he had since taught for several years. Browsing over a list of posts abroad, he had come upon the exchange offer from Pitt; trying for it on the hunch that they couldn't have the pick of his betters, he had found his divided talents suited them to a T. He would be a Fellow in English, but would also teach a course in mechanics on the side — what luck to find that his education, on the spotty side for home, had shifted about in a way they seemed to admire here. And after his year here, he ought to feel cheeky enough to jump ship, into the wider seas of industry.

To Alastair, third son of a colonial servant who had died in the service before rising in it — but not too soon to see his children reared as they should be, on the strong asses' milk of the imperial habit — it was normal beyond notice to have a brother in Malaya, another in Johannesburg, a married sister in Cyprus and an uncle in Accra. Hitherto, Alastair had been the one who had worried *them,* but now he rather pitied them, dogging along as they did, bewailing the loss of India, toward a half-pay retirement in Kensington — and all for a groundling lack-of-vision that had kept them from seeing the modern world as he had once been used to seeing it from his plane. At twenty thousand feet up, the technical lines of empire erased themselves; one saw that one might descend on the States as in other days one might have sailed to Kenya, but carrying a passport now, instead of a gun. And colonial sacrifices were still to be made; although in the modern way one might have to give up one's citizenship instead of one's health. Had to be done, unless one wanted to fizzle out in some corner, still denying that sahibs were passé. For, entering a country already in a high state of cultivation, and one in a certain sense already appropriated, the trick was to play it in re-verse, to go native as quickly as possible. Which he was fully resigned to do.

When he was met by his hosts at the end of his journey, they all took to each other at once. Dr. Mabie, stammering a pace behind his wife, expanded on being deferred to as "sir." Mrs. Mabie crimsoned with understanding when Mr. Pines referred to the bus as a charabanc. As for their guest, taking note of the man's jellyfish way with his wife, and the woman — hair right out of the flicks, and such an oddly nasal way of talking — he thought them as American as anything he'd seen yet.

It was close to two weeks before the professor, delaying happily in conferences and libraries, returned to Pittston alone, having left Hertha for a visit in Lansing. He spent Saturday night alone by choice, in one of those reflective lulls of the closely married, and, noting a card in the collected mail, went on Sunday afternoon to the McFarlands' opening tea of the academic season.

It was a lovely day, both crisp and smoky with autumn expectancy, and Weil, refreshed in perspective, leaned against Mrs. McFarland's wall with an enjoyment not yet dampened by the grapejuice-tea punch, watching the *Les Sylphides* advances between teacher and student, savoring a familiar, faculty-wife hat heightened inexplicably by a new feather. Then Mrs. McFarland bore down on him with a group, muttering names all round in her furry Scots. "Yeer to stay on, Mr. Pines," she said, tapping one young man on the shoulder, and passing by Weil, of whose worldliness she disapproved.

So this was young Pines. Listening with a pang of re-membrance, Weil docketed the accent: not quite Oxford or B.B.C., but within the gates — of Knightsbridge say, Kensington, or St. John's Wood. And could it be, yes, relaxing already into a certain Americanism? Looking, he saw what he used to think of as one of their *blended* faces, too browned and water-slapped for a man of intellect, too veiled for a man of sport.

He approached him, and they exchanged amenities on the wind and the weather, and on how Pines was settling in; it didn't occur to Weil that Pines might not have caught his name. Those around them, all students, melted back in deference to this faculty meeting. From a group across the room, Portia-Lou waved to Weil and called out an inquiry about Hertha. The young man included himself in her wave, and signaled back. "Hi!" he said.

To Weil's surprise, Mrs. Mabie's nod seemed sullen. "You are quite comfortable at the Mabies'?" he asked.

"Oh yes, rather. She's been incredibly, well — very kind really. Yes!"

"She seems a little — quiet," said the professor.

"Rather hard to take someone in, don't you know. Privacy, and so on," said Pines. "By the way, you pronounce it pri-vacy here, with the long 'i'?"

Weil nodded. "The great vowel change. Among others."

"Rather think I may have got her back up a bit, though. You see, I asked her to coach me in American. It was be-fore I knew that she, er well, that she —"

"That she was so very British?" said Weil.

Mr. Pines began to laugh, then thought better of it. "You

see — I hadn't the faintest. You see — I offered to *exchange*."

Weil grinned. "Poor Portia-Lou. When I was in London, I always felt one had to be *très bien élevé* to be able to say 'bloody.' "

Mr. Pines smiled, eyes hooded. "There during the war?"

"Yes."

There was a pause, during which Mr. Pines took a frail sip of punch, then set his cup decisively down.

"You drink wine?" asked Weil.

"When I can get it. But I was given to understand that one doesn't do, here."

"*They* don't," said Weil. "But I do." He smiled. "And if you play it right — I should think you could." He saw a clear path to the door. Clapping on his beret, he shook hands in adieu. "We must have a bottle, some night. See you in the department."

When Mr. Pines returned to his quarters at ten in the evening, the Mabies were still up. He passed them with a greeting, and went up the stairs. Mrs. McFarland's deafness had been rather exhausting; they had however established that his own father had once stayed at Dysart, not a stone's throw from her own town of Kirkcaldy on the Firth of Forth, at a time when she might very well still have been there. Curious how people insistently sought out these little fraternities of time and space; at the thought he went back downstairs, carefully making a noise, and stuck his head around the living-room arch. "Sorry to barge in, but would you mind telling me the name of a chap I met this afternoon," he said, looking at Dr. Mabie.

"If it's a student, they're all so *like*," said Mrs. Mabie.

"Oh no, no, no — a don." He thought the term might please her, but her regard remained cold. "Short, round sort of chap. Little Jew, with a beret."

"Why, that's Hans, Hans Weil. He's in your own department."

"Oh, that's Weil, is it? Stupid of me. Thank you very much." He turned to go.

"He may happen to be a Jew," said Mrs. Mabie, rising from her chair. "He's also very distinguished. And a refugee. And our very good friend."

"Charming fellow, very," said Mr. Pines. "Good night."

When he had gone back up the stairs, and she had listened for the sound of his door shutting, she turned back to Ernest. "I knew it. I knew there was something about that guy. All that going on about wonderful America — he's what *they* call smarmy. Maybe what they call a *spiv* — or worse."

"N-now, now," said Ernest.

"Well, if he's so top-drawer, what's he doing over here?"

"He never said anything about what he is," said Ernest, losing his stammer. "It's you. He just wants to be polite. And I think he's very straightforward."

"Oh-h — you. You didn't even have the spirit to stand up for Hans."

Upstairs, Alastair, whose frank estimate of himself would have been no closer to Ernest's than to Portia-Lou's, was looking in a mirror at his tongue. Yes, it had a boil on it, from the food here — not quite what Americans abroad had led him to expect. He touched the spot with iodine, then took out a pocket notebook in which, after chewing his pencil for a minute, he wrote, "Can't refer openly to origins, as we do. Affronts them." He was snoring by the time Mrs. Mabie, nudging Ernest, who had also begun to snore, wanted to know the name of that girl, the earl's daughter, the one who had fallen in love with Hitler.

A few days later, Weil, catching sight of Mr. Pines chatting with the pretty stenographer in the outer office, invited him for lunch.

"Righto. 'Bye, Janice."

" 'Bye, Mr. Pines."

"Ah now, remember," said Pines as they left. "Just call me Al."

They found a table in the cafeteria on the floor below. "Pretty girl," said Mr. Pines. "*She* don't mind teaching me American."

"Careful you don't teach her anything else," said Weil. "This is a pious campus."

"Not likely. Still, women are so much more irreligious than men, don't you think? Shocking, what some of them will do."

"Mm," said Weil. Though still liking Mr. Pines, he was beginning to place him rather more accurately than had the Mabies. "And how are you getting along in your quarters?"

"Oh, that's another cup of tea. Perhaps you can set me right on that, sir. Mrs. Mabie, would she be — a bit on the barmy side?"

"No-o. Just — exaggerated. Why?"

"Well, the last few days she's got very chatty, in a very odd way. I don't mind her wanting me to natter on about myself, where I've been, what I've done, politics and all that, but — it's as if she's trying to catch me out." Pines hesitated. "With what we've been told at home about things here — do you think she's trying to make me out a Communist?"

"Are you?" said Weil.

"No. Labor. But surely that — ?"

"Oh no, you are safe. Each visitor here is allowed certain national idiosyncrasies. That one happens to be yours."

"Well then, I wonder, I do," said Alastair. "You see, although I don't like to say this, I'm rather certain she's been going through my things."

Later, sometime after nine that evening, the Mabies and the Weils faced each other over the latter's dining-room table. Portia-Lou, sitting tall in the fullness of confession, had just refused a proffered slice of *Nüsstorte*.

"So," said the professor. "So Mr. Pines has skis from Garmisch, and his camera is an I.K.G. — as mine would be if I still had them. So he has, among souvenirs from Tangier and Castellammare, also some from Nüremberg — and among his billets-doux a bundle calling him Putzi. Ach, Portia! So during the war he flies over the Alps — and during the occupation he skis over them!" He flung up his hands. "So that makes this — this R.A.F. *Spitzbub'* — a *Nazi?*" He pushed his cup toward Hertha for more coffee. "Excuse me, I would laugh, if I could yet laugh at that word."

"But Hans, it's not just that — it's . . . other attitudes," said Portia.

"Ah, so, you are still sore at him because he does not act the way you expected. Excuse me again from your attitudes. I know them. *Arrières pensées,* ten or fifteen years behind the times. Like the Paris styles, by the time they come to Posen."

"*Na, na, Hans, halt dein Mund!*" said Hertha.

"Ernest," said Weil, "you will understand. We cannot have this gossiped in the college, on no provocation. Hertha and I have talked it over this afternoon. He will come to us, here."

"Oh, no!" said Portia. "Not to you, of all people. Tell them, Ernest."

"N-now, honey," said Ernest. "You're just building something up."

"Well then, I'll tell them. I'd hoped not to have to. But they can't let themselves in for that."

"For what, Portia?" Weil said.

"Your Mr. Pines. He's an anti-Semite."

Weil put a hand over Hertha's, which had just begun to tremble. "You have proof?"

"Something he said. About you."

"Hans," said Hertha. "Hans." Her hands gripped the table.

"*Du wilst gehen, Liebste?*"

"*Nein, nein.* I will stay."

"Repeat it then, Portia," said Weil, holding his wife's hands in his. "Repeat it exactly."

She repeated it.

"So," he said. "So." He got up, tucked the afghan around Hertha, and walked over to Portia. "Look at me." He leaned over her. "I am short, not? I wear now and then a beret?" He extracted two nods from her. "And I am a Jew?" She nodded again, head down.

"Ah," he said, "the muscles are a little stiff. So it is insult then, to be called a Jew." Drumming on the table, he brought his palm down flat. A cup turned on its side, spilling a stream of brown that seeped into the cloth. "*Ja,* the insult is there. Not in his mind. In yours."

He waved aside Ernest, who had moved to mop up the coffee. "The Jew is so sensitive, hah, and you want to be so sensitive too. So you will take special care not to notice what he is." He blotted at the coffee with a napkin. "I like better your Mrs. McFarland. She refuses me her house, because I drink wine. She is not afraid to include me in her prejudices, as she might any other man."

He went to the door. "Excuse me. Ernest. I am sorry. But maybe the evening is over."

When he had seen them out, he came back up the stairs to Hertha. "T-t-t," he said, "*was für ein Esel bin ich.* I make everybody cry." He sat down beside her. "Come, laugh. You know what she said to me at the door? She said, 'Hans, I wouldn't hurt *you* for the world. *You* of all people.'" He put his arms around her. "*Na, na,* it's all right. We are all here together." He pressed her head on his shoulder. "Come, it was no tragedy, just a little comic opera. Only — me — I still think I am *Heldentenor.*" He rocked her back and forth. "I spilled no blood, *hein?*" he said, rocking. "Just a little *Kaffee.*"

On the following Sunday, one of those honey-warm fall days that brought out summer habits like chilled bees, the professor and Alastair Pines sat over a bottle of wine in the Weil garden, a small high terrace overlooking the main highway that ran below. Alastair, member of the household for the past week, had already formed a gourmet's alliance with Hertha, who had taken to producing in triumph at dinner the *Wienerschnitzel* or *Knödel* over which Alastair would have reminisced so charmingly the day before. Now Weil uncorked the wine and set the bottle on the table in the middle of the picnic lunch — roast duck and beetroot *Salat*, that Hertha had left with them before going to Lansing.

"We let the wine breathe a little first, it will be better," he said, and sat back, thinking of how long it had been since he had said that to someone, and of how pleasant this was, this pause so male, so European.

Alastair leaned back, stretching his arms. "Soft berth, this," he said, smiling. "Very. You've both been so kind. Perhaps now you wouldn't mind telling me what was at the bottom of that business at the Mabies'. Not, of course, unless you want to."

"Not at all," said Weil. "It is very instructive." He explained some of Mrs. Mabie's suspicions.

"I say!" said Alastair. "How amazing! But I say, she can't be typical."

"Oh, no, no, she's a silly woman. One can't generalize about this big a country. Still, so often these unilateral fantasies about others. After two wars, still such an island."

"Hasn't done *us* all that much good," said Alastair. "To know all about the other fellow's cooking."

"Oh, they are very intelligent, very *sensitive*, the natives." Weil smiled, waving a hand vaguely at the highway. "Only sometimes the silly ones say what the smart ones, the nice ones do not even know they feel. She was for instance very hurt because you refer to me as a Jew."

"But, my word — you are, aren't you?"

Weil stretched his arms in a great, yawning arc, and brought his hands down together on the neck of the bottle. "Precisely. Let's have some wine."

He poured the wine and they sipped it.

"Jolly good."

"Moselle. Too light to travel very well. But then, nothing exports the same."

"Suppose I shall find that out, eh," said Pines, twirling his glass.

"You are planning to stay exported?"

Over a second glass of wine, a third, Pines confided his plans, some of his ruminations on the bus.

"Oh, no, no," said Weil. "My dear fellow, you will allow me to tell you something? Take out citizenship, yes, after all, it is owed. But don't study so hard to be American. Stay *echt* — you will have far more success."

"I suppose people do rather resent the expatriate."

"*Natürlich*. But here it is something more. Especially for an Englishman — they like you to stay as you are. They laugh a little but they admire. Maybe because they are not yet so sure of what they are."

"Ahha," said Alastair. "And is it the same for you?"

"With a difference. You see, you would be an *émigré*. I am a refugee — I have perhaps a few special privileges for humanity's sake." Weil laughed suddenly. "You know perhaps Mark Twain's angry essay against missionaries? On 'Extending the Blessings of Civilization to Our Brother Who Sits in Darkness'?" He poured some more wine. "I often think that for them I am a little 'the person sitting in darkness.'" He shrugged. "So, even in Pittston, I have my Moselle."

Alastair raised his glass. "Cheers."

"Cheers."

Suddenly Weil began to laugh again. " 'The clicks of the Hottentots,' " he said. With some difficulty, he stopped laughing, and explained.

Meanwhile Mr. Pines opened the second bottle, and poured. "'T' the Hottentots!" he said.

"To the Hottentots." The professor looked through his glass at the sun. "Maybe you will marry one, ha?"

"Oh, I've a sort of understanding with a girl at home — nothing restrictive. Joyce is very un — understanding. Good thing too, with all these — is it *drum girls?*"

"Drum majorettes."

"T-t. On the High Street, too. 'Straord'n'ry."

"Mm. But don't fool yourself you are at the Windmill Theatre. You may be, but they are not."

They drank to the Windmill.

" 'A night out on the tiles,' " said the professor. "Still say that in London?"

"Mmm."

The professor leaned back and dreamed, thinking obscurely that a traveler always brought to a foreign place something that wasn't really there. If he lived there long enough, he found that out. But luckily he hadn't lived long enough for that in London. So he might still dream on it. So he might still dream on it in yet another way, letting it bear the weight of all that he must no longer give to Dresden, to München, to Köln.

After a while he roused himself and sat forward, looking intently into the landscape. "Alastair — I may call you that?"

"Mmm. Call me Alastair. Definitely." The young man sat forward also, following Weil's glance, his lock of hair flopping down on his forehead. The two of them remained so for some minutes, staring at the same median point in the distance.

"Whatever you do, be firm," said the professor suddenly. "Don't give in. Even when you see the whites of their eyes."

"Oh, definitely."

They clicked glasses with casual aim, and drank. Sitting back, they mused sternly for a while on their mutual hardness. Raising their chins like muezzins, they looked easterly, looking into the air, into what might be assumed to be the direction of Europe, that old archipelago of ideas and emotions, which would fade and return for them, fade and return, coming out for them now and then like an odor reviving on a damp day.

"Still . . ." said Alastair. He leaned forward again, gazing down on the highway. "Still — everything's laid on very nicely."

"*Ja, ja.* Very."

Shoulders touching, they looked down on the highway, down to where the cars were flashing by like toucans, bright red, hot pink and high yellow, under the aboriginal sun.

A Christmas Carillon

ABOUT four weeks before Christmas, Grorley, in combined shame and panic, began to angle for an invitation to somewhere, anywhere, for Christmas Day. By this time, after six months of living alone in the little Waverly Place flat to which he had gone as soon as he and his wife had decided to separate, he had become all too well reacquainted with his own peculiar mechanism in regard to solitude. It was a mechanism that had its roots in the jumbled lack of privacy of an adolescence spent in the dark, four-room apartment to which his parents had removed themselves and three children after his father's bankruptcy in '29. Prior to that, Grorley's childhood had been what was now commonly referred to as Edwardian — in a house where servants and food smells kept their distance until needed, and there were no neurotic social concerns about the abundance of either — a house where there was always plush under the buttocks, a multiplicity of tureens and napery at table, lace on the pillow, and above all that general expectancy of creature comfort and spiritual order which novelists now relegated to the days before 1914.

That it had lasted considerably later, Grorley knew, since this had been the year of his own birth, but although he had been fifteen when they had moved, it was the substantial years before that had faded to fantasy. Even now, when he read or said the word "reality," his mind reverted to Sunday middays in the apartment house living room, where the smudgy daylight was always diluted by lamps, the cheaply stippled walls menaced the oversized furniture, and he, his father and brother and sister, each a claustrophobe island of irritation, were a constant menace to one another. Only his mother, struggling alone in the kitchen with the conventions of roast chicken and gravy, had perhaps achieved something of the solitude they all had craved. To Grorley even now, the smell of roasting fowl was the smell of a special kind of Sunday death.

Only once before now had he lived alone, and then too it had been in the Village, not far from where he presently was. After his graduation from City College he had worked a year, to save up for a master's in journalism, and then, salving his conscience with the thought that he had at least paid board at home for that period, he had left his family forever. The following year, dividing his time between small-time newspaper job and classes, living in his $27 per month place off Morton Street, he had savored all the wonders of the single doorkey opening on the quiet room, of the mulled book and the purring clock, of the smug decision not to answer the phone to let even the most delightful invader in. Now that he looked back on it, of course, he recalled that the room had rung pretty steadily with the voices of many such who had been admitted, but half the pleasure had been because it had been at his own behest. That had been a happy time, when he had been a gourmet of loneliness, prowling bachelor-style on the edge of society, dipping inward when he chose. Of all the habitations he had had since, that had been the one whose conformations he remembered best, down to the last, worn dimple of brick. When he had house-hunted, last June, he had returned instinctively to the neighborhood of that time. Only a practicality born of superstition had kept him from hunting up the very street, the very house.

He had had over two years of that earlier freedom, although the last third of it had been rather obscured by his courtship of Eunice. Among the girl students of the Village there had been quite a few who, although they dressed like ballerinas and prattled of art like painters' mistresses, drew both their incomes and their morality from good, solid middle-class families back home. Eunice had been the prettiest and most sought after of these, and part of her attraction for some, and certainly for Grorley, had been that she seemed to be, quite honestly, one of those rare girls who were not particularly eager to marry and settle down. Grorley had been so entranced at finding like feelings in a girl — and in such a beautiful one — that he had quite forgotten that in coaxing her out of her "freedom" he was persuading himself out of his own.

He hadn't realized this with any force until the children came, two within the first four years of the marriage. Before that, in the first fusion of love, it had seemed to Grorley that two could indeed live more delightfully alone than one, and added to this had been that wonderful release from jealousy which requited love brings — half the great comfort of the loved one's presence being that, *ipso facto*, she is with no one else. During this period of happy, though enlarged privacy, Grorley confided to Eunice some, though not all, of his feelings about family life and solitude. He was, he told her, the kind of person who needed to be alone a great deal — although this of course excepted her. But they must never spend their Sundays and holidays frowsting in the house like the rest of the world, sitting there stuffed and droning, with murder in their hearts. They must always have plans laid well in advance, plans which would keep the two of them emotionally limber, so to speak, and *en plein air*. Since these plans were always pleasant — tickets to the Philharmonic, with after-theater suppers, hikes along the Palisades, fishing expeditions to little-known ponds back of the Westchester parkways, whose intricacies Grorley, out of a history of Sunday afternoons, knew as well as certain guides knew Boca Raton — Eunice was quite willing to accede. In time she grew very tactful, almost smug, over Grorley's little idiosyncrasy, and he sometimes heard her on the phone, fending people off. "Not Sunday. Gordon and I have a thing about holidays, you know." By this time, too, they had both decided that, although Grorley would keep his now very respectable desk job at the paper, his real destiny was to "write"; and to Eunice, who respected "imagination" as only the unimaginative can, Grorley's foible was the very proper defect of a noble intelligence.

But with the coming of the children, it was brought home to Grorley that he was face to face with one of those major rearrangements of existence for which mere tact would not suffice. Eunice, during her first pregnancy, was as natural and unassuming about it as a man could wish; she went on their Sunday sorties to the very last, and maintained their gallant privacy right up to the door of the delivery room. But the child of so natural a mother was bound to be natural too. It contracted odd fevers whenever it wished and frequently on Sundays, became passionately endeared to their most expensive sitter or would have none at all, and in general permeated their lives as only the most powerfully frail of responsibilities can. And when the second one arrived, it did so, it seemed to Grorley, only to egg the other one on.

There came a morning, the Christmas morning of the fourth year, when Grorley, sitting in the odor of baked meat, first admitted that his hydra-headed privacy was no longer a privacy at all. He had created, he saw, his own monster; sex and the devil had had their sport with him, and he was, in a sense that no mere woman would understand, all too heavily "in the family way." Looking at Eunice, still neat, still very pretty, but with her lovely mouth pursed with maternity, her gaze sharp enough for *Kinder* and *Küche,* but abstract apparently for him, he saw that she had gone over to the enemy and was no longer his. Eunice had become "the family" too.

It was as a direct consequence of this that Grorley wrote the book which was his making. Right after that fatal morning, he had engaged a room in a cheap downtown hotel (he and Eunice were living out in Astoria at the time), with the intention, as he explained to Eunice, of writing there after he left the paper, and coming home weekends. He had also warned her that, because of the abrasive effects of family life, it would probably be quite some time before "the springs of reverie" — a phrase he had lifted from Ellen Glasgow — would start churning. His real intention was, of course, to prowl, and for some weeks thereafter he joined the company of those men who could be found, night after night, in places where they could enjoy the freedom of not having gone home where they belonged.

To his surprise, he found, all too quickly, that though his intentions were of the worst, he had somehow lost the moral force to pursue them. He had never been much for continuous strong drink, and that crude *savoir-faire* which was needed for the preliminaries to lechery seemed to have grown creaky with the years. He took to spending odd hours in the newspaper morgue, correlating, in a half-hearted way, certain current affairs that interested him. After some months, he suddenly realized that he had enough material for a book. It found a publisher almost immediately. Since he was much more a child of his period than he knew, he had hit upon exactly that note between disaffection and hope which met response in the breasts of those who regarded themselves as permanent political independents. His book was an instant success with those who thought of themselves as thinking for themselves (if they had only had time for it). Quick to capitalize upon this, Grorley's paper gave him a biweekly column, and he developed a considerable talent for telling men of good will, over Wednesday breakfast, the very thing they had been saying to one another at Tuesday night dinner.

Grorley spent the war years doing this, always careful to keep his column, like his readers, one step behind events. With certain minor changes, he kept, too, that scheme of life which had started him writing, changing only, with affluence, to a more comfortable hotel. In time also, that *savoir-faire* whose loss he had mourned returned to him, and his success at his profession erased any guilts he might otherwise have had — a wider experience, he told himself, being not only necessary to a man of his trade, but almost unavoidable in the practice of it. He often congratulated himself at having achieved, in a country which had almost completely domesticated the male, the perfect pattern for a man of temperament, and at times he became almost insufferable to some of his married men friends, when he dilated on the contrast between his "continental" way of life and their own. For by then, Grorley had reversed himself — it was his weekends and holidays that were now spent cozily *en famille*. It was pleasant, coming back to the house in Tarrytown on Friday evenings, coming back from the crusades to find Eunice and the whole household decked out, literally and psychologically, for his return. One grew sentimentally fond of children whom one saw only under such conditions — Grorley's Saturdays were now spent, as he himself boasted, "on all fours," in the rejuvenating air of the skating rinks, the museums, the woods, and the zoos. Sundays and holidays he and Eunice often entertained their relatives, and if, as the turkey browned, he had a momentary twinge of his old *mal de famille*, he had but to remember that his hat was, after all, only hung in the hall.

It was only some years after the war that Eunice began to give trouble. Before that, their double ménage had not been particularly unusual — almost all the households of couples their age had been upset in one way or another, and theirs had been more stable than many. During the war years Eunice had had plenty of company for her midweek evenings; all over America women had been managing bravely behind the scenes. But now that families had long since paired off again, Eunice showed a disquieting tendency to want to be out in front.

"No, you'll have to come home for good," she said to Grorley, at the end of their now frequent battles. "I'm tired of being a short-order wife."

"The trouble with you," said Grorley, "is that you've never adjusted to postwar conditions."

"That was your nineteen-forty-six column," said Eunice. "If you must quote yourself, pick one a little more up-to-date." Removing a jewel-encrusted slipper-toe from the fender, she made a feverish circle of the room, the velvet panniers of her housegown swinging dramatically behind her. She was one of those women who used their charge accounts for retaliation. With each crisis in their deteriorating relationship, Grorley noted gloomily, Eunice's wardrobe had improved.

"Now that the children are getting on," he said, "you ought to have another interest. A hobby."

Eunice made a hissing sound. "Nineteen-forty-seven!" she said.

In the weeks after, she made her position clear. Men, she told him, might have provided the interest he suggested, but when a woman had made a vocation of one, it wasn't easy to start making a hobby of several. It was hardly much use swishing out in clouds of Tabu at seven, if one had to be back to feel Georgie's forehead at eleven. Besides, at their age, the only odd men out were likely to be hypochondriacs, or bachelors still dreaming of mother, or very odd men indeed.

"All the others," she said nastily, "are already on somebody else's hearth rug. Or out making the rounds with you." Worst of all, she seemed to have lost her former reverence for Grorley's work. If he'd been a novelist or a poet, she said (she even made use of the sticky word "creative"), there'd have been more excuse for his need to go off into the silence. As it was, she saw no reason for his having to be so broody over analyzing the day's proceedings at the U.N. If he wanted an office, that should take care of things very adequately. But if he did not wish to live *with* her, then he could not go on *living* with her. "Mentally," she said, "you're still in the Village. Maybe you better go back there."

Things were at this pass when Grorley's paper sent him to London, on an assignment that kept him there for several months. He was put up for membership in one or two exclusively masculine clubs, and in their leonine atmosphere his outraged vanity — ("creative" indeed!) — swelled anew. Finally, regrettably near the end of his stay, he met up with a redheaded young woman named Vida, who worked for a junior magazine by day, wrote poetry by night, and had once been in America for three weeks. She and Grorley held hands over the mutual hazards of the "creative" life, and on her lips the word was like a caress. For a woman, too, she was remarkably perceptive about the possessiveness of other women. "Yes, quite," she had said. "Yes, quite."

When she and Grorley made their final adieu in her Chelsea flat, she held him, for just a minute, at arm's length. "I shall be thinking of you over there, in one of those ghastly, what do you call them, *living rooms*, of yours. Everybody matted together, and the floor all over children

— like beetles. Poor dear. I should think those living rooms must be the curse of the American family. Poor, poor dear."

On his return home in June, Grorley and Eunice agreed on a six-months trial separation prior to a divorce. Eunice showed a rather unfeeling calm in the lawyer's office, immediately afterward popped the children in camp, and went off to the Gaspé with friends. Grorley took a sublet on the apartment in Waverly Place. It was furnished in a monastic modern admirably suited to the novel he intended to write, that he had promised Vida to write.

He had always liked summers in town, when the real *aficionados* of the city took over, and now this summer seemed to him intoxicating, flowing with the peppery currents of his youth. In the daytime his freedom slouched unshaven; in the evenings the streets echoed and banged with life, and the moon made a hot harlequinade of every alley. He revisited the San Remo, Julius's, Chumley's, Jack Delaney's, and all the little Italian bars with backyard restaurants, his full heart and wallet carrying him quickly into the cameraderie of each. Occasionally he invited home some of the remarkables he met on his rounds — a young Italian bookie, a huge St. Bernard of a woman who drove a taxi and had once lived on a barge on the East River, an attenuated young couple from Chapel Hill, who were honeymooning at the New School. Now and then a few of his men friends from uptown joined him in a night out. A few of these, in turn, invited him home for the weekend, but although he kept sensibly silent on the subject of their fraternal jaunts, he detected some animus in the hospitality of their wives.

By October, Grorley was having a certain difficulty with his weekends. His list of bids to the country was momentarily exhausted, and his own ideas had begun to flag. The children, home from camp, had aged suddenly into the gang phase; they tore out to movies and jamborees of their own, were weanable from these only by what Grorley could scrape up in the way of rodeos and football games, and assumed, once the afternoon's treat was over, a faraway look of sufferance. Once or twice, when he took them home, he caught himself hoping that Eunice would ask him in for a drink, a chat that might conceivably lead to dinner, but she was always out, and Mrs. Lederer, the housekeeper, always pulled the children in as if they were packages whose delivery had been delayed, gave him a nasty nod, and shut the door.

For a few weekends he held himself to his desk, trying to work up a sense of dedication over the novel, but there was no doubt that it was going badly. Its best juice had been unwisely expended in long, analytic letters to Vida, and now, in her airmail replies, which bounced steadily and enthusiastically over the Atlantic, it began to seem more her novel than his. The Sunday before Thanksgiving, he made himself embark on a ski-train to Pittsfield, working up a comforting sense of urgency over the early rising and the impedimenta to be checked. The crowd on the train was divided between a band of Swiss and German perfectionists who had no conversation, and a horde of young couples, rolling on the slopes like puppies, who had too much. Between them, Grorley's privacy was respected to the point of insult. When he returned that night, he tossed his gear into a corner, where it wilted damply on his landlord's blond rug, made himself a hot toddy — with a spasm of self-pity over his ability to do for himself — and sat down to face his fright. For years, his regular intervals at home had been like the chewed coffee bean that renewed the wine-taster's palate. He had lost the background from which to rebel.

Thanksgiving Day was the worst. The day dawned oyster-pale and stayed that way. Grorley slept as late as he could, then went out for a walk. The streets were slack, without the twitch of crowds, and the houses had a tight look of inner concentration. He turned toward the streets which held only shops, and walked uptown as far as Rockefeller Center. The rink was open, with its usual cast of characters — ricocheting children, a satiny, professional twirler from the Ice Show, and several solemn old men who skated upright in some Euclidian absorption of their own. Except for a few couples strolling along in the twin featurelessness of love, the crowd around the rink was type-cast too. Here, it told itself, it participated in life; here in this flying spectacle of flag and stone it could not possibly be alone. With set, shy smiles, it glanced sideways at its neighbors, rounded its shoulders to the wind, turned up its collar, and leaned closer to the musical bonfire of the square. Grorley straightened up, turned on his heel, smoothed down his collar, and walked rapidly toward Sixth Avenue. He filled himself full of ham and eggs in one of the quick-order places that had no season, taxied home, downed a drink, swallowed two Seconal tablets, and went to bed.

The next morning, seated at his desk, he took a relieved look at the street. People were hard at their normal grind again; for a while the vacuum was past. But Christmas was not going to catch him alone. He picked up the phone. At the end of the day he was quite heartened. Although he had not yet turned up an invitation for Christmas Day, he had netted himself a cocktail party (which might easily go on to dinner) for two days before, a bid to an eggnog party on New Year's Day, and one weekend toward the middle of December. A lot of people did things impromptu. A phone call now and then would fix him up somehow.

But by Christmas week he was haggard. He had visualized himself as bidden to share, in a pleasantly avuncular capacity, some close friend's family gathering; he had seen himself as indolently and safely centered, but not anchored, in the bright poinsettia of their day. Apparently their vision of him was cast in a harsher mold; they returned his innuendoes with little more than a pointed sympathy. Only two propositions had turned up, one from a group of men, alone like himself for one reason or another, who were forming a party at an inn in the Poconos, and one from a waif-like spinster — "Last Christmas was my last one with dear Mother" — who offered to cook dinner for him in her apartment. Shuddering, he turned down both of these. The last thing he wanted to do on that day was to ally himself with *waifs* of any description; on that day he very definitely wanted to be safely inside some cozy family cocoon, looking out at *them.*

Finally, the day before Christmas, he thought of the Meechers. Ted was that blue-ribbon bore, the successful account executive who believed his own slogans, and his wife, a former social worker, matched him in her own field. Out of Ted's sense of what was due his position in the agency and Sybil's sense of duty to the world, they had created a model home in Chappaqua, equipped with four children, two Bedlingtons, a games room, and a part-time pony. Despite this, they were often hard up for company, since most people could seldom be compelled twice to their table, where a guest was the focus of a constant stream of self-congratulation from either end. Moreover, Ted had wormed his way into more than one stag party at Grorley's, and could hardly refuse a touch. And their Christmas, whatever its other drawbacks, would be a four-color job, on the best stock.

But Ted's voice, plum-smooth when he took the phone from his secretary, turned reedy and doubtful when he heard Grorley's inquiry. "Uh-oh! 'Fraid that puts me on the spot, fella. Yeah. Kind of got it in the neck from Sybil, last time I came home from your place. Yeah. Had a real old-fashioned hassle. Guess I better not risk reminding her just yet. But, say! How about coming up here right now, for the office party?"

Grorley declined, and hung up. Off-campus boy this time of year, that's what I am, he thought. He looked at his mantelpiece crowded with its reminders — greetings from Grace and Bill, Jane and Tom, Peg and Jack, Etcetera and Mrs. Etcetera. On top of the pile was another airmail from Vida, received that morning, picture enclosed. Sans the red in the hair, without the thrush tones of the assenting voice, she looked a little long in the teeth. Her hands and feet, he remembered, were always cold. Somehow or other, looking at the picture, he didn't think that central heating would improve them. "The living room is the curse," she'd said. That's it, he thought; that's it. And this, Vida, is the season of the living room.

He looked down into the street. The Village was all right for the summer, he thought. But now the periphery of the season had changed. In summer, the year spins on a youth-charged axis, and a man's muscles have a spurious oil. But this is the end toward which it spins. Only three hundred days to Christmas. Only a month — a week. And then, every year, the damned day itself, catching him with its holly claws, sounding its platitudes like carillons.

Down at the corner, carols bugled steamily from a mission soup-kitchen. There's no escape from it, he thought. Turn on the radio, and its alleluia licks you with tremolo tongue. In every store window flameth housegown, nuzzleth slipper. In all the streets the heavenly shops proclaim. The season has shifted inward, Grorley, and you're on the outside, looking in.

He moved toward the phone, grabbed it, and dialed the number before he remembered that you had to dial the code for Tarrytown. He replaced the receiver. Whatever he had to say, and he wasn't quite sure what, or how, it wasn't for the ears of the kids or the Lederer woman. He jammed on his hat. Better get there first, get inside the door.

Going up to Grand Central in the cab, he pressed his face against the glass. Everything had been taken care of weeks ago — the kids had been sent their two-wheelers, and he had mailed Eunice an extra-large check — one he hadn't sent through the lawyer. But at five o'clock, Fifth Avenue still shone like an enormous blue sugar-plum revolving in a tutti-frutti rain of light. Here was the season in all its questionable glory — the hallmarked joy of giving, the good will *diamanté*. But in the cosmetic air, people raised tinted faces, walked with levitated step.

In the train, he avoided the smoker, and chose an uncrowded car up front. At his station, he waited until all the gleaming car muzzles pointed at the train had picked up their loads and gone, then walked through the main street which led to his part of town. All was lit up here too, with a more intimate, household shine. He passed the pink damp of a butcher's, the bright fuzz of Woolworth's. "Sold out!" said a woman, emerging. "'S try the A & P." He walked on, invisible, his face pressed to the shop window of the world.

At Schlumbohn's Credit Jewelry Corner he paused, feeling for the wallet filled with cash yesterday for the still not impossible yes over the phone. This was the sort of store that he and Eunice, people like them, never thought of entering. It sold watches pinned to cards, zircons, musical powder-boxes, bracelets clasped with fat ten-carat hearts, Rajah pearl necklaces and Truelove blue-white diamonds. Something for Everybody, it said. He opened the door.

Inside, a magnetic salesgirl nipped him toward her like a pin. He had barely stuttered his wants before he acquired an Add-a-Pearl necklace for Sally, two Genuine Pinseal handbags for his mother-in-law and Mrs. Lederer, and a Stag-horn knife with three blades, a nailfile, and a corkscrew, for young George. He had left Eunice until last, but with each purchase, a shabby, telephoning day had dropped from him. Dizzy with participation, he surveyed the mottoed store.

"Something . . . something for the wife," he said.

"Our lovely Lifetime Watch, perhaps? Or Something in Silver, for the House?" The clerk tapped her teeth, gauging him.

He leaned closer, understanding suddenly why housewives, encysted in lonely houses, burbled confidences to the grocer, made an audience of the milkman. "We've had a — Little Tiff."

"Aw-w," said the clerk, adjusting her face. "Now . . . let me see. . . ." She kindled suddenly, raised a sibylline finger, beckoned him further down the counter, and drew out a tray of gold charms. Rummaging among them with a long, opalescent nail, she passed over minute cocktail shakers, bird cages, tennis rackets, a tiny scroll bearing the words, "If you can see this, you're too darn close," and seized a trinket she held up for view. A large gold shamrock, hung on a chain by a swivel through its middle, it bore the letter I. on its upper leaf, on its nether one the letter U. She reversed it. L.O.V.E. was engraved across the diameter of the other side. The clerk spun it with her accomplished nail. "See?" she said. "Spin it! Spin it and it says I. L.O.V.E. U!"

"Hmmm . . ." said Grorley, clearing his throat. "Well . . . guess you can't fob some women off with just a diamond bracelet." She tittered dutifully. But, as she handed it to him with his other packages, and closed the glass door behind him, he saw her shrug something, laughing, to another clerk. She had seen that he was not Schlumbohn's usual, after all. As he walked up his own street he felt that he was after all hardly anybody's usual, tonight. It was a pretty street, of no particular architectural striving. Not a competitive street, except sometimes in summer, on the subject of gardens. And, of course, now. In every house the tree was up and lit, in the window nearest the passer-by. Here was his own, with the same blue lights that had lasted, with some tinkering on his part, year after year. Eunice must have had a man in to fix them.

He stopped on the path. A man in. She was pretty, scorned, and — he had cavalierly assumed — miserable. He had taken for granted that his family, in his absence, would have remained reasonably static. They always had. He'd been thinking of himself. Silently, he peeled off another layer of self-knowledge. He still was.

He walked up the steps wondering what kind of man might rise to be introduced, perhaps from his own armchair. One of her faded, footballish resurrections from Ohio State U., perhaps: Gordon, this is Jim Jerk, from home. Or would she hand it to him at once? Would it be: *Dear*, this is Gordon.

The door was unlocked. He closed it softly behind him, and stood listening. This was the unmistakable quiet of an empty house — as if the secret respiration of all objects in it had just stopped at his entrance. The only light downstairs was the glowing tree. He went up the stairs.

In the bedroom, the curtains were drawn, the night light on. The bed was piled with an abandoned muddle of silver wrappings, tissue paper, ribbons. He dropped the presents on the bed, tossed his hat after them, let his coat slip down on the familiar chair, and parted the curtains. It had a good view of the river, his house. He stood there, savoring it. He was still there when a car door slammed and the family came up the path. The Christmas Eve pantomime, of course, held every year at the village hall. Georgie had on one of those white burnooses they always draped the boys in, and Sally, in long dress and coned hat, seemed to be a medieval lady. He saw that this year she had the waist for it. Eunice and Mrs. Lederer walked behind them. He tapped on the glass.

They raised their faces in tableau. The children waved, catcalled, and disappeared through the downstairs door. Mrs. Lederer followed them. Below, Eunice stared upward, in the shine from the tree-window. Behind him, he heard that sound made only by children — the noise of bodies falling up a staircase. As they swarmed in on him, she disappeared.

"You shoulda been to the hall," said Georgie, seizing him. "Christmas at King Arthur's court. I was a knight."

"Was it corny!" said Sally, from a distance. She caught sight of herself in a pier glass. "I was Guinevere."

"Had to do some last-minute shopping," said Grorley.

"I saw my bike!" said Georgie. "It's in the cellar."

"Oh . . . Georgie!" said Sally.

"Well, I couldn't help seeing it."

"Over there are some Christmas Eve presents," said Grorley.

"Open now?" they said. He nodded. They fell upon them.

"Gee," said Georgie, looking down at the knife. "Is that neat!" From his tone it was clear that he, at least, was Schlumbohn's usual.

"Oh, Dad!" Sally had the necklace around her neck. She raised her arms artistically above her head, in the fifth position, minced forward, and placed their slender wreath around Grorley's neck. As she hung on him, sacklike, he felt that she saw them both, a tender picture, in some lurking pier glass of her mind.

The door opened, and Eunice came in. She shut it behind her with a "not before the servants" air, and stood looking at him. Her face was blurred at the edges; she hadn't decked herself out for anybody. She looked the way a tired, pretty woman, of a certain age and responsibilities, might look at the hour before dinner, at the moment when age and prettiness tussle for her face, and age momentarily has won.

"Look what I got!" Georgie brandished the knife.

"And mine!" Sally undulated herself. "Mums! Doesn't it just *go!*" She stopped, looking from father to mother, her face hesitant, but shrewd.

"Open yours, Mums. Go on."

"Later," said Eunice. "Right now I think Mrs. Lederer wants you both to help with the chestnuts."

"No fair, no fair," said Georgie. "You saw ours."

"Do what your mother says," said Grorley. The paternal phrase, how it steadied him, was almost a hearthstone under his feet.

"Oh, well," said Eunice, wilting toward the children, as she invariably did when he was stern with them. Opening the package he indicated, she drew out the bauble. Georgie rushed to look at it, awarded it a quick, classifying disinterest, and returned to his knife.

"Oo — I know how to work those! Margie's sister has one," said Sally. She worked it. "If that isn't corny!" she gurgled. Eunice's head was bent over the gift. Sally straightened up, gave her and Grorley a swift, amending glance. "But cute!" she said. She flushed. Then, with one of the lightning changes that were the bane of her thirteen years, she began to cry. "Honestly, it's sweet!" she said.

Grorley looped an arm around her, gave her a squeeze and a kiss. "Now, shoo," he said. "Both of you."

When he turned back to the room, Eunice was looking out the window, chin up, her face not quite averted. Recognizing the posture, he quailed. It was the stance of the possessor of the stellar role — of the nightingale with her heart against the thorn. It was the stance of the woman who demands her scene.

He sighed, rat-tatted his fingers on a table top. "Well," he said. "Guess this is the season the corn grows tall."

A small movement of her shoulder. The back of her head to him. Now protocol demanded that he talk, into her silence, dredging his self-abasement until he hit upon some remark which made it possible for her to turn, to rend it, to show it up for the heartless, illogical, tawdry remark that it was. He could repeat a list of the game birds of North America, or a passage from the Congressional Record. The effect would be the same.

"Go on," he said, "get it over with. I deserve it. I just

want you to know . . . mentally, I'm out of the Village."

She turned, head up, nostrils dilated. Her mouth opened. "Get it ov — !" Breath failed her. But not for long.

Much later, they linked arms in front of the same window. Supper had been eaten, the turkey had been trussed, the children at last persuaded into their beds. That was the consolatory side of family life, Grorley thought — the long, Olympian codas of the emotions were cut short by the niggling detail. Women thought otherwise, of course. In the past, he had himself.

Eunice began clearing off the bed. "What's in those two? Father's and Mother's?"

"Oh Lord. I forgot Father."

"Never mind. I'll look in the white-elephant box." The household phrase — how comfortably it rang. She looked up. "What's in these then?"

"For Mother and Mrs. Lederer. Those leather satchel-things. Pinseal."

"Both the same, I'll bet."

He nodded.

Eunice began to laugh. "Oh, Lord. How they'll hate it." She continued to laugh, fondly, until Grorley smirked response. This, too, was familiar. Masculine gifts: the inappropriateness thereof.

But Eunice continued to laugh, steadily, hysterically, clutching her stomach, collapsing into a chair. "It's that hat," she said. "It's that s-specimen of a hat!"

Grorley's hat lay on the bed, where he had flung it. Brazenly dirty, limp denizen of bars, it reared sideways on a crest of tissue paper, one curling red whorl of ribbon around its crown. "L-like something out of Hogarth," she said. "The R-rounder's Return."

Grorley forced a smile. "You can buy me another."

"Mmmm . . . for Christmas." She stopped laughing. "You know . . . I think that's what convinced me — your coming back tonight. Knowing you — that complex of yours. Suppose I felt if you meant to stand us through the holidays, you meant to stand us for good."

Grorley coughed, bent to stuff some paper into the wastebasket. In fancy, he was stuffing in a picture too, portrait of Vida, woman of imagination, outdistanced forever by the value of a woman who had none.

Eunice yawned. "Oh . . . I forgot to turn out the tree."

"I'll go down."

"Here, take this along." She piled his arms with crushed paper. In grinning afterthought, she clapped the hat on his head.

He went to the kitchen and emptied his arms in the bin. The kitchen was in chaos, the cookery methods of *alt Wien* demanding that each meal rise like a phoenix, from a flaming muddle belowstairs. Tomorrow, as Mrs. Lederer mellowed with wine, they would hear once again of her grandfather's house, where the coffee was not even *roasted* until the guests' carriages appeared in the driveway.

In the dining room, the table was set in state, from damask to silver nut dishes. Father would sit there. He was teetotal, but anecdotalism signs no pledge. His jousts as purchasing agent for the city of his birth now left both narrator and listener with the impression that he had built it as well. They would hear from Mother too. It was unfortunate that her bit of glory — her father had once attended Grover Cleveland — should have crystallized itself in that one sentence so shifty for false teeth — "Yes, my father was a physician, you know."

Grorley sighed, and walked into the living room. He looked out, across the flowing blackness of the river. There to the south, somewhere in that jittering corona of yellow lights, was the apartment. He shuddered pleasurably, thinking of all the waifs in the world tonight. His own safety was too new for altruism; it was only by a paring of luck as thin as this pane of glass that he was safely here — on the inside, looking out.

Behind him, the tree shone — that *trompe-l'oeil* triumphant — yearly symbol of how eternally people had to use the spurious to catch at the real. If there was an angel at the top, then here was the devil at its base — that, at this season, anybody who opened his eyes and ears too wide caught the poor fools, caught himself, hard at it. Home is where the heart . . . the best things in life are . . . spin it and it says I. L.O.V.E. U.

Grorley reached up absently and took off his hat. This is middle age, he thought. Stand still and hear the sound of it, bonging like carillons, the gathering sound of all the platitudes, sternly coming true.

He looked down at the hat in his hand. It was an able hat; not every hat could cock a snook like that one. From now on, he'd need every ally he could muster. Holding it, he bent down and switched off the tree. He was out of the living room and halfway up the stairs, still holding it, before he turned back. Now the house was entirely dark, but he needed no light other than the last red sputter of rebellion in his heart. He crept down, felt along the wall, clasped a remembered hook. Firmly, he hung his hat in the hall. Then he turned, and went back up the stairs.

The Rabbi's Daughter

T HEY all came along with Eleanor and her baby in the cab to Grand Central, her father and mother on either side of her, her father holding the wicker bassinet on his carefully creased trousers. Rosalie and Helene, her cousins, smart in their fall ensembles, just right for the tingling October dusk, sat in the two little seats opposite them. Aunt Ruth, Dr. Ruth Brinn, her father's sister and no kin to the elegant distaff cousins, had insisted on sitting in front with the cabman. Eleanor could see her now, through the glass, in animated talk, her hat tilted piratically on her iron-gray braids.

Leaning forward, Eleanor studied the dim, above-eye-level picture of the driver. A sullen-faced young man, with a lock of black hair belligerent over his familiar nondescript face. "Manny Kaufman." What did Manny Kaufman think of Dr. Brinn? In ten minutes she would drag his life history from him, answering his unwilling statements with the snapping glance, the terse nods which showed that she got it all, at once, understood him down to the bone. At the end of her cross-questioning she would be quite capable of saying, "Young man, you are too pale! Get another job!"

"I certainly don't know why you wanted to wear that get-up," said Eleanor's mother, as the cab turned off the Drive toward Broadway. "On a train. And with the baby to handle, all alone." She brushed imaginary dust from her lap, scattering disapproval with it. She had never had to handle her babies alone.

Eleanor bent over the basket before she answered. She was a thin fair girl whom motherhood had hollowed, rather than enhanced. Tucking the bottle-bag further in, feeling the wad of diapers at the bottom, she envied the baby blinking solemnly up at her, safe in its surely serviced world.

"Oh, I don't know," she said. "It just felt gala. New York-ish. Some people dress down for a trip. Others dress up — like me." Staring at her own lap, though, at the bronze velveteen which had been her wedding dress, sensing the fur blob of hat insecure on her unprofessionally waved hair, shifting the shoes, faintly scuffed, which had been serving her for best for two years, she felt the sickening qualm, the frightful inner blush of the inappropriately dressed.

In front of her, half-turned toward her, the two cousins swayed neatly in unison, two high-nostriled gazelles, one in black, one in brown, both in pearls, wearing their propriety, their utter rightness, like skin. She had known her own excess when she had dressed for the trip yesterday morning, in the bare rooms, after the van had left, but her suits were worn, stretched with wearing during pregnancy, and nothing went with anything any more. Tired of house dresses, of the spotted habiliments of maternity, depressed with her three months' solitude in the country waiting out the lease after Dan went on to the new job, she had reached for the wedding clothes, seeing herself cleansed and queenly once more, mysterious traveler whose appearance might signify anything, approaching the pyrrhic towers of New

York, its efferverscent terminals, with her old brilliance, her old style.

Her father sighed. "Wish that boy could find a job nearer New York."

"You know an engineer has to go where the plants are," she said, weary of the old argument. "It's not like you — with your own business and everything. Don't you think I'd like . . . ?" She stopped, under Rosalie's bright, tallying stare.

"I know, I know." He leaned over the baby, doting.

"What's your new house like?" said Rosalie.

"You know," she said gaily, "after all Dan's letters, I'm not just sure, except that it's part of a two-family. They divide houses every which way in those towns. He's written about 'Bostons,' and 'flats,' and 'duplexes.' All I really know is it has automatic heat, thank goodness, and room for the piano." She clamped her lips suddenly on the hectic, chattering voice. Why had she had to mention the piano, especially since they were just passing Fifty-seventh Street, past Carnegie with all its clustering satellites — the Pharmacy, the Playhouse, the Russian restaurant — and in the distance, the brindled windows of the galleries, the little chiffoned store fronts, spitting garnet and saffron light? All her old life smoked out toward her from these buildings, from this parrot-gay, music-scored street.

"Have you been able to keep up with your piano?" Helene's head cocked, her eyes screened.

"Not — not recently. But I'm planning a schedule. After we're settled." In the baby's nap time, she thought. When I'm not boiling formulas or wash. In the evenings, while Dan reads, if I'm only — just not too tired. With a constriction, almost of fear, she realized that she and Dan had not even discussed whether the family on the other side of the house would mind the practicing. That's how far I've come away from it, she thought, sickened.

"All that time spent." Her father stroked his chin with a scraping sound and shook his head, then moved his hand down to brace the basket as the cab swung forward on the green light.

My time, she thought, my life — your money, knowing her unfairness in the same moment, knowing it was only his devotion, wanting the best for her, which deplored. Or, like her mother, did he mourn too the preening pride in the accomplished daughter, the long build-up, Juilliard, the feverish, relative-ridden Sunday afternoon recitals in Stengel's studio, the program at Town Hall, finally, with her name, no longer Eleanor Goldman, but Elly Gold, truncated hopefully, euphoniously for the professional life to come, that had already begun to be, thereafter, in the first small jobs, warm notices?

As the cab rounded the corner of Fifth, she saw two ballerinas walking together, unmistakable with their dark Psyche knots over their fichus, their sandaled feet angled outwards, the peculiar compensating tilt of their little strutting behinds. In that moment it was as if she had taken them all in at once, seen deep into their lives. There was a studio of them around the hall from Stengel's, and under the superficial differences the atmosphere in the two studios had been much the same: two tight, concentric worlds whose *aficionados* bickered and endlessly discussed in their separate argots, whose students, glowing with the serious work of creation, were like trajectories meeting at the burning curve of interest.

She looked at the cousins with a dislike close to envy, because they neither burned nor were consumed. They would never throw down the fixed cards. Conformity would protect them. They would marry for love if they could; if not, they would pick, prudently, a candidate who would never remove them from the life to which they were accustomed. Mentally they would never even leave Eighty-sixth Street, and their homes would be like their mothers', like her mother's, *bibelots* suave on the coffee tables, bonbon dishes full, but babies postponed until they could afford to have them born at Doctors Hospital. "After all the money Uncle Harry spent on her, too," they would say later in mutually confirming gossip. For to them she would simply have missed out on the putative glory of the prima donna; that it was the work she missed would be out of their ken.

The cab swung into the line of cars at the side entrance to Grand Central. Eleanor bent over the basket and took out the baby. "You take the basket, Dad." Then, as if forced by the motion of the cab, she reached over and thrust the bundle of baby onto Helene's narrow brown crepe lap, and held it there until Helene grasped it diffidently with her suede gloves.

"She isn't — she won't wet, will she?" said Helene.

A porter opened the door. Eleanor followed her mother and father out and then reached back into the cab. "I'll take her now." She stood there hugging the bundle, feeling it close, a round comforting cyst of love and possession.

Making her way through the snarled mess of traffic on the

curb, Aunt Ruth came and stood beside her. "Remember what I told you!" she called to the departing driver, wagging her finger at him.

"What did you tell him?" said Eleanor.

"Hah! What I told him!" Her aunt shrugged, the blunt Russian shrug of inevitability, her shrewd eyes ruminant over the outthrust chin, the spread hands. "Can I fix life? Life in Brooklyn on sixty dollars a week? I'm only a medical doctor!" She pushed her hat forward on her braids. "Here! Give me that baby!" She whipped the baby from Eleanor's grasp and held it with authority, looking speculatively at Eleanor. "Go on! Walk ahead with them!" She grinned. "Don't I make a fine nurse? Expensive, too!"

Down at the train, Eleanor stood at the door of the roomette while the other women, jammed inside, divided their ardor for the miniature between the baby and the telescoped comforts of the cubicle. At the end of the corridor, money and a pantomime of cordiality passed between her father and the car porter. Her father came back down the aisle, solid gray man, refuge of childhood, grown shorter than she. She stared down at his shoulder, rigid, her eyes unfocused, restraining herself from laying her head upon it.

"All taken care of," he said. "He's got the formula in the icebox and he'll take care of getting you off in the morning. Wish you could have stayed longer, darling." He pressed an envelope into her hand. "Buy yourself something. Or the baby." He patted her shoulder. "No . . . now never mind now. This is between you and me."

"Guess we better say good-by, dear," said her mother, emerging from the roomette with the others. Doors slammed, passengers swirled around them. They kissed in a circle, nibbling and diffident.

Aunt Ruth did not kiss her, but took Eleanor's hands and looked at her, holding on to them. She felt her aunt's hands moving softly on her own. The cousins watched brightly.

"What's this, what's this?" said her aunt. She raised Eleanor's hands, first one, then the other, as if weighing them in a scale, rubbed her own strong, diagnostic thumb back and forth over Eleanor's right hand, looking down at it. They all looked down at it. It was noticeably more spatulate, coarser-skinned than the left, and the middle knuckles were thickened.

"So . . . ," said her aunt. "So-o . . . ," and her enveloping stare had in it that warmth, tinged with resignation, which she offered indiscriminately to cabmen, to nieces, to life. "So . . . , the 'rabbi's daughter' is washing dishes!" And she nodded, in requiem.

"Prescription?" said Eleanor, smiling wryly back.

"No prescription!" said her aunt. "In my office I see hundreds of girls like you. And there is no little pink pill to fit." She shrugged, and then whirled on the others. "Come. Come on." They were gone, in a last-minute flurry of ejaculations. As the train began to wheel past the platform, Eleanor caught a blurred glimpse of their faces, her parents and aunt in anxious trio, the two cousins neatly together.

People were still passing by the door of the roomette, and a woman in one group paused to admire the baby, frilly in the delicately lined basket, "Ah, look!" she cooed. "Sweet! How old is she?"

"Three months."

"It *is* a she?"

Eleanor nodded.

"Sweet!" the woman said again, shaking her head admiringly, and went on down the aisle. Now the picture was madonna-perfect, Eleanor knew — the harsh, tintype lighting centraled down on her and the child, glowing in the viscous paneling that was grained to look like wood, highlighted in the absurd plush-cum-metal fixtures of this sedulously planned manger. She shut the door.

The baby began to whimper. She made it comfortable for the night, diapering it quickly, clipping the pins in the square folds, raising the joined ankles in a routine that was like a jigging ballet of the fingers. Only after she had made herself ready for the night, hanging the dress quickly behind a curtain, after she had slipped the last prewarmed bottle out of its case and was holding the baby close as it fed, watching the three-cornered pulse of the soft spot winking in and out on the downy head — only then did she let herself look closely at her two hands.

The difference between them was not enough to attract casual notice, but enough, when once pointed out, for anyone to see. She remembered Stengel's strictures on practicing with the less able left one. "Don't think you can gloss over, Miss. It shows!" But that the scrubbing hand, the working hand, would really "show" was her first intimation that the daily makeshift could become cumulative, could leave its imprint on the flesh with a crude symbolism as dully real, as conventionally laughable, as the first wrinkle, the first gray hair.

She turned out the light and stared into the rushing dark. The physical change was nothing, she told herself, was easily repaired; what she feared almost to phrase was the death by postponement, the slow uneventful death of impulse. "Hundreds of girls like you," she thought, fearing for the first time the compromises that could arrive upon one unaware, not in the heroic renunciations, but erosive, gradual, in the slow chip-chipping of circumstance. Outside the window the hills of the Hudson Valley loomed and receded, rose up, piled, and slunk again into foothills. For a long time before she fell asleep she probed the dark for their withdrawing shapes, as if drama and purpose receded with them.

In the morning the porter roused her at six, returning an iced bottle of formula, and one warmed and made ready. She rose with a granular sense of return to the real, which lightened as she attended to the baby and dressed. Energized, she saw herself conquering whatever niche Dan had found for them, revitalizing the unknown house as she had other houses, with all the artifices of her New York chic, squeezing ragouts from the tiny salary spent cagily at the A & P, enjoying the baby instead of seeing her in the groggy focus of a thousand tasks. She saw herself caught up at odd hours in the old exaltation of practice, even if they had to hire a mute piano, line a room with cork. Nothing was impossible to the young, bogey-dispersing morning.

The station ran past the window, such a long one, sliding through the greasy lemon-colored lights, that she was almost afraid they were not going to stop, or that it was the wrong one, until she saw Dan's instantly known contour, jointed, thin, and his face, raised anxiously to the train windows with the vulnerability of people who do not know they are observed. She saw him for a minute as other passengers, brushing their teeth hastily in the washrooms, might look out and see him, a young man, interesting because he was alone on the platform, a nice young man in a thick jacket and heavy work pants, with a face full of willingness and anticipation. Who would get off for him?

As she waited in the jumble of baggage at the car's end, she warned herself that emotion was forever contriving toward moments which, when achieved, were not single and high as they ought to have been, but often splintered slowly — just walked away on the little centrifugal feet of detail. She remembered how she had mulled before their wedding night, how she had been unable to see beyond the single devouring picture of their two figures turning, turning toward one another. It had all happened, it had all been there, but memory could not recall it so, retaining instead, with the pedantic fidelity of some poet whose interminable listings recorded obliquely the face of the beloved but never invoked it, a whole rosary of irrelevancies, in the telling of which the two figures merged and were lost. Again she had the sense of life pushing her on by minute, imperceptible steps whose trend would not be discerned until it was too late, as the tide might encroach upon the late swimmer, making a sea of the sand he left behind.

"Dan!" she called. "Dan!"

He ran toward her. She wanted to run too, to leap out of the hemming baggage and fall against him, rejoined. Instead, she and the bags and the basket were jockeyed off the platform by the obsequious porter, and she found herself on the gray boards of the station, her feet still rocking with the leftover rhythm of the train, holding the basket clumsily between her and Dan, while the train washed off hoarsely behind them. He took the basket from her, set it down, and they clung and kissed, but in all that ragged movement, the moment subdivided and dispersed.

"Good Lord, how big she is!" he said, poking at the baby with a shy, awkward hand.

"Mmm. Tremendous!" They laughed together, looking down.

"Your shoes — what on earth?" she said. They were huge, laced to the ankle, the square tips inches high, like blocks of wood on the narrow clerkly feet she remembered.

"Safety shoes. You have to wear them around a foundry. Pretty handy if a casting drops on your toe."

"Very swagger." She smiled up at him, her throat full of all there was to tell — how, in the country, she had spoken to no one but the groceryman for so long that she had begun to monologue to the baby; how she had built up the first furnace fire piece by piece, crouching before it in awe and a sort of pride, hoping, as she shifted the damper chains, that she was pulling the right one; how the boy who was to mow the lawn had never come, and how at last she had taken a scythe to the knee-deep, insistent grass and then grimly, jaggedly, had mown. But now, seeing his face dented with fatigue, she saw too his grilling neophyte's day at the foundry, the evenings when he must have dragged hopefully through ads and houses, subjecting his worn wallet and male ingenuousness to the soiled witcheries of how many landlords, of how many narrow-faced householders tipping back in their porch chairs, patting tenderly at their bellies, who would suck at their teeth and look him over. "You permanent here, mister?" Ashamed of her city-bred heroisms, she said nothing.

"You look wonderful," he said. "Wonderful."

"Oh." She looked down. "A far cry from."

"I borrowed a car from one of the men, so we can go over in style." He swung the basket gaily under one arm. "Let's have breakfast first, though."

"Yes, let's." She was not eager to get to the house.

They breakfasted in a quick-lunch place on the pallid, smudged street where the car was parked, and she waited, drinking a second cup of coffee from a grainy white mug while Dan went back to the station to get the trunk. The mug had an indistinct blue V on it in the middle of a faded blue line running around the rim; it had probably come secondhand from somewhere else. The fork she had used had a faint brassiness showing through its nickel-colored tines and was marked "Hotel Ten Eyck, Albany," although this was not Albany. Even the restaurant, on whose white, baked look the people made gray transient blurs which slid and departed, had the familiar melancholy which pervaded such places because they were composed everywhere, in a hundred towns, of the same elements, but were never lingered in or personally known. This town would be like that too; one would be able to stand in the whirling center of the five-and-dime and fancy oneself in a score of other places where the streets had angled perhaps a little differently and the bank had been not opposite the post office, but a block down. There would not even be a need for fancy because, irretrievably here, one was still in all the resembling towns, and going along these streets one would catch oneself nodding to faces known surely, plumbed at a glance, since these were overtones of faces in all the other towns that had been and were to be.

They drove through the streets, which raised an expectation she knew to be doomed, but cherished until it should be dampened by knowledge. Small houses succeeded one another, gray, coffee-colored, a few white ones, many with two doors and two sets of steps.

"Marlborough Road," she said. "My God."

"Ours is Ravenswood Avenue."

"No!"

"Slicker!" he said. "Ah, darling, I can't believe you're here." His free arm tightened and she slid down on his shoulder. The car made a few more turns, stopped in the middle of a block, and was still.

The house, one of the white ones, had two close-set doors, but the two flights of steps were set at opposite ends of the ledge of porch, as if some craving for a privacy but doubtfully maintained within had leaked outside. Hereabouts, in houses with the cramped deadness of diagrams, was the special ugliness created by people who would keep themselves a toehold above the slums by the exercise of a terrible, ardent neatness which had erupted into the foolish or the grotesque — the two niggling paths in the common driveway, the large trellis arching pompously over nothing. On Sundays they would emerge, the fathers and mothers, dressed soberly, even threadbare, but dragging children outfitted like angelic visitants from the country of the rich, in poke bonnets and suitees of pink and mauve, larded triumphantly with fur.

As Dan bent over the lock of one of the doors, he seemed to her like a man warding off a blow.

"Is the gas on?" she said hurriedly. "I've got one more bottle."

He nodded. "It heats with gas, you know. That's why I took it. They have cheap natural gas up here." He pushed the door open, and the alien, anti-people smell of an empty house came out toward them.

"I know. You said. Wait till I tell you about me and the furnace in the other place." Her voice died away as, finally, they were inside.

He put the basket on the floor beside him. "Well," he said, "this am it."

"Why, there's the sofa!" she said. "It's so funny to see everything — just two days ago in Erie, and now here." Her hand delayed on the familiar pillows, as if on the shoulder of a friend. Then, although a glance had told her that no festoonings of the imagination were going to change this place, there was nothing to do but look.

The door-cluttered box in which they stood predicated a three-piece "suite" and no more. In the center of its mustard woodwork and a wallpaper like cold cereal, two contorted pedestals supported less the ceiling than the status of the room. Wedged in without hope of rearrangement, her own furniture had an air of outrage, like social workers who had come to rescue a hovel and had been confronted, instead, with the proud glare of mediocrity.

She returned the room's stare with an enmity of her own.

Soon I will get to know you the way a woman gets to know a house — where the baseboards are roughest, and in which corners the dust drifts — the way a person knows the blemishes of his own skin. But just now I am still free of you — still a visitor.

"Best I could do." The heavy shoes clumped, shifting.

"It'll be all right," she said. "You wait and see." She put her palms on his shoulders. "It just looked queer for a minute, with windows only on one side." She heard her own failing voice with dislike, quirked it up for him. "Half chick. That's what it is. Half-chick house!"

"Crazy!" But some of the strain left his face.

"Uh-huh, *Das Ewig Weibliche,* that's me!" She half pirouetted. "Dan!" she said. "Dan, where's the piano?"

"Back of you. We had to put it in the dinette. I thought we could eat in the living room anyway."

She opened the door. There it was, filling the box room, one corner jutting into the entry to the kitchenette. Tinny light, whitening down from a meager casement, was recorded feebly on its lustrous flanks. Morning and evening she would edge past it, with the gummy dishes and the clean. Immobile, in its cage, it faced her, a great dark harp lying on its side.

"Play something, for luck." Dan came up behind her, the baby bobbing on his shoulder.

She shook her head.

"Ah, come on." His free arm cinched the three of them in a circle, so that the baby participated in their kiss. The baby began to cry.

"See," she said. "We better feed her."

"I'll warm the bottle. Have to brush up on being a

father." He nudged his way through the opening. She heard him rummaging in a carton, then the clinking of a pot.

She opened the lid of the piano and struck the A, waiting until the tone had died away inside her, then struck a few more notes. The middle register had flattened first, as it always did. Sitting down on the stool, she looked into her lap as if it belonged to someone else. What was the piano doing here, this opulent shape of sound, five hundred miles from where it was the day before yesterday; what was she doing here, sitting in the lopped-off house, in the dress that had been her wedding dress, listening to the tinkle of a bottle against a pan? What was the mystery of distance — that it was not only geographical but clove through the map, into the heart?

She began to play, barely flexing her fingers, hearing the nails she had let grow slip and click on the keys. Then, thinking of the entities on the other side of the wall, she began to play softly, placating, as if she would woo them, the town, providence. She played a Beethoven andante with variations, then an adagio, seeing the Von Bülow footnotes before her: ". . . the ascending diminished fifth may be phrased, as it were, like a question, to which the succeeding bass figure may be regarded as the answer."

The movement finished but she did not go on to the scherzo. Closing the lid, she put her head down on her crossed arms. Often, on the fringes of concerts, there were little haunting crones of women who ran up afterward to horn in on the congratulatory shoptalk of the players. She

could see one of them now, batting her stiff claws together among her fluttering draperies, nodding eagerly for
notice: "I studied . . . I played too, you know . . . years
ago . . . with De Pachmann!"

So many variants of the same theme, she thought, so
many of them — the shriveled, talented women. Distance
has nothing to do with it; be honest — they are everywhere. Fifty-seventh Street is full of them. The women who
were once "at the League," who cannot keep themselves
from hanging the paintings, the promising *juvenilia*, on
their walls, but who flinch, deprecating, when one notices.
The quondam writers, chary of ridicule, who sometimes,
over wine, let themselves be persuaded into bringing out
a faded typescript, and to whom there is never anything to
say, because it is so surprisingly good, so fragmentary, and
was written — how long ago? She could still hear the light
insistent note of the A, thrumming unresolved, for herself,
and for all the other girls. A man, she thought jealously,
can be reasonably certain it was his talent which failed him,
but the women, for whom there are still so many excuses,
can never be so sure.

"You're tired." Dan returned, stood behind her.

She shook her head, staring into the shining case of the
piano, wishing that she could retreat into it somehow and
stay there huddled over its strings, like those recalcitrant
nymphs whom legend immured in their native wood or
water, but saved.

"I have to be back at the plant at eleven." He was smiling
uncertainly, balancing the baby and the bottle.

She put a finger against his cheek, traced the hollows under his eyes. "I'll soon fatten you up," she murmured, and held out her arms to receive the baby and the long, coping day.

"Won't you crush your dress? I can wait till you change."

"No." She heard her own voice, sugared viciously with wistfulness. "Once I change I'll be settled. As long as I keep it on . . . I'm still a visitor."

Silenced, he passed her the baby and the bottle.

This will have to stop, she thought. Or will the denied half of me persist, venomously arranging for the ruin of the other? She wanted to warn him standing there, trusting, in the devious shadow of her resentment.

The baby began to pedal its feet and cry, a long nagging ululation. She sprinkled a few warm drops of milk from the bottle on the back of her own hand. It was just right, the milk, but she sat on, holding the baby in her lap, while the drops cooled. Flexing the hand, she suddenly held it out gracefully, airily, regarding it.

"This one is still 'the rabbi's daughter,' " she said. Dan looked down at her, puzzled. She shook her head, smiling back at him, quizzical and false, and bending, pushed the nipple in the baby's mouth. At once it began to suck greedily, gazing back at her with the intent, agate eyes of satisfaction.

Little Did I Know

AT night, Florence has no tourists. All along the tables dotted in front of this particularly famous café, people sat close together in the half-light, musing, chatting — though it was midnight — in little infernos of talk that celebrated the hour. On the pavement before the tables an unending line of strollers repeated its themes; how many times, for instance, had there not seemed to pass the same pair of high-stepping, black-crepe-and-honey women — or were they girls? — the pout of their calves and pompadours drawn by the same dusky brush, between shoulder and chin always the same long, half-agonized line of throat? Both sitters and promenaders were alike in that each line thought itself audience to the other; for each, its side was the land of the living, the other side the stage.

"I must have been about your age, about nineteen"— the woman speaking, hidden in the shadows beyond the high-backed chair of her invisible vis-à-vis, either thought them both concealed, or did not care who saw or heard — "maybe nineteen and a half, for we were still counting our years in halves then. That gorgeous spring I spent whirling through first love with a boy named Ben. And planning to murder a professor named Tyng. You ever notice, incidentally, that 'gorgeous' has quite dropped out of the language? Must have gone during the depression; we all came out of those years so very stripped and staccato, cleansed of everything from fake Renaissance furniture to the acting style of Sir Henry Irving. And slang had to be just like the plays — short words, full of compasssion.

"Anyway . . . it was the spring of my junior or senior year. I'm not good about dates and time, and that goes for geography too; facts of when or where don't interest me. A person like me's memory is likely to be long, but schoolbook accuracy is seldom its forte. Right in the middle of a conversation, an experience, it goes on selecting, exaggerating, and what we're doomed to remember — believe me, *doomed* — is . . . Oh, well, not so much the facts as the *feeling*. . . .

"But that's just the sort of thing you have to keep in mind about people like us, about me . . . in what I seem to be going to tell you. Yes, I know you're interested, or you wouldn't have looked me up. Just remember, though, that even when we're at our quietest — and we can be quiet — words are our reflex. We spend our lives putting things into words."

Contrarily, before the voice began again — not with a sigh, for there seemed no sighs in this clear-thinking reed — there was a silence. And then the voice again.

"For instance, I'm willing to bet when you go back home you'll have a far better idea of where this terrace was in Florence, and of what we saw today at the galleries, than I — and I've been here before. How I'll remember, dunno — not till I sit down someday to write about it. And then maybe it'll turn into a dialogue between two women of different ages, sitting here watching the other unaccompanied women go by, and wondering which of the well-dressed ones are — see that ladylike one; she's a very well-known one — and pinning us all down in our separate terms."

The occupant of the chair opposite the speaker must have leaned forward, uncurling feet that had been tucked under, for there was now visible one pale slipper of uncertain color, of the kind known as "ballerinas" — a tentative, young shoe.

"Or," said the voice, "I might use *you* discovering Italy, turning you round and round, seeing you with Italy at your edges, or Italy vice versa — though I won't necessarily use what you told me happened between you and the boy in Stamford. . . . Hmm? No, of course I won't. If I'm lucky, you'll be true to life, that's all. Not necessarily true to yours. And I shan't apologize; the odds are I'll be in there too somewhere, on just as sharp a pin.

"Notice I'm not the least interested in what you'll remember. My way of talking's a habit I can't shake. Keep that in mind, won't you, that I warned you? For I've reached an age, you see, where I notice people try to undazzle the young. . . .

"Thank you, you're very sweet, but I'm almost forty-one. There are women who falsify their age and women who ask you to guess; I'm too old to be the first sort and not old enough to be the other. And if you think *that* remark has been made before — well, it has! Oh well, thanks. The hair's a tint of course, but at least I started out a real blonde. And we small-boned types wear better than average; I'll live till ninety and die of a broken hip. And of course nobody who *is* anybody fattens anymore. A social comment, that — maybe you'll use it someday when you use *me*.

"Anyway, there are at least a half dozen of us who might

be me. All of us have done enough to be looked up, the way you looked me up, all about forty, forty-five. All with at least two husbands too, although mine were better than most. A painter so handsome you wouldn't believe his work could deserve such success — until you saw it — and a banker of such charm that nobody minded his money. Too good to have let go, both of them. And of course *I* didn't, though they let me think so, right up to the end. Absolute opposites, those two men were, never even met; yet when they left, it was with the same parting words. . . .

"Don't flinch. You said you wanted to be one of us, didn't you? From the pieces you showed me, maybe you will be. That's why I'm telling you this. Get it straight, though — I loved them, and they me. My first used to say he'd *never* seen a woman as pretty and sexy as I was who was so tough to paint. Maybe you're thinking that's because one can't paint a verbal shimmer. But I don't talk very much with men actually, and I never talked at all in bed; I knew enough not to do that, even before I'd read about it. And I suppose it's not surprising they both made the same remark when they left — after all, they were both expressing the same thought. Of course, it wasn't my intelligence that bothered my husbands, though I'm grateful people think so. When asked, I take the line that the painter wouldn't cope — engage — with it, and I couldn't stand that. And that the banker wanted to promote it — and of course I couldn't stand *that* either. That's the line I take."

In the chair opposite, the one pale slipper, twisting, was joined in its movement by the other; then both were set flat, suggesting that the chair's occupant was nervously in thrall.

"So," said the voice quickly, "at last, back to that spring.

Couldn't do without the preamble, though; you'll see why, if you haven't begun to already. In fact, because you're so smart — so much smarter than I was at your age — I'll even give you the key to it all, though I expect it'll sound like kitchen-maid stuff to your collegiate ear. *That spring was the last spring she really lived.* Sorry, this is one of those. What I call 'little did I know' stories. Anyway — in case I made you uneasy back there — I still haven't *quite* murdered Professor Tyng.

"William Tenney Tyng. He was a tall, monk-skulled Anglophile, who opened his Daily Theme course every year by reciting 'The policeman's lot is not a happy one.' In private life he was known to be writing an epic poem. He hated to see the student eye in a fine frenzy rolling, and his highest accolade — I never got it — was to put 'Neat but not gaudy' on modest little themes about cats. I suppose his real trouble was he wanted to be teaching young Oxonians, not second-generation American girls who were floundering in a tumescent passion for the language and spoke it mostly in the accents of the Midwest or the Bronx. And I suppose I should feel sorry for him, now that I know he directed his irony at us only because he didn't dare direct it at the sublime. But I can't. Oh, I've used him, now and then, as people like me will use, over and over, those who have humiliated them, and I once said he didn't 'teach the young idea how to shoot,' as the quote says; he *shot* it, wherever, green and trembling, it arose. Let that stand.

"For you see, I'd set myself to handing in poems as themes. Five a week we had to hand in — and almost always I was his target. And I was drunk on language, the way you see kids get on jazz at Birdland. I ran all over the pasture, wondering how I could ever eat all the books there were; I was out of my mind with delight at what some people had been able to do to the world with words. And the words! I collected them in all shapes and sizes, and hung them like bangles in my mind. To this day I've never seen a snaffle, but I remember sitting for hours once wondering what made it twinkle — twinkle — on the page; a lot of those double-consonant words do it. Lots of times I never even knew how the words sounded out loud, and I rarely looked up the meanings — the words simply hung up there, waiting. It wasn't a bad way, really; you don't have much of value to say at that age; what can anybody do but hang up the words and wait?

"So, of course, I was a setup for Tyng. If he hated, as he did, the exotic in Sir Thomas Browne, De Quincey, Coleridge, what couldn't he do with me! 'Now, let us see what our young wallower in the beauties of English literature has for us today! Hmm, a sonnet: "Let me touch the terrace of the dream, /Soft set foot upon the fragile stair . . ." Hmm. I'm rather a stupid man. Perhaps the author will explain this to me. Most of the terraces I'm familiar with happen to be in Scarsdale.'

"I might have cut his classes — we had free cuts — but I found I couldn't; I had to sit there, in defense of I didn't quite know what. He wasn't just preaching against excess; I knew that. He was saying that all ardor, aspiration, was a disgrace.

"When I was most sunk, I started reading detective stories. Dostoevski and Baudelaire were too much for me; in their company I didn't need Tyng to tell me I was a serf. I don't know how the idea of writing a theme in which a professor was safely murdered merged with the idea of murdering a professor — maybe because the plot was so close to hand. During vacations Tyng had us mail themes to him with a self-addressed envelope enclosed for their return. He was a bachelor with no secretary, and the themes always came back marked in his own crabbed script. If one could find a strong poison to put under the flap of the return envelope — a delaying poison, of course, which wouldn't be fatal until the envelope was safely away in the mail — then 'twere done. Of course, one would have to gamble that Tyng didn't use a sponge.

"You laugh; I don't blame you. I would too, if I didn't know how close I came to the deed. I scared myself, because I knew the intense way I brooded on it wasn't normal. And I had a girl friend whose father ran an untidy, neglected drugstore; we often stopped by of an afternoon and made sodas for ourselves. I found myself one day looking up poisons in the pharmacopoeia, and I tried to reassure myself by recalling that, no matter how many times I'd read *Crime and Punishment*, I'd always hoped that Raskolnikov *wouldn't*. Still, why had I avoided the school library and gone to the city one downtown?

"Then, one day when Tyng stood up to dismiss me after having been particularly vicious to me in the conference hour, he said: 'Easter vacation coming up. Such a strain on poets. Perhaps you might curb your *élan* a little, during the Lenten season. Try not to drink quite so deep of the Pierian spring. Otherwise ——' Then he shook his head, licked the flap of an envelope he'd been fiddling with, and set it on the desk, as if for me to see. REPORTS, it said. RETURN to REGISTRAR.

"I walked out of there holding my breath, but not because I was worried about the mark. I'd done the work, and for all its spotty precocity it wasn't the kind he could openly give an F or D; what he'd do would be to purge me with mediocrity as he'd done last term, cupping my overheated blood with a C.

"No, what made me shiver, even as I passed girls in light jerseys on the tennis courts, was that licked envelope, falling to my lot as the knowledge that the old woman would be alone fell to Raskolnikov's. Dozens of times I'd heard someone say, as we left Tyng's course in Room 242: 'Couldn't you *kill* him?' Now I realized that what I'd been saying to myself was 'I *could* kill him.' I don't know what I'd have gone on to do if Ben Bijur hadn't been waiting for me at the dorm — as he usually was, in spite of his best resolutions, almost every other day. He was waiting, though, in one of those chintzy cubicles they made boys wait in. In a way it was like being saved from jumping out the bedroom window by happening to be in the center of the room, thinking about it, when the plaster falls.

"I suppose I was in love with Ben Bijur because he was the first man who'd ever touched me. In later years I've seen words swarm about an idea just the way my spongy dreams clustered about Ben Bijur's head the minute he put a hand on me and I let it stay. At home, in Ontario, I'd been a day student at a convent in a small town; the few local boys I'd known had been as fair and corn-fed as myself. This boy was enticingly swart and world-weary; he had splendid teeth and a fine baritone, but at twenty-two he was already losing his hair — a fact that he and I both looked upon, at the time, as an effect of character — and he was fond of saying quietly that he had been born old.

"The sad truth was that he had; his was one of those temperaments that never, even in senility, take the form of youth. At twenty-two, he was already a disappointed man, sulking at authority instead of flying at its eyes, carrying his hypersensitivity around with him the way a would-be suicide carries a knife — hoping to hurt himself. Even his frustrations seemed secondhand, as if he'd got them only through reading of Prufrock and Leopold Bloom. But at the time I was much impressed by the experiences at which Ben hinted — though he was, no doubt, as virginal as I — and when he repeated his fantasies of affairs with older women, I smoothed his poor, shedding scalp in awe. He was a word collector too, and used to tell me mournfully that he was afraid he was already putting life into footnotes without ever having enjoyed the text. Whereas, he used to say, there was something about me, young as I was, which marked me for the success that would pass him by. Sometimes he drew little word pictures of how, when ten years had passed, I would open the door of my penthouse and find him fainting on the doorstep, his feet wrapped up in burlap bags.

"Ben called me four or five times a week and dropped by during the day, but he would never make a date ahead, and he had a way of not phoning on Saturday night — this was to preserve his freedom and keep me from knowing where I stood. Marriage was never mentioned, of course — he was getting his Ph.D. on an allowance from his father — but neither of us saw anybody else. Nights when he hadn't called, I hung near the phone in agony; when he did call, and we went somewhere to neck, it often ended with me crying like mad on his shoulder — I didn't know why. Sadness interested him, and he treated mine with great deference, kissing me with a kind of scientific respect and muttering words like *Sehnsucht* into my ear. The farthest he'd ever gone was to lean against my blouse and quote into it, but this seemed to me very far.

"I'd never told Ben about Tyng, and I didn't this time; I was in such a high state of dejection I hardly noticed him. He'd got me out of the cubicle, bought us both hot dogs, and walked me to our favorite stretch along the river, before I realized that he was hanging on to my arm and looking at me with a humility I'd seen on the faces of young husbands walking their pregnant wives.

"I wasn't noticing *him*, you see; it must have been clear to him that I was swept up in some powerful emotion that was bigger than I. And for people like — well, like Ben — the sight of another person in the throes, divorced from reason, offering a breast for the eagles to pick at and so on, has an attraction just as strong as sex. That's why lots of times you'll see a weak man or an ugly woman with an entourage otherwise hard to explain; it's because they have this talent for letting life blow through them, for seeming to be swept away. And the people who hang around them don't even hope to get into the act; all they ask is to get close enough to be shaken a little themselves — something like kissing the Pope's ring, or being touched by the king for pox.

"Of course, there's another, simpler explanation for the way Ben acted — that he thought I was thinking of some other boy. Whichever it was, between it and the evening, he was done for.

"It *was* a gorgeous evening, one of those butterfly-blue ones. Every once in a while the river gave a little shantung wrinkle and then lay still; there was one sailboat low in the foreground, like Whistler's signature. Behind us, the windows of the Alpha Delt house were open, but there was nobody in them; everybody was off for the Easter holidays. Ben knew the grad student who acted as janitor in exchange for an apartment in the basement, an older man who was doing some kind of endless project on the Risorgimento and went off now and then with the merchant marine, until he had enough funds for another go at research. His door was always unlocked, and we'd been there once or twice alone. That evening there was a note tacked to the door: 'Back next Wednesday at eighteen hours.'

"Ben led me inside, murmuring, 'Say something, darling; you look so sad. I've never seen you look so sad!' By this time I wasn't, of course — he'd never called me darling before, and I knew that for him words spoke much louder than action — but I had the sense to hold my tongue and keep my sad expression, and on a young skin I suppose the wish to murder and the wish to love look much the same.

"He took off my dress, and the sight of me in my long cotton slip sent him down on one knee, his arms flung wide; it was a pose like the gallants in those slightly shady, illustrated editions of *Mademoiselle de Maupin* or the *Heptameron* — both of which Ben had. I was in an odd rig for seduction; there was a fashion on then for Oxford glasses, silver-rimmed ones that snapped open like lorgnettes, and mine hung down over my chest on a chain. My shoes were much too sedate for me too — terribly long, pointed ones, like dachshunds' muzzles — and my stockings, heavy gunmetal silk, were rolled. Despite all this, we were able to lose our heads. Or at least we thought we had — this generation can have no idea of the innocence of mine. When we left the apartment, I was under the confused impression that I had been seduced — an assumption that wasn't corrected until two years later, when I was. Ben must have been under the same misapprehension, because he insisted on taking me back to the dorm, ten blocks away, in a cab. And on the way he asked me for a date — for Saturday night.

"And when Saturday night came, he surprised me by taking me to the Baxter. Unlike the campus joints where we'd always gone for Coke or coffee, the Hotel Baxter was downtown, dull and semiofficial; couples went there dutifully the minute they got engaged, for a splurge a la carte. Poor Ben! It was only his way of saying that if necessary he'd do right by me, but I was as insulted as if he'd bought the ring without asking me. It seemed humiliating that only sin had got me to the Baxter — and besides, I wasn't dressed for it.

"To this day those starlight-roof places always make me think of babies born out of wedlock, for of course that's what was on Ben's mind. He ordered Alexanders — in those days that's what you started girls drinking on — and when I said mine made me feel positively sick he turned white, not knowing I'd said it only because at home in Ontario my grandfather had taught us early to disdain anything but Scotch. 'What — what about *Banjo?*' he said.

"Banjo was one of those terrible whimsies that lovers

have, like those letters beginning 'Dear Poodles . . .' that
stockbrokers always seem to get held up for; you and your
Stamford boy probably shared something of the same. Ben
was always plying me with anecdotes I didn't yet know
were cliché, and once — after he'd told me how Isadora
Duncan wrote Bernard Shaw suggesting what a paragon
any child of theirs would be — we'd spent an afternoon
concocting a paragon of our own. It was to have Ben's teeth,
my hair, and — since this was still a very feminist era —
both our brains. We'd dubbed it Ben-Jo, corrupted in time
to Banjo.

"And for some reason that wasn't clear to me at the Baxter, his choosing that way to ask me infuriated me. Why
did he always have to remove himself from everything,
from the most important things, by putting them into
quotes!

"'Oh you!' I said. 'You're so literary you make me spit!'
Then I stood up, burst into tears, and we went home.

"Extraordinary, isn't it? There it was, a warning out of
my own mouth, and I passed it by, the way you can speed
to your death right past a warning from Burma-Shave.

"During the next few weeks Ben scarcely left my side.
Vacation was well under way, but by this time I was glad I
hadn't had the money to go home; I couldn't have borne
being at home feeling like Hardy's Tess. Day after day
went by and — it must have been nervous strain or self-
hypnosis — I still couldn't assure Ben we weren't going to
have a baby. Luckily I had term papers to do, and Ben had
his thesis; we spent most of our time in the library or walking by the river, holding hands numbly but not kissing. I
was finding out how the world both heightens and darkens

under a single, consuming anxiety; normality goes on rattling around you, and your trouble is like a goiter in your gullet that no one else can see. Ben and I couldn't bear to be out of each other's sight; it was such a relief to be with someone who *knew*. At the same time, I couldn't help feeling a certain excitement at being one with several heroines of history. Once, when we were down by the river, I referred darkly to *An American Tragedy* and, to my surprise, Ben gave me a dreadful look and dropped my hand. It hadn't occurred to me until then that he might be having heroic feelings of his own. I wasn't afraid of them, but I was rather miffed at the idea of his enjoying them, and for the first time I wondered whether it would be a bore to marry someone whose reference books were the same as mine.

"Meanwhile, I'd forgotten all about Professor Tyng. Then, the last night before school began again, I remembered I hadn't sent him my ration of themes. I'd enough back poems to choose from, and after Ben and I had parted, I sat up until three retyping them. As I slugged them out I kept thinking of how I might never have been in the situation I was in, if it hadn't been for Tyng. When I'd finished, I went down the hall to wash out some underwear, and in the bathroom I saw the bottle of stuff the maids used for the drains. It was marked POISON in large, navy-blue letters.

"I picked it up and read the fine print on the label: *Antidote: Drink teaspoon or more of magnesia, chalk, whiting or simple wall plaster — or small pieces of soap softened in water — in milk, or raw egg.* Quite a rhythm the first phrases had, each with its feminine ending, then that nice little dactyl: *or raw egg*. Neat, but not gaudy. I went back for the envelope I'd addressed to myself, carefully used an old toothbrush to paint some of the stuff from the bottle onto the underside of the flap, carried the envelope back to my room, and set it on the blotter to dry. I never once thought of using the poison on myself. Indeed, I had never felt more surgingly alive, and for the first time in days I fell asleep like a lamb.

"And the next morning I discovered I wasn't going to have Banjo after all. The world immediately lost that intent, outlined look and went back to being its usual astigmatic blur; I'd never before felt how glorious the ordinary was. Ben had a nine-o'clock in philosophy; I raced over there to tell him.

"The elevator in Philosophy Hall was one of those old-fashioned wire-cage ones that held only about six people. I'd squeezed in and faced the door before I saw that Professor Tyng was one of the six, his height looming over us all. I must have looked wild. My hair was tousled, and I'd just remembered the envelope on my blotter in my room.

" 'Ah, good morning, Miss — er,' he said. He had a very commanding voice. And you know that conscious stillness people have in elevators. 'Tell me,' he said. 'Have you quite deserted poetry?'

"The elevator girl, an old university hand, closed the door softly and waited; she knew as well as I did that he hadn't finished. I lowered my eyes, but I could feel the mass smile all around me.

" 'Ah, well,' said Tyng, 'I always say that one's poetry is a solace to oneself and a nuisance to one's friends.'

"That elevator must have been the slowest in the city; it rose in exact time with the blood in my ears. I didn't answer Tyng and I didn't look him in the face. I just stared at the cords in his neck. Someday I'll murder you, I thought, but not with poison. No, I'll remember what you taught me, that only irony is safe. Just you go on talking, and someday I'll murder you — with words. Some day I'll hang you by the neck with them, until you are *alive*.

"Classes were already on, but I got Ben out of his; he was an awful color and kept saying, 'What is it? What is it?' out of the side of his mouth as we went down the hall. When we got outside on the steps, I told him. At that moment, all I felt was a horrible, female embarrassment at having to tell him.

" 'It's Banjo,' I said. 'He isn't.'

"The most peculiar expression crossed his face. There was relief there first, of course, but then something else took its place. Regret after catharsis is the only way I can describe it — the way people's faces sometimes look when they come out of the theater after a wonderfully harrowing play.

"I didn't understand it until later that afternoon, when we were sitting quietly together over a Coke, in the rear of the soda parlor.

" 'You know,' Ben said, 'when we were so worried, back there . . . Nevertheless that was *living*, though, wasn't it? That was real.'

"I knew what he meant, of course; I'd seen the world shift that morning too. But to *say* it, to put it into . . . maybe even while it was all going on . . . or even before! Poor footnoter, I thought, poor self-murderer. At the same time I shrank back from the table, from him — the way one leans away from someone with a bad cold.

" 'I'm alive!' I said. 'I'm *still* alive.' I stood up. 'Afraid I've got to run,' I said. And I ran.

"The minute I got back to my room I sat down and wrote him a letter saying I didn't want to see him again. I didn't understand quite why yet myself, so I lied and said I was in love with another man.

"Two weeks later, Ben came to see me; I suppose he thought it just another dodge to bring him to his knees. Anyway, that's just what he did — went down on his knees again, without even saying hello first, and asked me to marry him. Later he told a friend of mine that from the way I'd refused him — I *knew* I hadn't been sad enough — it was clear I'd never be a woman of the world. I haven't seen him since, but now and then I hear he's around somewhere, technically alive. I sure don't want to see him. Little does he know the very particular way he could crow over me — fainting on my doorstep or not, with or without his feet in those burlap bags. . . ."

An intensity of silence reigned now, a contest of quiet in which the speaker herself must have been wondering if she was to be allowed to get away with it like that — or whether the girl across from her was going to let her know that she was not.

We can be quiet too, the silence said now. People like us . . .

"What?" Was the voice relieved at not being let off? "Don't mumble so. . . . Ah, you want to know what it was — what both my husbands said when they left. Now, really! The listener ought to do some of the work. I've been telling you, actually, all the way along. OK, guess, then. Don't be shy; go on, try.

"Oh. You think it was more or less what I said to Ben — just before I ran? That's very clever of you; you're a very clever girl. That would be a twist, wouldn't it? You've *got* talent, no doubt about it. Well, I shan't say, but you listen now. You listen very carefully.

"After I'd sealed that letter to Ben and put it into the mail slot in the hall, I came back to my room. The envelope for Tyng, stained brown and shriveled, was lying where I'd left it. I picked it up, rolled it in some tissue from an old stocking box, and threw it into the basket. Then I went to the window and leaned on the sill. It was the holy time, a beautiful evening. A dusky wind was blowing, and the west was the color of a peach. I could feel the cold touch of the pearls at my throat, the warm cuddle of the jersey I'd just thrust my arms into; I thought I could even feel the lovely tickle of the blood running in my veins. It was spring, and my whole future was opening up again, full of oysters, music, lovers. A few foghorns were sounding on the river, and I wondered idly whether I would ever be able to set down exactly the emotion that sound always called up in me — as I had tried and failed to do so many times before.

"And after a while, as I leaned there, the words came, began to shimmer and hang in the air about me. There they were, armies of them, ready to be made into ropes for necks, ready for lovers to be put into, husbands, life. They danced in my mind like wild ponies that moved only to my command, with hooves sharp enough to kill, but forelocks meek enough to me.

"It had been a day. All in one day I'd found out I wasn't going to have Banjo, marry Ben, poison Tyng. It had been a day full enough for anyone. Except me — and perhaps you. . . ."

Was she leaning forward? The voice was low now, farther back in its own mists than it had ever been, yet near enough for the quick of any ear.

"So I sat down at the desk again — what I wrote was published the next year. The world stretched all before me that evening, in profuse strains of unpremeditated — life. But I left the window, and began to write about it. . . ."

No, it was the girl, leaning back, away, now stealthily rising. For a moment the figure stayed, a series of soft, dark ellipses lapsing to that poised, no longer tentative shoe. Then it ran. On the edge of the promenade it halted; then the wind, or a gesture of its own, tossed back the free-swinging hair and it was gone.

Did the voice know it was alone now? Had it planned it that way — to be left addressing that perfect, illimitable audience of one? For it was still speaking.

"So I left the window," it said, "and began to write about it. Beginning with the word 'I.'"

The Gulf Between

TURNING their backs on the last fanfare of sunset over the river, Hester and Kinny Elkin, side by side, skated laboriously up the hill, toward Broadway. Ordinarily, they would have kept a more cynical distance between elder sister, gone past twelve, and younger brother, but today, in the sprawling ten-room apartment which had always been their home, the shape of things was being dismantled for removal to a sunless five rooms in the rear of the building, on the same floor. Neither was anxious to return to the uneasy place now revealing itself as no longer theirs.

For Hester, it was hard to believe that things back there would not be the same as they always had been at this hour, full of the settled ease of women from both sides of the family, dropped in for their afternoon coffee — white tablecloth, the cake plates with angels painted in their centers, cocoa for the children; to think of all this as not there to return to was like trying to hold in the ear two separate chords. Surely, when Josie, the maid, opened the door, her hectic look, both shaky and starched, would advise that the usual assortment of aunts and cousins was already sitting within, the two clans politely opposed as always, joined only on such topics as their common opinion of the Elkin maid. Silent on the things that mattered, they would be exchanging crumbs of agreement on whatever didn't, across a little neutral sea where innuendo slid like eels; this was what adult "politeness" was. For the half-grown like herself, its counterpart was: to say, and appear to see — nothing. To rest on the yet safer swells of a bottom dark was what it had been to be a child.

Meanwhile, in the exchanges that had gone on above, the women of her father's family, no longer rich or beautiful, older than her mother by the same some twenty years as her father, had always held the upper hand. Allied closest to the household by their dependence on Mr. Elkin, on a business just large enough to be sometimes in important difficulties — and until recently, by their deference to her grandmother, the six-months-dead monarch of them all — something they owned had nevertheless kept them always the winners over her mother, and the family on her mother's side.

Her mother's people, when momentarily left to themselves, to the thriftier gossip of their own smaller businesses, households, smaller everything, could often be heard to cluck a "T-t-t"ing disapproval of this quality, whatever it was, and — in the dead waits between those murmurs — to admire. As later comers to the country from a rural part of Bavaria, after fifty years here the men of her mother's people still had fingers thick at the root, the women a strong village-sense of disaster. The Elkin lot, born in the laziest part of America, sometimes wasted time, and, on occasion, fortune — they knew how to waste. Her mother's people were drawn daily to the comfort of it. Yet, if on those slow afternoons the Elkin women still triumphed, it was by the others' subservience to what could be seen most clearly in the two lots of unframed family pictures, enemies tumbled together in an old breakfront's drawer. For while her mother's aunts and cousins were always taken at their rigid best, in full-length, marble-finish studies by Sarony — within the faultless drape of ballgown or teagown, perhaps gazing at a long dinner-ring on a forefinger, or all unconscious of a highlighted necklace — the Elkin women (by her mother's comment and Hester's own admission *"foolish* dressers") were invariably shown to the waist only, emerging from that photographer's mist which gave predominance to the face, these upheld proudly, as if something within, flowering from neck to brain, to hair wild or confined but always luxuriant, said, "We are more than we *have*. We *are*."

Ordinarily, Hester held both sides under advisement, and knew too well their estimate of her — on her case, as on Josie's, they were joined. Today, however, she wished against hope that she might find them all there taking their comfort, however divided, as a sign to her that it was still there to take.

"Race you down the new sidewalk," said Kinny.

On Fort Washington Avenue, the top of the hill, they wheeled sideways and rested, wheezing for breath. Before them, seen through the sidestreet, the blinding bronze of the high windows on Broadway flashed like cymbals turning away from light, faded floor by floor, and went out. Here, the pebbly tan stone of the pavement changed to a smooth concrete, more dangerous to skate on, of a kind which slid under wheel silkily with a high, singing sound.

"Ah no. Let's not race." Mostly, she let him win, not minding. It was the contest she minded. "Want to go down holding on, no knee-bend?" This was more dangerous, but a trial against the hill, not between themselves. But Kinny whizzed ahead, crouched over, shouting low insults to that imaginary combatant boys always carried with them, and disappeared around the corner.

Knees straight, Hester, insolently balanced, clasped her hands in front of her and rolled down the hill after him, almost persuading herself that while she was immovable, the houses were being pulled past her on an endless tape. As she flew around the corner, another change in the sidewalk threw her forward, almost on her face, but she saved herself with a few hacking steps and slid down on the stoop of the corner house, pulling at her skate-straps with fingers numbed by the darkening air. During the moment in which she had turned the corner, the dusk had become palpable, in that gradual surge she could never arrest with her eyes.

"Got the key?" Kinny swooped down beside her. She dug in her pocket and handed him the skate-key. From the curls of its broken, grayish string, a nickel fell out and rang on pavement speckled here with particles which would prickle into silver when the streetlights went on.

"Buy us a chocolate bar?" said Kinny.

"Let's get a frank, and divvy." Recently, her greediness had shifted away from the sweet to the sour. Herder's frankfurters were served with a gamboge daub of mustard and a fringe of kraut. She picked up the nickel and spun it on the stone.

"It'll go down the grating," he said.

"We could fish for it with a magnet." Between the dim edges of a pervading sadness, she saw herself looking for the magnet in the topsy-turviness of her room as she had left it this noon, bureaus emptied, bed stacked against the wall. Over her protests, the rattan toy chest had had its contents dumped into a carton, and had been packed with linen.

She kicked off her skates and stood up. Swinging them by the thongs, she walked with him back up the hill on the Broadway side, feeling deflated and set down, her legs wobbling oddly on the suddenly still ground. All the interstices of the city were deepening with a chill color and people were passing quietly, their faces softened and reminiscent. She had a feeling that if she wet her finger and drew it through the air it would return stained with the dye of dusk. Even Mr. Mishnun, the old stationer, emerging from his stunted store to shoo out a small boy who had been snitching candy, paused for a minute, looking upward, abashed by the dumb, violet passage of the city into evening.

Herder's dairy was warm, insulated from the transit of the day by bright, particolored shelves and a smell of breads and peppercorns. She and Kinny ate slowly, served absent-mindedly by Mrs. Herder, who stood behind the counter, talking to a woman customer.

"*Ja*, that's the way it is," said Mrs. Herder, nodding her head, smoothing together the crumbs and poppyseed on the cutting-board with her raw, boiled-looking hand. "That's the way it is."

"Comes to everybody," said the customer, grasping her bundle stolidly before her.

"Sooner or later," said Mrs. Herder, still nodding. Looking

past them all into some mournful middle distance, she let out her breath in a long, confirming sigh. The nodding, like the last effort of a pendulum, quivered into ever shorter arcs, and stopped.

To Hester, reared among so many elderly and middle-aged of both clans, these sad conversational cul-de-sacs of the grown had a sound both familiar and elusive. Though unable to define that central foreboding which, lurking always under the oblique talk, was acknowledged and propitiated by all, she recognized that some hovering bird, whether of time or death or doom, circled over all the grown, and that even while they confirmed its presence with this rallying of voices, each hoped secretly that this would forestall the moment when it would notice *him* in his cranny of safety — and pounce. Each said to himself cannily: "As long as I can speak of it to others, it is not yet here for me."

Kinny had darted out of the store, but Hester, chewing speculatively, stared at Mrs. Herder until the woman looked at her, inquiring.

"Th — thank-you," muttered Hester, and left, closing the door behind her with special care. As she stepped outside, the streetlamps went on, with their succinct "Now!" and the night was there.

Far down the block of small old-fashioned shops still bare of neon, Kinny was peering into the weakly shining window of Pachmann's jewelry store on the corner.

"Looka here!" he called.

She ran over and knelt down next to him. Against the darkened inner store, a single bulb in the window burned over rows of square cards spaced on humped-up red velvet, each card holding a single, gleaming nugget of lure. Behind them, a row of clocks told various times of day, all false except the large moving one in the center.

"Keep looking in sideways!" Kinny knelt in front of the window, hooking an arm around its side. She knelt beside him. Through the glass corner she saw, refracted and shimmering, an airy replica of the whole display. Kinny's plump fingers, exaggeratedly curved, poised over a man's watch, dipped recklessly through it and alighted again, this time over a heart-shaped locket with an enameled American flag blowing in its center.

"Want it?" Pinching the image between thumb and forefinger, he tossed it to her. She cupped herself, almost expecting to receive it. The locket remained. If she shifted her head past a certain angle of interception, it blinked out, on. In the window, the real one had a solidity almost disappointing. Outside it, very slightly double-edged, the other bloomed with an added shine. She stretched out her own hand.

"Holy mackerel!" said Kinny. "Will we catch it. Look at the time!"

Grabbing up their skates, they scurried down a sidestreet into the doorway of their own apartment house. Its lobby had the deserted look of dinnertime. Far above them, the elevator hummed dispiritedly in its shaft, and came to a jouncing stop on some upper floor.

"Wish we didn't have to go in." Kinny kicked glumly at the carpet, his ruddy face chapfallen and aggrieved under the jaundiced tan light here. Against the Oriental splendor of the lobby, his rotund figure in its eternally battered clothes caught at her sympathy like a humpty-dumpty version of herself.

"Let's walk up," he said at last.

Toiling up the stairs in front of him, past each hallway, past the closed doors of the Shoemakers, the Levys, the Kings and other residents she didn't know, she visualized each family, unchanged and comfortable at their white-draped tables, behind them the maids serving unhurriedly from massive sideboards on which were ranged, permanent and secure, the tureens, the candlesticks, and the bowls of fruit. Only at the Elkins' was there distortion beyond repair but not yet complete, where one groped absently for the displaced chair, the drawer that had been "there," caught in the painful torsion of contexts not quite yet shelved into retrospect.

"Wish we were leaving here altogether," she said, as they reached their own floor. She put a hesitant hand on the bell.

"Go on. Ring." Kinny goosed her from behind. Swatting back at him, she was almost comforted, half convinced that behind the door everything would be unchanged. At this hour, her father would open it, crying, "Good God in heaven, where have you two been!" and even before they got their jackets off, her mother's honing recitative against dirt would be at them to wash their hands. Hester, once she had slipped into the place at table marked by her own dented napkin ring, could then slip into her childish role of culprit permanently arraigned, in which, comfortably abraded, suspended between her parents' personalities, she could regress into her revery with herself.

Hester's mother opened the door. Against the grotto

welter of piled goods looming behind, her head, covered with a white hand-towel pinned at the nape, had an air of heroic resolve, coifed for the worst, like the nurses in the recruiting posters that hung on the walls at school. She snapped on a brighter light, as if to bring their lateness into surer focus.

"No consideration whatsoever — none at all!" she said. She shook her head, but her face had an abstracted look, and her hands, whose usual cleanliness in the midst of the grimiest task was to Hester half an attractive riddle, half a reproof, were dusty, and left a smear on the head-towel as she patted it irritably.

"Daddy home?" asked Kinny.

"Yes," said his mother, looking at him sternly. "He came home early." Kinny slipped past her.

"Where's Josie?" asked Hester.

"You know Josie went to find a room in Yorkville," said her mother. "We won't have room for a sleep-in girl in the new place. Can't you get it through your head that — ?" She broke off in the long, exasperated sigh that was almost a reversion to her native *Ach!* To Hester, her mother's face, formed with a beautiful inevitability of bone, much resembled a head of Venus in her Latin book, or would have, had it not had also the lurking contour of a plaintiveness everready for some disaster sure to occur. Tonight, as always in time of crisis, her face had the triumphant look of disaster confirmed.

For a moment she looked at Hester significantly, searchingly, in a way she had been doing of late, as if the fact of Hester's being a girl, almost a woman, should make her rise to the stature of confidante. Then, as if what she saw only confirmed the impossibility of such an alliance, she threw up her hands and went back toward the kitchen.

Hester went into the dining room. The polished table shone emptily.

" 'Lo, darlin'," said her father. He was bent over the sideboard, tussling ineffectually with the rope bound around its doors in preparation for tomorrow's moving. He patted her absently.

"Where's the sherry, Hattie?" he called.

"Sherry!" Her mother reappeared at the door to the kitchen. Behind her Kinny lounged, already munching a roll. "Table's set in the kitchen!"

They had never before eaten in the kitchen, too small except for scratch lunches or the solitary, clinking meals of the maid.

"Look, Hattie," said her father, frowning, "why don't I take you all out to dinner?"

"Hmmph!" said her mother. "Delmonico's, perhaps?"

"No need to grind it in," said her father, flushing. His teasing account of their engagement dinner — when he, the so much older man of the world, had found himself at Delmonico's with a girl made tipsy by one glass of champagne — was known to all.

Mrs. Elkin sat down at the kitchen table and began to eat. Set out were cheeses still in their cartons, cold sliced meat in butcher's paper, everything haphazard and at odds, as if she, normally a heckler of maidservants on table detail, would forcibly show her family the ugly pattern of tomorrow.

"Get your father some coffee," she said to Hester, pointing to the pot on the stove.

Hester waited, warily. Her mother had a habit of urging her to activity, then stopping Hester's clumsy efforts midway.

"Let the child alone. I'll get my own coffee," said Mr. Elkin, his face red and miserable above a dandified tie and jeweled stickpin which contrasted queerly with the stove, as he bent over it.

"Time they realized their father isn't a millionaire," said Mrs. Elkin. Kinny had already tiptoed away.

"Now look here, Hattie . . ." said her father. He brought his cup to the table and sat down, sighing. Suave afterdinner raconteur, he was completely lacking in the vocabulary of dissension. Time after time, Hester had watched his superior verbal elegancies falter and dry up before the thrust of his wife's homely tongue.

"They've never wanted for anything so far," he said. "And neither have you."

Mrs. Elkin's lips tightened. Large-boned, calmly moving, she had few fussy mannerisms; it was only her voice that fiddled. "Time they realized their father isn't getting any younger."

In the silence, the percolator chortled on the stove. The cup shook in her father's veined hand, and a drop fell on the waxy linen of his cuff, near the lion-headed cuff link. He set the cup carefully down.

Mrs. Elkin's cheekbones and eyelids reddened. It was known that she lived among dreamers who could be educated for the worst only by her savage ability to get under the skins of those she loved and must awaken; this was why she was compelled first to tear down the self-deceptive veils with which they wreathed themselves and only afterwards could poultice up their wounds with love — with the tray of food brought to the banished boy, the party dress ironed to perfection for the girl who had given up going. All this was known, and now contemplated.

"Joe . . ." said Mrs. Elkin.

Raising his head, Mr. Elkin took off his noseglasses and rubbed at the inflamed prints on either side of his nose. The luxuriant up-twirl of his dated moustache looked suddenly too jaunty for his exposed face. He slid the glasses into their case, which popped shut with a snap, and looked at his wife. "For God's sake, Hattie, take that damn *thing* off your head!"

Hester, chewing a soda cracker, heard the sound twice: the dry champing heard by their ears, at the same time magnified in her head. Wishing that she might melt from the room, carrying her dislocation with her, she started to tiptoe from the table.

"Come on back now, and finish your supper," said her father, pleading, anxious as always to deny the ugly breach, to cover it over with the kindness that bled from him steadily, that he could never learn not to expect in return.

"I'm sleepy." With the word, sleep fell on her like a blow. Seeing herself already in a mound of blankets, folded impervious in her own arms until tomorrow, she turned away, down the hall to the haven of her room.

She was halfway into the darkened room before she felt the alteration in it. Thinking that some of the furniture must be ranged along the walls, she moved confidently toward the island of the bed. Her body passed through its image with the ease of fingers passing through a locket. A moving reflection from the headlights of a car going by in the street below traveled up one wall, trembled watery on the ceiling, and swept down the other wall, leaving a scene fanned into an instant's being, and gone. There was nothing in the room.

She turned and ran back down the hall, cracking a knee against chairs stacked one-over-one, as in restaurants in the early morning. Lumpily shrouded barriers extended all along the walls. She felt down them, hunting a cream-colored bed with insets of caning, the surely discoverable scallop-shape of a mirror, the bureau with bow-front swagged in wooden roses, in a pattern that was like a silly friend.

Holding onto the bruised knee, she limped back to the kitchen and confronted her mother. "Where's all my room?" she said.

"What?" asked her father, puzzled.

"Oh, I meant to tell you," answered her mother, composedly. "You're to sleep in Grandma's old room. Your nightgown's there on the bed."

"But where's my furniture?"

"You're to have Grandma's old set. You know that. How many bedrooms do you think we'll have, in the new place!"

"What have you done with the child's things!" Mr. Elkin's face was already shrunken with a warding-off of the answer.

Mrs. Elkin hesitated, but only to trim a note of triumph. "I — sold them."

"I might know you'd start dramatizing," he said. "There's no need to act as if we were down to our last penny."

"Are we?" Hester saw it, copper-bright and final, in the linted seam of his pocket.

For answer, he pulled her onto his lap. She perched

there awkwardly, conscious of her gangling legs, but savoring the old position of comfort. "Almost forgot what I brought you from downtown," he said, fumbling in the pocket and bringing out two objects. "New compass for Kinny," he said, laying it on the table. "And this — for you." In his palm, he held a tiny, round vanity-case of translucent, rosy enamel and painted flowers, its cover fitted with a golden latch.

"Fellow brought it in the office," he mumbled.

Mrs. Elkin, for whom the extras of life had a touch of the dissolute, turned her head aside.

Hester, warming the pink gift in her hand, stood up between them, in the gap between her mother, immovable on her plateau of the practical, and her father, wavering curator of intangibles he could assert but not protect. All this was known, yet there was never a way to say it. She aligned her free hand on his shoulder. "I wonder what I would have looked like," she said in a hard voice, "if you had not married her." Without waiting for an answer to what was not after all a question, she left the kitchen again.

In the doorway of her room, she stopped, waiting until she could half-see in the darkness. The nude walls poured from ceiling to floor, regarding her. Refracted in her mind, she saw the room as it had been, its objects spaced with the exact ruler of remembrance but already blurred with the double-edge of the past. Wading carefully into its center, she set the gift down on the bare floor. She knelt over it a moment. Then she walked out and closed the door.

In her grandmother's room, she flipped the light switch

on and off just long enough to see the odd note of her own sprigged flannel gown on the huge bed. The room, shrouded in dust-covers since its owner's death, had the reserve of disuse. Ordinarily Hester would have tried the locks of the trunks which held the vestees of *broderie anglaise* and the threadlace shawls, and run a scuttling finger through bureau drawers still full of passementerie rejected by the raiding relatives six months ago. Tonight, she had begun to understand the mechanics of desecration. She stepped out of her clothes and into the nightdress, feeling as strange here as on the one night she had spent in the hospital. Crouched down under the comforter, she gripped her ankles with her hands. Burrowing her head into the blackness between her knees, listening to the purling of her own breath, she slept.

Sometime during the night she woke, her heart hammering up from a dream in which two hands, smooth, anonymous and huge, emerging wrist upward from mist, wrestled with one another, the great fingers twining in silent, marble struggle. From beneath a coverlet of stone, she waited for the mushrooming spaces of the dream to settle and ebb. Through the open door of the bathroom connecting with her parents' bedroom, she heard their voices, locked and vying.

"No!" said her mother, in a whisper as long-drawn as a scream. "I won't let you have it. What should be kept for your own children. To let it go down the family drain, like all the rest."

"By God," said her father's voice, "how would you have it,

except for me? How many women are there who can buy ten thousand dollars' worth of stock out of their household allowance?"

"Sixteen years," said her mother, still in that shuddering whisper. "Licking their backsides. Being the *Ausländer*. Being the responsible one. Carrying the bedpans to your mother, so your sisters could visit, and drink cream. . . . And the miles and miles of fine words, of fine *feelings* that the Elkins have such a talent for — as long as someone else underwrites them . . . Someone crass — like me."

"No one asked you to martyr yourself. Who do you think I work for, if not for you and the children?"

"For anyone who gets to you first with a few cheap words to make you feel big Ike. For anyone who will say 'dear Joe.'"

"Now listen, Hattie —"

"You corrupt people," said her mother, her voice rising. "Because you are too weak to refuse them."

"For the last time . . ."

"No!" said her mother. "Not this time," the words pulling from her as if she spun them one by one from a pit of resolve. "Not if you go down on your knees."

"God, what kind of woman are you, to make a man abase himself so? Over *money*," said her father, his voice ratchety and breathy.

"Family of leeches, leeches," intoned her mother. "Sister Flora's husband can't get a job in anyone else's business, but dear Joe will give him one. Sister Amy can't live with her rotter of a husband, but she can talk about his aristocratic Leesburg connections, as long as dear Joe will help her out. And the bookkeeper you won't accuse of stealing from you, because he is your sister-in-law's brother. Even your brother's widow, that low Irish, complaining about the settlement you gave her. What was he but a shoe sales-man until he brought her from Chicago, and dear Joe gave him the factory to manage. Fine manager."

"Leave the dead alone!" Her father's voice had an empty sound. There was a pause, in which the edges of silence rubbed together.

"Ask the dead for your collateral," said her mother.

From beneath the stone coverlet, Hester heard that last, faceless word sink into the quiet. After a time, someone shut the connecting door.

In the hollow of the bed, the dream waited to grow again. With an effort, she pushed up the rim of stone, and slipped out of bed. Dragging after her the comforter, suddenly light and threatless in her hand, she felt her way down the corridor to Kinny's room. Always in a state of embattled flux, even packing day had scarcely dislodged it from the norm, and its shadows had the clutter of homeliness.

She sat on the edge of his bed and drew the comforter around her, nestling toward him, feeling him warm and insensate beside her, smelling of boy-sweat and grubbi-ness, and infinitely removed. From behind them, the moil-ing quarrel between her parents pierced through her, past her, into the world beyond. All of it had been known, but she could now see, as never before, the exact angle of its interception. On the one side stood her mother, the deny-ing one, the unraveler of other people's façades, but resolute and forceful by her very lack of some dimension; on the other side stood her father, made weak by his aware-ness of others, carrying like a phylactery the burden of his kindliness. And flawed with their difference, she felt herself falling endlessly, soundlessly, in the gulf between.

On Kinny's shoulder, rounded in sleep, a lozenge of light wavered. She put out her hand hopefully, but she had lost the trick of playing with such semblances. She tried to cry, but could not summon that childish scald. Though she could not name the bird now hovering, she knew its nature. Slowly the bird descended, and chose. She began to weep the sparse, grudging tears of the grown.

Songs My Mother Taught Me

SOME ten years ago when I was for the first time in London — when, as a rather elderly innocent abroad, I was for the first time *any*where outside New York City except Rochester, Elmira, Binghamton, the Eastern Shore, a few summer resorts in New England and, at the age of twelve, Asbury Park, New Jersey — I attended a semi-diplomatic dinner party at which, after we had all drunk considerable amounts of several delightful wines, one of the ladies present suddenly peeled off her blouse.

Since the other guests, though moist and perfervid, were still upright in their chairs and conversation, the incident caused, even in that imperturbable company, a certain silence. Chitchat, suddenly quenched, faded off into one of those pauses where isolated sentences stand out sharply. The man on my left, whom I had placed tentatively as either a connoisseur of heraldry or a baiter of Americans, had been lecturing me on the purity of lineage maintained by German nobility up to the last war. "Where else," he had just inquired, "can one find, even now, a person whose line shows sixteen quarterings?" Then he stopped short, as if contradicted by circumstance. Headily I reassured myself that quite without knowing it — and in the first week too — I must have scaled one of those dizzily international heights of society so often promised the provincial: a set so patrician that queens had no legs, emperors might be clothed exactly as they said they were, and ladies appeared in their quarterings without shame.

She was an exceedingly pretty young woman of about twenty-five with masses of blond hair arranged ingénue, and a pair of truly enormous blue eyes swimming in some Venus-lymph, clear natural nacre in which a man, or indeed any onlooker, might well sink. Words like "truly" came inevitably to mind as one regarded them. As I did so, they spilled over pellucidly. Casting a reproachful look at her partner (later it was understood that he had dared her), turning down the corners of a lovely mouth rosied with wine and — though one hated to think it — stupidity, she gazed at us, clutching the discarded portion of her costume, then hung her head and let fall on her lavishly ruffled *broderie anglaise* corselet two neatly schooled tears.

"Why, Lady Catherine!" our host said at once, and rising, he went round the table to her and poured her more wine, murmuring what I thought to be "How very sporting!" and capping it with — as he raised his own glass — "Bravo!"

Other gentlemen took up the plaudit. Lady Catherine, shyly consoled, raised her head, and I remembered her patronymic, ducally familiar even to me: one of her ancestresses, whom she was said to resemble, had been a wife of Henry the Eighth. From her round eyes two more pearls dropped, but this time surely with retrospective art — I wondered whether Henry, watching her ancestress' head fall, might not have thought to himself, "None of my other wives looked that good upside down."

What happened next I can only recount, not explain. It is true that, while we were only fourteen at table, the number of empty bottles ranged testimonially behind us must have totaled more than twice that. I have a vague impression that the male applause may have attained an ethnic intensity. Also that our host, bending over Lady Catherine, was assuring her that she looked smashing, and rather more respectable than the portrait of his grandmother as lady in waiting to Queen Alexandra. And that she, though retaining a disconsolate posture, was looking smug. What I know for sure is that when I next glanced at our hostess — a bishop's daughter — she too had peeled.

"She's upset the gravy boat, Mother!" I murmured delightedly, but of course no one paid any attention to me, or would have understood the reference if they had. No one there was likely to have heard of Mrs. Potter Palmer, much less of my mother. I shall shortly explain — for the benefit of readers who, although they may have caught the allusion to American social history, cannot possibly know anything of mine. But first let me complete the *mise en scène* of a moment in which were to be brought home to me all the old saws of my girlhood — a moment of truth in which, across so much water and over the ten years of my mother's sojourn in Mrs. Grundy's heaven, I could at last exclaim to her, "Mother, you were right!"

Of the seven women at table, six, including myself, were wearing the version of the currently fashionable (and easily doffable) "separates" known as "evening sweaters." There was nothing coincidental about this; the best houses were cold, even for London; rationing was still on and the English were burning an ineffectual sludge called, with their usual talent, "nutty slack." The one exception to the sweaters was also the only one of the others who was neither chic nor pretty, a vast, untidy woman opposite me — Frau Ewig, a noted anthropologist, recently returned from Sierra Leone — whose dress, showing so many possible means of separation that the eye was unable to choose the probable, looked somewhat as if, in order to appear in it at the party, she had first chopped several natives up. She, like the rest of us, had forgotten Lady Catherine in the sight of our hostess, who sat revealed, with the air of a prioress who had removed her wimple, in a rock-pink, ten-guinea model by Berlé.

In the silence that followed I heard the clink of crystal — the gentlemen, according to their needs and natures, were either taking another drink or putting down the one they had. A muted cry of protest was heard — from Lady Catherine. I could have seconded it — for another reason. For glancing round at the other ladies, I sensed something infinitely feminine glissade from eye to eye. In prescience I closed mine. When I opened them, what I saw confirmed it. Every remaining lady — except the anthropologist and the American — had the upper part of her costume in her hand.

Now there was nothing essentially risky in the tableau before us: a number of ladies sitting, modestly swan-necked, in their foundations, is a sight familiar to every window-shopper. Besides, the temperature being what it was, I thought I could discern, between various lacy interstices, the fuzzier-than-flesh-tone of what Debenham & Freebody's (where I bought one the next morning) called a vest. No, the riskiness is often in the eye of the beholder. And this composite eye, twelve times magnified and stern as that of a nudist group eyeing the indecency of a visitor's

clothing, was now fixed on my pied vis-à-vis and on me.
Leave me there now, while we make our way back — by
gravy boat and a sneaky trail of safety pins — to my mother.
We shall return.

Moral instruction by moral illustration has long since disappeared from the training of the young. Metaphor itself is
considered untrustworthy — likely to weaken the facts of
what already is a pretty slippery reality — and every
good parent knows that the parable is too "punitive" by far.
My childhood was full of them, from boogieman to Bun-
yan, my parents belonging to a generation still very sure of
its facts. And my mother's specialty was what might be
called the "social" allegory. Obvious in design, single in
target, it was part of the process by which she hoped to
transform the unpromising grub at that very moment
scratching its knee-scabs in front of her into something
pretty and marriageable, destined to preside, with some of
her own graces and others she aspired to, at a table even
more elaborate than her own.

Under a codex possibly marked "Accidents, Dinner" —
for, as will be seen, a good proportion of my mother's tales
revolved on accident — reposed Mrs. Potter Palmer. Famous arbiter of bygone Chicago society, she may be the
model for performances slightly more rarefied than the one
I know her for — as for me, I see her only in the attitude of
one. Eternally she presides at her exalted dinner table,
from whose foot, in the worm's-eye view of my mother's
imagination, she is all but obscured by the gravy boat suited
to her station — to my mind about twice the size of our
largest tureen. In her historic moment she knows noth-

ing of us, but all is open to posterity — hovering above her now like helicopters, like damsel flies, we see all. Then it happens. Far down the length of the gilt-encrusted table — exactly center I make it for drama — a guest jars a servingman's wrist. A great gout of gravy erupts on the cloth.

My mother pauses; I return her look of high seriousness. Extrasensory perception or what you will, with not a word said between us, our images of that cloth are the same. As a superb embroiderer, my mother's chef d'oeuvre is her banquet cloth. Loaded with eyelet, scallop, punchwork, Valenciennes, fringe and insertion, lying even now on its cardboard cylinder between sheets of preservative blue paper, five years in the making, never used and none like it in the world — yet there on that august table, with a terrible brown blot on its middle, lies its twin.

The guest hangs his head, and no wonder. In unavoidable *frisson* the other guests, well-bred as they are, avert theirs. We gloat over the dreadful moment, knowing rescue is nigh. Mrs. Palmer, whose eagle eye — exactly like my mother's at her half-yearly dinner parties — sees everything while appearing to register nothing, pauses for a fraction in her elegant conversation. Then she makes her gesture — irreparable and immortal. I see her elbow, plump, white and shapely, a noble *fin-de-siècle* elbow suited to its duty, not covered with chicken-skin like mine. Carefully careless as Réjane, no doubt chatting gaily the while, she has swept it outward. Hail Mrs. Palmer, heroic hostess, who, in the imitation that is the ultimate of good manners, is seen now to have overturned, on that cloth, the tureen!

With years of reflection, this tale of my mother's, like another even more pertinent, came to have as many holes in

it as the cloth had eyelets. Was it quite the thing to be so
exemplary so publicly? Wouldn't the real acme of taste have
been not to notice — had the guest felt better, or worse? It
came to me that Mrs. Palmer's manner might someday
merit the same comment as her money: too much of it. As
a matter of fact, if they were being served by footmen,
what was the tureen doing in front of her at all?

But at eleven or so, yes, moral illustration, when taken literally, can be dangerous. We were a family of many guests
and many, though infrequently regal, dinners at which,
since our household was small, I was often allowed up.
Time went by while I waited for someone to have his accident, so that I might pridefully watch my mother's aristocratic amends. For months we seemed to feed no one but
aunts and uncles; I knew my mother too well to think she
would waste that sort of high style on them. But at last one
of our guests obliged. He was a Dr. Nettel, fresh from a
twenty-year stint in Egypt, who had once been one of my
mother's suitors — perhaps it was my father's still sardonic
eye on him that caused him to drop a fork into a vegetable
dish that splattered wide.

To me, seated at my mother's left, all augured well; the
cloth was damask only, but the vegetable was beet. I
looked at my mother expectantly; when she did nothing I
nudged her, pointing to the service dish of beets which,
since it was maid's night out and we were short of footmen, reposed, family-style, in front of her. "Don't be ridiculous," she whispered, her lips sealed, her gaze on the horizon.

I had just been through my eighth-grade graduation —
"Into thy hands we give the torch"— the noblesse of our
house, it would seem, rested with me. I crooked my sharp

elbow, bending my hand backward from the wrist as if it held a little pinch of something, meanwhile elegantly averting my head, as if to chitchat, toward Dr. Nettel, but since I could think of nothing to say I remained thus, bas-relief — perhaps he thought I was assuming an Egyptian pose just for him. "Stiff neck?" said my father. My mother, knowing better, grabbed for the elbow; absorbed in the mental picture, profile, of myself, I jumped at the touch; between us we upset the ice pitcher. Diversion was thus created, though not as symmetrically as it would have been via beet. Later, before I went to bed, I was whacked. "Because you are so smart," said my mother between whacks, "and because you are absolutely unteachable." She was wrong. I had just learned for sure what I had always suspected— that we were irretrievably middle-class.

Meanwhile, allegory still pursued me, though from another corner. Other girls my age were becoming women, flirts, sirens — at least girls — without trouble, and some avidly; it was my mother's cross that I had to be nagged there inch by recalcitrant inch. Daintiness, my mother said, was its essence; once a woman's daintiness got through to a man, all consummations devoutly to be wished for — such as a trousseau of one's own triple-monogrammed tea napkins — soon followed. To me the word was "daindee," as our German cook crooned it — "Oooh, so daindee!" over anything fancy — and as she looked on her day off, a clumsy veil of white obscuring everything human, excess of starch in the blouse, powder on the neck, fish-net gloves on her honest, corned-beef hands. To me even a bath was an assault on one's boundaries. Cleanliness was hypocrisy, dirt "sincere." Still the other ethic followed me, ruthlessly inserted in my ear along with the morning and evening soapings, and always with some elaboration peculiar to my mother — witness her *divertissement* on the Safety Pin.

I belong to the tail end of the button-traumaed generation. The embarrassments of the zipper-reared are quite otherwise — gaps in the memory or the metal, a fear of being locked in. We lived in the opposite fear of — the very words still have a blush and a hush to them — things "dropping down." Camisoles, panties and petticoats, even when snapped or hook-and-eyed, still required ceaseless vigilance with the needle — and thread was fallible, not nylon. Hence the reign of the safety pin, now used only by cleaners and babies. But the protocol of its use was strict. Emergency supply was always in the purse — in my mother's a chain of small gold ones. In case of "accident" one retired somewhere — to the washroom at Wanamaker's for instance — pinned "things up" and rushed home in a pink state of guilt, praying all the while that one would not be knocked down by a car on the way. For the core of the ethic — known, as I found later, to almost every girl of the era — was: "What if you are rushed suddenly to the hospital, and *there they discover* . . . ?" Dream sequences often finished the line, sung above our shrinking forms by hosts of angelic interns forever lost to us: "She has a safety pin in her corset cover!" The worst offense, of course, against sense as well as neatness, was to start the day or the journey already pinned. Hence my mother's variation, known to me always as The Gentleman from Philadelphia.

There was once a girl who was being courted by such

a gentleman. Whether there was any significance in his origin, I don't know; perhaps — this being the unsolicited detail with which my mother often fleshed a fable — he just was. *She* was one of those girls (not unknown to me) who were hastily groomed on the surface, at the cost of squalor below. For a while, said my mother, the girl was able to string him along. But, said she, you can't string them along forever — tangentially I tag this as the single allusion she had hitherto made to sex. There came a day when he arrived with intent to propose. It was a warm occasion; the girl was wearing a peekaboo blouse. Perhaps it was warm enough, say, for him to take off his driving goggles and lean closer. Anyway, just as he was about to declare . . . he saw that her shoulder strap was attached with — you've got it. The gentleman went back where he came from. And the girl is single yet.

It has since struck me that she was well shet of him. But at the time — "*Now* do you see?" said my mother, and I mumbled back, "Yerse."

In time of course, through vanity and the sly connivance of the lingerie-makers, I became as "insincere" as any other "nice" woman, although I never quite convinced my mother of it — or myself. "Fine feathers, *on top*," she would greet a new costume of mine, and sure enough, within minutes, some detail of my toilette would mysteriously unravel. I scrubbed my wedding ring until some of the stones fell out, because she had a habit of murmuring, "Dirty diamonds," whenever she saw an overdressed woman, and I primped for hospital visits as courtesans once may have for their levées. Wanamaker's was torn down, but I sometimes still dreamed myself in its washroom, standing there

with the top button gone from my skirt waistband, holding one gaunt safety pin the size of a salmon's skeleton.
And I never was able to look a real safety pin straight in
its fishy, faintly libidinous eye.

But now — let us return to that table in London. There
sit the ladies, swan-necked and squinting — what does the
slightly piscine shape of their squint remind me of? — at
me. And there, somewhat blue-lawed about the jowl at the
very plurality of the situation, sit the men. And me — what
I am thinking? As any woman would be, of course, of
what I have on underneath. Being me, I am also thinking
that I am after all the child, at last the Good Child of my
mother, and that the scene before me — although of course
she could not possibly countenance it — is the accident we
have both been waiting for all my life.

For what I happen to have on underneath — nothing
more of course, or less, than what thousands of Rockefeller
Center secretaries, window mannequins and ladies out for
the evening in Rochester, Elmira and Binghamton are
wearing — is a La Belle Hélène Walzette, Model 11A56,
Merrie Widowe Waiste Pincher, nyl. lce. blk., size 36 B. Edwardian it may be, but not in execution; no amount of wine
will unravel me — Seventh Avenue expertise has machine-
tooled me into it and only the hotel chambermaid will get
me out. And its modesty is unimpeachable — is, in fact,
Mail Order. This, indeed, is the accident. For what I had
ordered, in the rush before sailing, was the nyl. lce. wht. —
in the catalogue very daindee, with the usual sprig of
mashed ribbon rosebuds in the décolletage. But what I
have got on — sent me by one of the Eumenides brooding

darkly in Best's warehouse — is the blk. And the blk. is not with rosebuds. Blissfully I feel, beneath my sweater, what it *is* with — something to end traumas forever. There, centered where once button or pin might have resided, now lies, locking me in by patents pending, a round red cabochon glass jewel about the size of a nickel, La Belle Hélène's star ruby clasp, my order of merit, winking rosy and waiting for the light.

Or is it? Dare I? I look heavenward, seeing at first only a dim, brackish ceiling in St. John's Wood. But in dreams one does not always rehearse only one's anxieties. Sometimes one dreams that one is walking downtown in one's Walzette, and wakes to find — that one is. And better yet — that Mother is watching. Here I am then, I say upwards. See me now, met with my accident just as you warned me, but in what aristocratic company! There sits Lady Catherine, who began it, surrounded by several others who may well count sixteen quarterings, whatever that is, among them — if not all in one. There indeed sits Mrs. Potter Palmer modern version, with her sweater-tureen in her hand. Mother, you were right. And now, if I do what it appears I must, aren't I?

And immediately I am answered. Nothing supernatural about it — if there is any moral to this fable it is that, unbecoming as we at first may seem to our parents, in the end we become them. At the moment, however, I prefer to think that the suggestion comes via the grate, where a piece of nutty slack slides down, *sotto voce.* "Ask the lady across from you."

I do so. I tip Frau Ewig a wink toward the others, signaling, "Shall we join them?" She seems larger and redder

in the face than when I last noticed her. Not to my entire
surprise, she shakes her head imperceptibly. Under my
stare her face empurples further. *"Kann nicht!"* she murmurs at last, her lips unmoving; and as her seams stretch
with her breathing, I see why — underneath each of her
vast arms, a baleful, metallic winking-back. I look the
other way. More's the pity! Anthropologist or no, Frau
Ewig was reared in Vienna, and I think I know how. Like
me. But I don't see how I can help her. Still, a pity that in
every apotheosis of the Good Child, there must be, clinging
to the bottom of the ladder and gazing upward, a Bad.

My mother's face, up there like a decal through which I
can still see the ceiling, is of course seen by no one but me.
She has her eyes closed, knowing, as usual, just what I am
about to do, and she cannot quite approve this modern ending to her fable. But she also cannot help smiling. Listen to
them, the heavenly host, not of angels but of interns, as
leaning down with her in the center of the circle they sing
it to me *a cappella, con amore* . . . "and now we discover . . . she has got . . ." (soft Gilbertian surprise) "No!
She has not! . . . Yes she has, yes she *has,* she has got
. . ." (*pianissimo, ma non troppo*) "a roo-oo-ooo-ooooby
. . . yes, a ruby, ruby, ruby, ruby, ruby . . . a Star Ruby
in her corset cover!"

And as, with my hand bent a little at the wrist, I make
my gesture, all the company, leaning forward with interest
— and perhaps even my mother — may see that I have.

If You Don't
Want to Live
I Can't Help You

MARY PONTHUS stepped outside, into the straw-colored June morning, from the Fifth Avenue entrance of the bank to which, as administratrix of her nephew's trust fund, she had just paid her usual call when in New York. In her size forty-two Liberty lawn and wide ballibuntl hat set firmly on unshorn white hair, she might have just stepped off a veranda in Tuxedo or Newport, from one of those corners where the dowagers affixed themselves. It would be a corner, perhaps, smelling pleasantly of Morny bath soap and littered with playing cards, over which the pairs of blue-veined hands with the buffed, pale nails would pass expertly, pausing to dip now and then into the large Beauvais handbags — hallmarks of Parisian honeymoons of forty years ago — that had outlasted the husbands and were likely to outlast the owners as well.

In fact, Mrs. Ponthus had not been on such a veranda since a morning thirty years ago, when news had been brought to her there of the drowning of her husband and son, while out sailing, in a sudden squall. Her summers, ever since, had been spent in a house on the grounds of the New England college from which she had been married and to which, desperate for occupation, she had returned to teach within a year after the news. Occasionally the summers had varied, with trips abroad to university friends made through correspondence over the slowly published critiques which had earned her a more than scholarly repute during those years when, while teaching, she herself had learned — and had finally brought her the honorary doctorate of letters that she was to be awarded here later in the day.

She walked south on the Avenue, reluctant to complete her errand, to keep her appointment with her nephew and her old acquaintance, the doctor who had once more been summoned to treat him. If she thought, momentarily, of her husband now, it was not of the tall young man standing in the boat in that aura of lost grace and virility with which the youthfully dead surrounded themselves. His influence had survived in other ways — in the money he had left her, which had not only exempted her from that professorial scratching for preferment out of which so many theses were born, but had allowed also her dearest extravagance, the subsidizing, now and then, of some young person of promise. It had survived too in the income siphoned through her to the son of his dead brother — the nephew Paul she was on her way to see. And for him, Paul, it had been, blameless in itself, perhaps the touch of ruin.

She turned down Lexington Avenue toward the old brownstone where Paul and Helen, or rather just Paul now, had the second floor front. Here the street had a nineteenth-century breadth which only pointed up the dullness of the façades on each side, houses without resurrectible charm, that still had escaped the ash-can vibrancy of a slum. Really, Paul had a homing instinct for the vitiated, the in-between. In a city where almost no place was any longer this way depersonalized, he had managed to find a street still as inconclusive as himself, this byway that neither stank nor sparkled but merely had a look of having been turned, like the collar on an old shirt. Here and there the lights of some marginal enterprise glistened indeterminately on a parlor or a basement floor, but in general, if the street had any character at all, it was that of the "small private income." Opposite Paul's corner there was a vestigial hotel with an open-cage, curlicued elevator, potted plants at a few of its bays and a permanent roster of vintage guests. On her last visit she and Paul had breakfasted in its coffee shop in the company of two of these — an elderly theatrical relic in wing collar and Homburg, and a hennaed old woman, fussily ringed and dressed as if for some long-superannuated soirée, leading a dachshund that had settled down to sleep at once in an accustomed spot. The talkative waitress had fed scraps to the dog, provided saccharin for the old man and inquired about Paul's last X rays, performing a function that, in a brisker neighborhood, might have been that of the neighborhood bartender.

She walked up the steps of Paul's house and hunted for the bell in the dimness of the not quite seedy vestibule. It was no wonder that Paul had gravitated here, to the acquiescent company of other pensioners. In an age which demanded that money be accompanied by personal achievement, a young man with a small private income was an anachronism, unless he had other directives or talents that made the money only accessory. And for Paul, with neither, and a pensioner since twenty, it had indeed been the touch of ruin. He had made the grand tour of the talents in a time when the mere possession of the means to do so was already antiquated. He had dabbled in painting in southern Italy, had written for and later supported a magazine in the Village, where he had been pitilessly marked for exploitation by those with greater needs and coarser drives, and all along the way he had dabbled in women and in wine, not so much out of lechery or a compulsion to alcohol as because these were good ways to pass the time — and of time he had so much to pass. Whatever his inner lack, his lack of need had enlarged it, making of him, at thirty-six, a "young man" whose every activity, foredoomed to the dilettante, was tolerated by his elders and suspect to his contemporaries. So finally, as some might say, he had dabbled in disease. And if so, even here he had been lucklessly dilettante too, for tuberculosis, that mordant parlor wound which had once bred so many gallantly ethereal heroines and interesting, smoking-jacketed heroes among the people of his class of another day, had now become, for such people, almost an anachronism too.

Mrs. Ponthus pressed the bell next to the nameplate, which still said "Paul Ponthus — Helen Bonner," although Helen had been gone for months. Helen had been Paul's "girl," as Paul's crowd would have put it, in the way they had of using the catch phrases of juvenility to convince themselves that they had all remained indecorously young. In and out of Paul's life for years, although he had never married her — perhaps because he hadn't — Helen had been one of those girls who yearly assaulted the city with a junior-executive energy, quickly learning to adulterate their wheaten, somewhat craggy good looks with a certain uniformity of style — women who, if they did not conventionally marry or brilliantly succeed, plodded hopefully

along at the careers that kept them girls, often with some at-
tachment in the background, some man with a talent to be
nourished, a weakness to be supported, who always seemed
to be earning less money than they.

Mrs. Ponthus pressed the bell again, with a longer ring.
Paul usually slept late, in the drugged burrowing of a man
without pressing appointments. Poor Helen, she thought. To
her, at first, Paul's aimless round would have seemed Bo-
hemian, their illicit affair cosmopolitan. With the pitiable
eagerness of those who seek love she would have mistaken
for passion what might never have been much more than
the heightened sexuality of the man without a job; later,
too deeply entangled, she would have refused to face the
fact that Paul's variety of joblessness was for life. With
him she had gone through all the fantastic travail of the
woman's end of such an affair, his rebellions against possessiveness, his ego-driven nights out with other women, his
reluctance to give her any certainty except the abject one
of his return. And her Griselda devotion had had its re-
ward. For even as she became that background against
which he could most serviceably revolt, her lap had become the confessional in which his head felt most at home.
She had become that familiar woman who stands behind
the "artistic" man, patches up his vagaries and explains
him to a misunderstanding world — particularly, in Paul's
case, to those malicious ones who noted that Paul had all
the sufferings of the artistic personality without having anything to show for it. And finally, now that she had left him
— for he had always before done the leaving — she had
achieved wifely status at last, as the person by whom he

was most misunderstood. For now that she had found the will to leave him, they no longer said of her, "Poor Helen." "Poor Paul," they said now. Poor, poor Paul.

The buzzer rang suddenly, stopping before she had time to press in the door. Then it rang again, a long, sustained ring. She walked slowly up the stairs. Remember not to be disarmed this time, she told herself. Not this one time. He had never let her be the conventional aunt but had wooed her knowingly, as a confrere, drawing out her own susceptibility to that, attaching her to him with her own sticky, spidery thread. For, knowing so much about weakness, he disarmed people with his delicate appreciation of theirs, and before they knew it, like a child pressing his one grubby treasure into their hands, he had given them his own weakness to hold.

His hall door was open. She stepped inside and closed it. Dusty sunlight from the avenue ribbed the empty front room. Back of her, the high, sliding doors to the bedroom were almost completely closed.

"Helen!" said a bemused voice from behind the doors. "Helen?"

She bit her lip, already disarmed. "No, it's Mary, Paul," she said. "No, it's Mary."

She walked toward the doors, letting him hear her footfalls on the bare floor, waited, then slid the doors back.

He stared at her, raised up on one elbow in bed, the other hand still pressed near the buzzer, against the wall. Then recognition woke him and he dove back under the covers, so that she could only see the back of his head. "Don't look at me," he said, muffled. "Don't look at me for a minute."

She turned her back on him. After an interval she heard him get up and turn on the shower in the bathroom. She walked over to the window and looked out, feeling as if she were collaborating in the byplay of a child. This was his talent perhaps, that one could collaborate with him only on his own basis, drawn in a trice into his world of willful charm and egocentric fears, forgetting that this was a dangerous juggernaut of a child with the body and impulses of a man.

"Sorry, Mary. I had a rough night." He had come from behind her, putting his hands lightly on her shoulders and turning her around. She inclined her cheek, but he shook his head, stepping significantly back with the courtesy of his disease.

"Were you sick again?"

He twisted the towel he held. "No more than usual. As a matter of fact — I broke training. Went on a party."

"Oh. Oh, Paul!" She knew those parties, which he ferreted out with professional desperation, calling up all over town, hoping to catch all the other busy, busy people on the prong of some momentary idleness, persuading them to take time out with an ardor like that of a drunkard who feels better when others are drinking.

He shrugged and sawed the towel back and forth on his wet hair.

"Ought you to get your head wet like that?"

"Now, don't go auntie on me. You women — at bottom you're all nannies."

"So I've heard," she said. "Usually from some man who's looking for one."

"Touché," he said, sitting down rather too quickly in a

chair and smiling up at her. Certainly no special weakness appeared, Lombroso-like, in that face, in the wide brow, firmly jutting nose, the cheekbones joined to the square jaw by the long, concave dimple of his illness. How wrong we are, she thought, to believe that character always sneaks into the lineaments of a face. This is what people would call a strong face, whose strength was only sapped if you knew its age. Then, indeed, it seemed almost criminally young.

"Come on," he said, "take off your hat. Such a nice, sensible hat. Ah, I'm glad to see you, Mary." He stood up and lifted the hat lightly from her head, bent to set it on a table wooled with dust, blew futilely at the table and finally hung the hat on the finial of a chair that held a pile of clothing. "Sit down, if you can find a spot. And don't say I ought to have a woman in. I'm working on that. Hard."

"I've no such intentions, Paul." She felt suddenly weary and sat down.

"I know, I know," he said, hovering above her. "But don't declare them, whatever they are, till I've had coffee. Have you had breakfast?"

"Of course I've had breakfast."

"Of course," he said. "Such a sane, sensible hat!" His voice faded, and he had to sit down on the nearest chair. She started toward him, but he waved her back. "Not what you think. It's just a dirty old hangover."

They looked at each other from chair to chair. "You fool," she said. "You fool!"

"Ah, Mary, you *are* good for me," he said.

Here it comes, she thought. The sweet bait that works on any age, any sex. The terrible, tricksy intimacy of another's

need, saved up just for you. Thus is the thread spun —
and to any comer. "I'll make you coffee," she said.

She crossed the room and opened the folding shutters of
the kitchenette. Its sparse equipment, ranged stiffly, was
grimy with disuse. On the drainboard a dishcloth, frozen
into a contortion of days back, gave off an odor of mildew.

"Smell it?" he said. "The odor of celibacy. Varied by an
occasional woman — and an occasional mouse."

"Spare me the details," she said, her back to him.

"No, that's one of the reasons you are so good for me.
You and Helen. You're the lucky ones. You don't have to
be spared."

"We have our limits," she said. "Such as making coffee
when there is none." She picked up her bag. "I'll go get
some. You better stay to let Jamie in."

"He's not coming. He's washed his hands of me."

"But I spoke to him yesterday! Yesterday morning."

"So did I. Yesterday afternoon, in his office. He wanted
me to go back to that magic mountain of his. No, that's not
for me. What'll they do? Patch up the lesion in my chest?
So I can hang around a little longer, to rot of the one in
my head?"

"Paul." She sat down again, heavily. The handbag slid to
the floor. "Paul . . . what *is* for you?"

"You tell me." His short laugh turned into a cough. He
leaned forward and took her hands in his, staring at her
with the mesmeric shine of the devotee. "It's Helen. I
know that now. I haven't any shame about it. I'll turn
somersaults. I'll lie, I'll be honest, just so she comes back.
But she won't see me. I haven't even talked to her in five
months. I don't even know where she's living, and when I

call her office she's got them primed to say, 'Miss Bonner's not in.' 'Miss Bonner's not at her desk.' I've written, I've had friends badger her . . ." He sat back, closing his eyes. When he opened them again she saw that the shine in them was actually tears. "She let me lean on her for years," he said, in a voice almost without breath. "She got me into this straitjacket. Now she can damn well get me out of it."

For a moment she was rigid with anger, on the part of a woman she had never known well. "Perhaps she has other plans."

"No," he said. "I was her first. I'll be her last. Without me she doesn't feel the need. That's why she's afraid to see me, don't you see that?"

"I'd rather not tell you what I see."

"Oh, go on," he said, "tell me I'm a bastard. I don't know why I have such trouble getting people to believe it."

Because they see the real straitjacket, she thought — and know it in part for their own. Because, locked in yourself, you are to the nth degree that sad monstrosity which we are all in part. "No . . . you're not a bastard."

"No?" he said. "Sometimes my own cleverness sickens me. Your coming today — I was pretty sure Jamie had asked you to stop the money unless I went up to that place. And you know what I thought?" He gave her the intense, open stare of the man who, despairing of gulling one with lies, tries the truth. "I thought, all right, let them turn the house cat into the jungle. Then he'll really touch bottom. Then Helen will take him in." He gripped her hands again. His own were burning hot. "She'll listen to you. Just do that for me. Just get her to see me — see the spot I'm in. I'll take it from there."

She stood up, wrenching her hands away, and walked to the window. One of the shades was uneven. She straightened it without seeing it. "I wish to God the money'd been left to you in one sum. So you could have stood or fallen on it. As it is, I blame myself. For not stopping it. Years ago."

"Oh, let's face it, Mary. No matter what chances I'd have had — something's been left out. I can't manage. The best I can do is to cling to someone who can."

She turned from her view of the meager street in time to see him stand up, take a step toward her and falter with a look of surprise. "As now," he said. His knees buckled and he slid to the floor. She ran toward him. "Blankets . . ." he said through chattering teeth, but by the time she had torn them from the bed and helped him into a chair, the chill had subsided and his pajamas were dark with sweat. She went to the phone and dialed the doctor's number. When she had finished she sat down at Paul's side and put her hand on his forehead.

"He won't come." His whisper held a note of satisfaction. "He's given me up."

"He's coming right away. On his way to the hospital." After a few minutes she looked secretly at her watch, which said two. She was due at the university at three-thirty, robed and in her place for the procession.

"What's the time?"

"Two, Paul."

He nodded gravely, as if she had given him a fact of importance. "Helen used to say I watched the clock more than anyone she knew." He moved his head from side to side. His hurried breathing was like a pulse in the room. "You and Helen, most people, you get up in the morning, you go through the day — as if . . . there were a plan. Maybe you don't know what it is either, but you all act . . . *as if . . .*"

She found herself breathing with him as one did leaning over the feverish bodies of children. "Better not talk."

He rolled his head impatiently. "When I was a kid — I used to think grown people had some gimmick that kept them pushing through their days — it was a gimmick they had and I would get it too." He turned his head away from her and was silent. There fell between them that suspended communion of the sickroom, in which conversation was only a recitative against the forces of dark. Street noises crowded into the room, poignant with health. She raised her head and found him looking at her.

"What is it?" he said.

"That — ? A car. A truck."

"The gimmick," he said. "I meant the gimmick."

"Sh." She put her finger against her lips, with the ticlike smile with which one cajoled the sick. For if now, in his fever, he brought up truth like phlegm, there was no way to treat it except as fever.

The bell rang curtly, bringing an image of Jamie downstairs, grizzled hair, sandy face lively with impatience, feet shuffling in the way he had of always seeming to be treading water. His was a cathartic presence that comforted, not with calm but with the energy of an annoyance that barked peremptorily at the forces of ill: I won't have this. I simply won't have it. She walked the length of the room and leaned against the buzzer with a sigh of relief.

On her way back Paul caught at her hand. A blue smear

of beard on his upper lip and on the round of flesh under his chin gave him the culprit look of a boy long since too old to be told to wash.

"Call her," he said. "Promise."

She detached her hand, even flexed her white, wrinkled palm to show that it was still empty, still free. "Yes," she said, "I promise," and went to open the door.

Jamie stumped past her, dropped his bag on the floor near Paul and stood looking down at him. He bent, flipped back Paul's blankets and straightened up, still looking at him. Neither spoke.

She took up her post at the window again. Behind her the small, diagnostic clinkings went on, and she could hear the separate breathings that haunted a room at such times — the heavy intake of the patient, the quiet, judging respiration of the doctor, and her own breath, held. Then Jamie's voice, brusque at the phone, ordered an ambulance. He joined her at the window, lit a cigarette and puffed at it angrily. Behind them Paul seemed to doze. A Good Humor wagon went slowly down the street, pricking at the heat with its feeble icicle of sound, but no children came from the elderly doorways and it puttered on out of sight.

"There it is," said Jamie. He opened the window and motioned to the orderlies, who were drawing the stretcher from the ambulance.

"Pleurisy," said Paul's voice behind them. "Isn't it?" The doctor, shutting his bag, did not answer. "Where you taking me?"

"Lenox Hill. You'll need a tent."

"Is that routine?"

The doctor reddened. "I told you yesterday. Your condition's routine. But you seem to want to distinguish yourself by dying of it."

Paul's eyelids flickered. "I'm just like everyone else. I don't want to die." His voice tremored defiantly, like that of a man presenting doubtful credentials at a bank.

She put her hand on Jamie's arm. He was glowering at Paul as if they were enemies. "Maybe not," he said. "But if you don't want to live I can't help you."

There was a knock and a shuffling at the door. She opened it. "This it?" said one of the men, and with a joint, hard glance at Paul they pointed the litter inside. They moved quickly, two vacant-faced nullities, one that chewed, one that did not, and when they had finished, Paul, neatly cocooned in gray, was a nullity too. But as they swung him toward the door his hand came imperiously out of the gray cowl, and they paused, holding him slung between them, two indifferent caryatids, smelling faintly of dishwater and iodoform.

"Mary!"

"Yes, Paul. Yes, I will. Yes!"

His hand touched his smile, saluted, and let them bear him off. It was the gesture of a hero borne wounded from the field — but on the winning side.

She turned to find Jamie watching her as if he saw something telltale, symptomatic, in her. "Going uptown?" he said. "I'll drop you."

"I better find the key." She found it, in the pocket of the trousers collapsed on a chair. Holding it in her hand, she looked around the room, feeling that she must tidy it, but already its disorder had the subtle, irreparable flavor of desertion. *No one here by that name now. The policy has changed.* "How quick trouble is!" she murmured, and for a moment felt the thirty-year-old shock turn and reverberate in her heart. They left, locking the door behind them.

In the car he offered her a cigarette like a truce. "Will he be all right?" she asked.

He was silent until they had pulled away from the curb and were part of the traffic. "They're hard to kill."

"People with TB?"

He shook his head. "Sometimes I think I could go down the file in my office and tick them off. The ones who want to, and the ones who don't."

"Die, you mean?"

"No. Live."

She ground out her cigarette. "Pretty subtle distinction."

"No!" He kept his eyes on the traffic. "We're all subject to the normal human damnations. We're all 'afraid to die.'" His voice was a faint, savage mimicry of Paul's. "But these people make their whole lives a deathbed — and expect the rest of us to gather round." He flicked her a glance. "And we do. We do."

"I can think of a lot of books, a lot of art, came out of some of them."

"No. Those were the ones who wanted to live most of all. Wasn't Keats a lunger? And still able to make such an expression of interest in the world?" His voice softened. "No — that's the crux of it — when you see that."

"Oh, if Paul had found his talent . . ."

He grunted. "I oughtn't have blown up at Paul yesterday — but the man in before him was an old patient, a graduate of Dachau — and gangrene. Long since turned him over to an orthopedist. Fitted with a hand four years ago. He sells soap — but he wants to go back to being a printer. Barged in full of excitement to show me his new hand. Untied my tie — and tied it again."

He dug down on the gas pedal and they spurted ahead of the parallel traffic. "No, this is pre-Freud, something in the egg. Maybe we'll get so we can calibrate it in the kindergarten. The ones who are willing, and the ones who will have to be dragged. Try it on your friends sometime."

She looked out the window. The day was in full blare now, the air like an agar through which the outlines of people vibrated and doubled. "You're pretty arbitrary."

"No," he said. "The egg is arbitrary."

She was silent until they reached the university. "Anywhere along here."

He let her out at a corner. She thanked him, leaning for a moment on the car door. "And the others, Jamie? What do we do about them?"

He patted her hand and gave it back to her. "What do you do? What do I do?" He shrugged. "Visit as usual," he said, and tipped his hat and drove off.

She walked into a drugstore opposite the main building and ordered a sandwich and coffee. This place was a student haunt well known to her: three years ago she had been a visiting professor at the university. Even this late in the year it was packed with glossy boys and girls, talking and lolling with that combination of urgency and unpremeditated time for which they would be nostalgic the rest of their lives. She ate hurriedly, sitting among them with the sad anonymity of the outsider — a feeling as familiar to her home ground as here. With them, any age past their own was the outsider; any skin that had made its concessions or eye that had veined with memory was both beneath their notice and beyond it. One sat with them, skeletal at their feast, knowing something about them that they would be incapable of believing, that the skeleton, if challenged, would be unable to describe.

An hour later, however, seated on the platform in the immense white daze of the stadium, she felt closer to them than to her colleagues sitting on the dais with her in their annual empurplement of heat and dignity. So many of these were such dry faggots as collected wherever intellectual pursuits went on, kindling to occasions like this one with an inescapable air of having been rejected at better fires. Now the chancellor was making his address, and out into the air floated all the baccalaureate cognates — "war . . . goal . . . peace . . . aspiration . . . from our failing hands" — in a style that just skirted iambic pentameter, leaving one doubtful as to whether it ran from it or toward it. On his head he wore a little pillow of scarlet plush of whose heraldry she was ignorant, unless it signified an eminence that no longer bent the knee but rather must be protected from the jagged points of the stars. Now he spoke directly to the graduates, telling them, with the easy teleology of the safe, that certain wars were sacred, certain generations — perhaps theirs — divinely lost, and they lifted their faces toward him in a thousandfold ovoid innocence. If some among them saw privately that the emperor had no head but a pillow, ten years from now they would be less sure.

Hearing her own name, she raised her head, but bent it quickly, for her own citation had begun. "For achievement in the world of letters . . . for yeoman service to young candidates for that world . . ." The university had already approached her with a plan for its administering, as scholarships, the money she used for her own scattered benefices, but the citation, laying no indelicate emphasis on these, circled fulsomely around her own work. *Timeo Danaos,* she thought, but the praise lapped her with shameful warmth.

At a benedictory signal from the chancellor she went forward, bending to receive the brilliant capelet on her shoulders. He shook her hand, turning it with practiced dismissal, so that for a moment she faced her audience, a speaker who was not to be allowed to speak.

As she returned to her seat, Sweet, the head of the department, shot out a hand as if it had been tapped with a mallet and beamed violently, making a noise like a bubbling kettle, but already his face was angled toward the next to be honored, as were all the young faces before her. Tipped and oval, a thousand eggs of unknown impulse, they waited, dressed in their rented black, as if the old could not quickly enough take the young into the dark seminary of responsibility. If she had been allowed to speak, she thought, what would she have told them? That life gave no baccalaureates? That there was always the visit to be paid as usual, always the telephone call to be made?

At last the ceremony was over. With one final fanfare it smashed and dispersed, scattering its components over the grounds like bright and drab bits of glass from which no further pattern could be expected that day. She walked slowly, through family groupings, toward the Faculty Club, where her presence had been requested at tea and where there was a phone.

In the booth she dialed the number of Helen's office. It was not quite five o'clock.

"Manning and Coe, good afternoon."

"May I speak to Miss Bonner, please?"

She gave her own name, spelling it out. After an interval a second voice spoke. "What is it, please?"

"Helen? Is this Miss Bonner?"

There was a pause, then the voice spoke again. "Miss Bonner is no longer connected with this office."

It was close in the booth but she suddenly found herself shivering. "Can you tell me where I can reach her?"

Again the voice waited. "No," it said finally. "I'm sorry — but I cannot."

She drew a long breath. "If she — gets in touch with you, perhaps you'd give her a message?"

"What is the message." It was less a question than a statement.

"I'm calling for my nephew, Paul Ponthus. He is seriously ill in Lenox Hill Hospital. He would like to get in touch with her."

Over the wire she could hear the breathing of the other woman. She waited. "Yes," the voice said, and its weary inflection made her certain. "I'll see that she gets the message. If she calls. But I doubt if she will call."

When she left the booth she was still shivering. She hadn't seen Helen in over a year. But she was good at voices, good at inflections. The second voice had been Helen's.

In the Faculty Parlor she held herself apart from the chattering groups, drank two cups of hot tea and took a third to a seat in a corner. I caught a chill, she told herself, and knew that she had not. Most of us are such drifters, she thought, leaving our fates to erosion, our amputations to death and accident. When we see someone his own surgeon, we are filled with awe.

Through an open window at her side she heard children playing outside the chapel gates, exchanging the familiar twilight calls: "Where are You?" . . . "I'm anyplace, where are You?" The cries rose gawkily, the sound of viols played by amateurs for whom the opulent instrument was yet too much. For an insistent moment she wished herself back there with them, with the sun going down in a clash of skates. Not to be here in this tea-colored room where the old condescendingly relaxed with the young, and the young were so ruddy and unaware of how powerfully they could condescend to the old. Not to be sitting here, an elderly voyeur, holding in my lap, like knitting, the severed nerve ends of two lives. But not quite yet the voyeur. There is still the visit to be made.

Someone turned on the lights, the dusk at the window snapped to a sharper blue, and people, blinking in the orange brightness, plunged again into the rubble of talk. She looked down the room as one did at funerals, reunions, all the roll calls at which one took stock of the assessments of time. Chester, that sorry sufferer from the worst of academic diseases, had retired into some cranky shade, taking with him his disappointment in himself. But Conway was gone too, the tall, bearded medievalist whose mind had been of such an opaline goodness that, staring into it, one almost saw striations of goodness that were one's own.

"Felicitations! Felicitations!" Sweet teetered on his heels before her, his clasped hands cherishing his tweed belly. "How does it feel, eh? How does it feel?" Having founded a career on repetition, he was not one to desert it for lesser purposes. "But they'll be wanting to meet you," he added. "Come take your turn at the urn. Ha! Turn at the urn."

He led her to the long table and installed her in front of the tea service. "Young chap you must meet," he whispered. "Just back to the graduate school from the Army. Did some brilliant emendations on *The Pearl* before he left. 'S matter of fact — if you should see your way clear — hm — he'd be one of our first candidates. Used to be a protégé of poor Conway." She watched him shamble over to a group and detach a young man from it. She had always piqued him with her preference for Conway, a man of no great departmental or secular distinction. But the patronage of the dead, if useful, would not offend.

She looked at the boy Sweet was bringing toward her, a nice enough young man with his hair cut in that neat furze they all affected, his face still that printless mask which nature affected for them. For the first time she could not summon the friable tenderness, that perverse sense of her own youth whereby she seemed to herself really only a prisoner, caught in some gargantuan trap of flesh and years. For the first time she felt the great disinterest that was age. They keep coming, she thought, another and another. It's time I stopped running toward them, poking at them for whatever it was I was seeking. Perhaps it's time to admit what that was too — nothing much more than the bawling of an old cow with caked udders, lowing for a calf thirty years gone. I'll let the college have the money, let them handle it any way they wish. I'll take on Paul, for whom nothing can be done, and it will at least be better that the nothing be done by me than by Helen. People like Paul can be looked after quite easily out of duty; the agony comes only when they are looked after with hope.

Sweet intoned a name she didn't catch. "Great fan of yours, this young man. Great fan." He beamed impartially at them and departed.

"You don't have to *say* anything." She smiled up at the young man.

"It's true, though." He spoke with a bluntness past having to be put at its ease. "Charles Conway put me on to your work."

"Yes?" she said. She looked down the room. "I miss him here."

He too looked down the room. "I loved Conway," he said. "Even if you were only a student, he made you feel that you counted."

She glanced at him more sharply. One seldom heard them use the word "love" in the quiet sense that he had used it — it was contrarily the one four-letter word they still spoke with a sense of shame.

"Yes," she said. "He was a good man."

"They never made too much of him here."

"No," she said. "I guess the good don't dramatize easily."

"That's true!" he said with a rush. "True in books too, isn't it?"

She nodded, smiling. "So then — you're going to special-ize in Medieval?"

He grinned at her and, grudgingly, she felt the familiar

rictus of interest. Intelligent, of course, she warned herself, but then the room was full of intelligence, beady-eyed with it, full of quick-billed birds, and if the eyes of the younger ones seemed more luminous, it was only because they hadn't quite learned when to drop the secondary lid, the filmy lid of conformism.

"No," he said. "I'm giving up the graduate school. I haven't told anyone yet. I've — I've got some notes for a book."

"Oh?"

He bent his head, flushing. "Actually . . . I wrote a book. While I was in the Army. But I chucked that too. I had just enough sense to see how derivative it was." He brought out the phrase, as they so often did, like a password.

"But we're all that," she said, hearing in her voice a melting note that she decried.

"But this wasn't just style," he said, raising his head. "It was full of the best prime anxiety — and all secondhand. It had everybody's fingerprint on it except mine."

"And your fingerprint?" she said. "What will that be?"

He drooped again. "Oh, I'm still in boot camp. I know that!" But his doldrums were only those of the young, easily routed by the tensing of a muscle, or rain drying on a pane. He reached toward a plate on the table and popped several pallid triangles into his mouth. "This lost-generation stuff we were tossed this aft — you believe that?"

"I'm not sure," she said. "I've never been sure. It's more important whether you believe it. All of you."

"We get so confused," he said. "They've got us staring at their navels, not our own. And we've got nothing to answer them with — yet." He cast her a desperate smile and concentrated on an empty cup and saucer, pushing them back and forth on the table. "Guess I'm a freak or something. But I like being in the world. And if I write, oughtn't it to have some — some of that in it? Oh, I was in the Army — I know there's enough trouble to go around. But I have to earn mine — not inherit it!" He cast her another agonized glance and bent again to his game with the saucer. "Speech, speech," he said.

"No," she said slowly, "you're not a freak," and caught an echo of what she had said to Paul. No, you're not a bastard. But what they are, she thought, I can't tell them.

"Anyway, that's why I'm leaving," he said. "I told myself, okay, I helped mop up a war for them. But I'm damned if I'll write their books for them."

His voice was loud and she looked apprehensively around the room, but it had emptied and they were alone.

"I guess I shouldn't get so angry," he said, averting a cheek that was as mild as a child's.

She leaned forward, peering at him with the habit of a lifetime. It's just the glow they all have once, she told herself, nothing special. It's like the gaudy light that clings to their first poems; one must always be suspicious of it, for it may be simply the peak of freshness attained at least once by everyone, like the transitory skin bloom on a plain girl.

"I seem to be angry practically all of the time," he said. But his eyes, before he slanted them away again, were proud.

She looked at him. Maybe, she thought. But in any case why do I watch for it, why have I spent my life watching for it? The Freudians would say I was still looking for a son. She drew a deep breath and leaned back. And if so, she thought, we are all, at any age past a certain one, hunting hopefully for our sons.

He'll think me odd, she thought, staring at him this way without speaking. But she saw that he stood there dreaming, lost in a dream of his own oddness.

Yes, they keep coming, she thought — another and another. And some of them will be the Pauls, who dramatize so easily, to love whom is the worst dead end of fate — for they will knock at every door and never be able to unlock their own. But these others will be coming too. They'll keep coming, the angry ones, another and another, and when they hold out, they are the bright specks on the retina of the world.

He turned. He had picked up the cup and saucer and was holding them out to her with a tentative smile.

She took them and held them, staring down into the cup. I can't help it, she thought; I'm of the breed that hopes. Maybe this one wants to live, she thought. *Maybe this one wants to live.* And when you see that — that's the crux of it. We are all in the dark together, but those are the ones who humanize the dark.

Pouring the cold tea into the cup, her hands trembled so that the cup clinked against the saucer, but when she held out the cup, staring up at him, her wrist was firm.

Extreme Magic

OVER the rolltop desk, in the handsomely remodeled barn which Guy Callendar used for antique shop and home, he had hung, among other things, a present once given him by another dealer for obvious reason — a thinnish old almanac whose heavily scrolled frontispiece bore the title, in letters to suit: *The Resourceful Calendar* — for 1846. Printed McGuffey reader style on the good old paper of the era, its blunt, steel-engraved homiletic for weather, crops, and the general moral behavior taken for granted by its readers, had withstood the finely manicured air of the Hudson River shoreline some miles above Garrison, New York, for almost as long as he had — seven years. He liked to see it hanging there, a tightly integrated little universe whose assumptions were only as yellowed as its paper — including that flourished motto which, despite its missing "l," seemed indeed intended for his life, for him. He had never known whether or not the giver had known his history.

At the moment he was busied in converting an old Rochester lamp, object and task both rather out of line for a shop owner who seldom bothered with the humbler Victoriana and had his own finisher, but these pretensions were his trade's and the neighborhood's, not his own. The lamp belonged to a neighbor — if one could give that name to

Sligo and his wife Marion, proprietors of an old waterfront "hotel" ten miles up the shore, really a restaurant-bar of the kind smartened up with horse brasses for the Saturday afternoon country squires. And Callendar liked any task which let him look continually up and out at any one of the weathers of his own acreage, modest in size, but vast in trees through whose ancient swirl, layer upon layer toward the river, he could see, like a natural fence that gave him the limits he still so needed, glimpses of the waterline, even of the sky — but not of the opposite shore. For this he had bought the barn on a day's decision, and the barn, in turn so neglectedly beautiful, so rescuable and then so emptily waiting, had brought him by gentle nudges to a trade that was no more out of line than any other for a man so nearly out of life.

Ten years ago, he had been an ordinary young man of thirty-one, living with wife and three children — an infant, a boy of seven and a girl of two, in a split-level cottage in one of the developments outside Hartford, Connecticut, working as a company man for the largest in the constellation of insurance underwriters in that city, and doing well enough. Born nearby, married to a town girl, he had come of that lower-middle native stock, in name often resonantly Anglo-Saxon, which the boys from the great schools studding New England called "townies" — a class that, with the will, the luck and the proper scholarships, frequently ended up years later socially alongside of those same boys. With some of the luck, two army-earned years at an obscure business college, and no will beyond that of someday having his own agency, he had been contented enough, unlikely to end up anywhere except much as he was. But that year, while he had been away at the company's convention plus special classes for men of his caliber, his house, catching fire at dead of night in a high November wind, four miles from the nearest hook and ladder and no waterpower when they got there, had burned, with all his family, to the ground. Two owners of badly scorched houses adjacent had urged him to join their suit against the contractor whose defective wiring had already been the subject of complaint. Even if he had been able to overcome his horror, there had been no need; as a model employee, he had had Ellen, little Chester, Constance, and even the baby heavily overinsured in every available form from straight life to special savings plans, college plans, mortgage, fire and endowment. He had managed to survive all the obsequies, the leaden vacation in Bermuda insisted upon by his office manager, even the return to a furnished room and restaurant meals in the best businessmen's residence club in Hartford. It was only when the indemnity money came in, thousands upon rolling thousands of it, that he had gone out of his mind.

The phone rang. "Guy? Polly Dahlgren here. How are you?"

"Hi, Poll, how are you?" An Englishwoman, widow of a Swedish ceramist, she had continued to run their gift shop at Orient Point, the farther tip of Long Island, a place he imagined to be a seashore version of Garrison, in terms of quiet estate money ever more fringed by a louder suburbia, with here and there an air pocket for people like themselves. He had been careful never to see it, though now and then she asked him down, and he liked Poll. She liked him too much for a man who could only like. "What's on your mind?" He'd said it too fast, sad for them both because he already knew.

"Those silver luster canisters you said you'd seen a set of someplace, a dealer's. Near where you fish."

"The Battenkill." It was the first place he'd gone from the hospital, in the beginning with another patient, the stockbroker who'd taught him flycasting, then, for every one of the years since, on his own. "But that was last April."

"Collector down here went wild when she heard about them. Pay anything, if they're what she wants."

"They wouldn't cost all that much," he said. "About two hundred for the four of them. If they're still there. They just might be. I could find out for you. Or she could go see."

"Invalid, can't. I do a little legwork for her now and then, expense-paid of course. Nice old gal."

"Well, why don't you?" he said. "Beautiful country in August. And five or six dealers strung out along one lovely road. Not too far for a three-day weekend. With the parkways."

"Where is it, did you say? And the name?"

"Vermont – New York border," he said, "the Battenkill." He couldn't keep the dream of holy peace out of his voice, the years of gratitude. "The most beautiful trout stream in the world." He'd never seen any other.

"I might just do that," she said. There was a pause. Then she spoke brusquely. "Like to go with me?" Into his silence, she said abruptly, "For the fish."

"Thanks, Poll, but I can't—" Get away. She knew he could, any time. He plumped for the truth, at least some of it. "It's particularly a place where I like to go alone." As he went most places.

"Right!" she said at once. "Nice of you to tell me that." She understood that he had given her an intimacy. He did like her. "And now, give on those names."

He gave her the lot, extra warmly. This was what he was good at, and where he could be generous. "Don't bother with the Graysons if you're in a hurry. Retired couple, he'll want to talk and she'll want to show her collection. Goes in for ruby hanging lamps and anything doll-size, from tea sets to iron cookstoves. Has some good glass, but none of it for sale. One of those. Then, along the road north there's a tidy little farmer's wife, barn stuff mostly, woven comforters and moss-rose china et cetera, but cheaper than most. Doing it to send the older girl through beautician's college." He stopped, at a snort of amusement from the other end. "Hmm?"

"Nothing," she said. "Just that you can't sell your specialty either. A pity. You're so good at it."

"I know." He smiled at her. "Don't hold it against me. And listen now. The lady you want is named Katrina Bogardus — and she is a lady. Gets the early stuff from the big houses when they break up. Has a couple herself. Looks like a little French marquise and is a retired superintendent of schools."

"Record of sale then, if she's sold. Or she'll remember." Poll's voice was her business one, to remind him that though not strictly in the trade she knew as well as he the range of its characters from junkyard on — as varied as its stock and as severely appraisable.

"Decidedly." He hesitated, then warmed to his specialty. "And look, Poll, if you do have time, hit there on a Thursday, when her son-in-law visits. He's a parson, I guess you'd call him, but you never saw anything like him in America, though he is one — minister, up-Hudson way. Dresses high Anglican and calls her *mater* — she must have had him refinished somewhere. Right out of a British movie, the kind they don't make any more."

"*Barchester Towers*," she said.

"Never saw it."

"A book." Her voice risked tenderness again.

He covered this with a rush. "And Poll, if she likes you — which I'm sure she will — she'll take you upstairs to see the drawing room. Paneled. Moved from somewhere. Lowestoft to match. Your cup of tea, as I've heard you say."

"Pennies to pounds she liked you," she said. "Well, I might do. And shall I mention your name?"

"Oh, she wouldn't know it," he said. "I was just there once. And I don't buy, you know — when I go up that way."

"I know," she said. "You just go — for the fish."

"Ah, come on now."

"The way you go almost anywhere," she said crossly. "Wonder you stay in business." At once she was contrite, but too nice to say so. "I mean —" She knew he didn't need money, and why. "Never you mind," she said quickly. "Go on and do what you like to do, why not. And *be* grandmother to the rest of us. We can use it, all right, all right. . . . Well, good-by, Guy m'love, and thanks."

"Good-by, Poll." There came the final, impossible silence in which he waited for her to hang up, and she didn't.

"Fancy," she said, very soft for her. "And you were only there once. . . . Well. See you sometime. Cheerio."

"Tell you what, Poll," he said desperately. "On your way up there, why not stop by for — lunch. I'll gather in some people. Or better still — on your way back, then we can have a gas about it."

"Right," she said promptly. "Let you know. Or if not, you drop down here. Oh, no fear, I remember what you said about weekends. For the day. I'll — gather some people." One more pause. "Good-by, you bloody old fisherman, you," she said very rapidly, and rang off.

During his two years in the first-class establishment — its rolling golflands not thirty miles from here — into which relatives and the company had been able to put him on all that money (at a yearly maintaining fee of twice his former salary, and in the company of others similarly able to be as expensively aberrant or agonized) he had been led through the gentle craft world of the sanitarium, toward its own necessary fantasy of the goodness and wholeness entirely residual in the world. In that selective company of Wall Street alcoholics, matrons at the climacteric, schizophrenic young nymphs in riding habit, and highly placed failures of the barbiturate, even the other patients had been extra gentle with him, often — as the doctors were quick to see and use — extra reachable by him.

At first he had been in no condition to notice this. Later on, under the constant encouragement from above to help one another, he hadn't questioned it. Sitting alongside one of the "Park Avenue" matrons, whose hair had been freshly hyacinthed in the on-grounds salon that morning, he and she had learned how to French-polish furniture; on leaving she had sent him — from an address that wasn't Park but at another altitude he hadn't yet been aware of — a box of the books on furniture and china which were still the best he owned. The exquisite young rider — who dressed to the nines at every hour of the day, was mortally afraid of men at less than a yard's distance, and always had an animal beside her — had been willing to dismount from her horse, leave her Doberman behind, and walk with him — he had taken it to be because as a man he was still so nullified. The flycaster had taught him golf also, and like a legendary rich uncle turned up in a poor young man's thirties, had opened to him, in the wistful after-dinner talk of a drinker on cure, a whole Barmecide's feast of bon vivant living; this man, now lapsed between bed and occasional club window, Callendar still visited, and unlike the man's own nephews, was received. He understood why now of course, long since grown used to that special kindness which in the hospital he had taken for the good manners the rich had been bred to even in their own sickness, awarded even to him who could teach them nothing, not even — as in the one try which had given him a setback — a knowledge of insurance. Only on leaving had he understood what he was to them, to anyone. Against their ills, mostly fugitive from the world, casualties from within, his case had the ghastly health of the man whose coup de grace had come from life itself, from outside. Against his accident, they still had hands to cross themselves. He was their extreme, the triple amputee at the sight of whom even the single-legged may still take heart.

The phone rang.

"Is this the *eminent*, the res*ource*ful —"

"Hello, Quent." He prepared to laugh with Quentin

Paterno, to join in with the preliminary conversation tic, a stutter of courage rather than larynx, with which his earliest customer-friend always had to start.

"*Spoils*port! Now I'll have to begin all over." He could hear the little man clear his throat, see the pudge of fist kneading potbelly, the bright brown eyes straining under nobly bald brow.

"Is this the powerful *schattchen,* goodman extraordinary — ?"

"I dunno, Quent. What's that?"

"Marriage broker, you Christian." Joke. So was Quentin. "Yop, you did it again, matchmaker. And I suppose you'll say without even knowing it, like always."

"Ah, come on now." Because he thought about people a lot generally, those introduced by him — anywhere from dinner guests, to the fellow who'd had a letter from him to a dealer-correspondent in the Rome where Callendar had never been himself, and had married her — almost always clicked, and sometimes paired off.

"It's just like any statistics, Quent," he said. "Nobody remembers the ones that don't come off."

"Well, this one did. The party was last night. I suppose they didn't even call you, those young ingrates."

"No. But I can't think who." He shouldn't have said that. Quent might take it to mean, who in *Quent's* crowd? It was hard to think of them without the italic in which they thought of themselves.

"Cast your mind back, in fact *turn* back, O Callendar." No offense given then, except, in that painful laugh at his own joke, by Quent to Quent, who hurried on with the doomed rapidity of a man who had absolute pitch for the way he was sounding. "To a freezing night a nice guy, a *Guy*, is nice enough to come all the way in to hear my concert. A fall guy, in fact, for anyone his broken-down friends writes a play, paints a pitcher."

"Quent. Give." If he was a faithful, even grateful audience, always using the tickets, not just buying them, he'd learned not to dwell on the fact that he was always audience.

"Sorry." If stopped in time, Quent could tune his delicate pitch to others. Exerted, it at once eased him. "After the concert, Guy. Carnegie Taproom. Remember our kid harpist, Violet? The one the orchestra boys were teasing? 'Nobody-violates-me Violet,' they call her. And the couple you bumped into at intermission, they run a shop in an old mill down in Bucks somewhere."

"New Hope," he said. "Joe and Milly Pink." The stuff they sold was terrible.

"They had a son with them, a Princeton boy."

He barely remembered a boy who sat back, who should have been with the younger crowd. Yes, now. The Princeton boy, day boy probably, scholarship surely, who sat well back from all of them, most of all from his all-wrong parents, the mother in squaw blouse and skirt and no bridgework, the father wearing a huge free-form silver ring of his own design. "Yes, I remember now." And the shy girl, from Oberlin, Ohio. Farm girl probably, or — if they had them out there — a townie. Who sat back. He had gone over and introduced them.

"Those two," said Quent. "That boy, that girl."

"Why, that's fine!" he said. "They — they should do well together."

"Yeah, you have a fatality. Or a green thumb. And I have a headache. From the party."

"Nice of you to call me, anyway," he said. And waited.

"Matter-of-fact —" Quent said. "I'm in the slough, slow, sloo — of despond. Or how do you pronounce it."

"I dunno. If that's what you called me for." A pause.

"Tell me," said Quentin. "You heard of people named Benjamin? Must be near neighbors of yours."

"Two doors down," said Guy, grinning. "And a half a mile away. Yes, I've heard of them. They own the house between us too, but keep it empty. A sort of buffer state between them and a commercial."

"Not now they don't. They got the grandmother in it, Phoebe Jasper Aldrich. The Aldrich Chamber Concert Mrs. Aldrich. Library of Congress, and points west. You wouldn't know."

"I read the papers."

"Then you know. They blow a horn in heaven, she hired the hall. Lucky the composer gets to feed at that trough. Trow. Troo. Give her credit, most the good ones do get."

"Oh?" he said, puzzled. Quent, rich enough by inheritance to own the house in Turtle Bay for which he kept Guy still buying, was too proud-poor in another ever to ask this kind of favor. "No — I'm afraid I don't know them."

"Don't anticipate, guileful Guy. I *been* asked. A little late in life, it's true. To make music in that celestial company. This coming weekend." When the mock accent dropped, then they were near.

He picked it up. "So?" And waited. It came as expected. "William."

As usual.

"How?" he said, finally.

"Pills . . . Oh, he's all right. Resting quiet. We got to him."

As usual.

"I knew in my bones last night, when he wouldn't go with me. Always a sign, when he won't leave the house. But I felt I had to go. It's such a bind, you're not supposed to show worry. Y'know?"

"Mmm." He knew.

"You have to be tough with them," said poor Quentin. "Especially when you're *family*."

For this he had no answer. "He wasn't asked up here?" he said. "To go with you."

"Oh, nothing *personal*," Quentin said quickly. "Nobody gets to bring anybody up there. Not even *wives*. I told him. But he wouldn't believe me. You know William."

"Yes." Yes, he knew William. A swag of still true-blond hair over the high, narrow cranium of an underfed child — of which William had been one. A mouth set like a cherry pit in the slender jaw. And a nameless talent, or only the desire for one, harbored like a wound. William, barbiturate failure, still only a year away from true boy when first met.

"Yes, I know William." He had been the patient to whom Guy had tried to teach insurance. "Quent —" If I came down to stay — would he let you go? He already knew the answer, which would be given even now with pride: No. Only me. "No," he said aloud, "I don't suppose."

"Well anyway, that's really why I called you. To get a line on them. I had some wild idea, maybe she would ask him up. But I can see now how ridiculous." Quentin expelled a long, relieved sigh.

"No, I don't know a thing, I've never seen them. Except that they have cats." One was nosing the screen door now.

"Give me that high-class excuse of yours," Quent said suddenly. "The one *you* use to beg off weekends with. You know. The one you give *us*."

He laughed, and gave it. "I say I like to be alone too much. Then they say 'Oh, we'll leave you alone!' Then I say the simple truth, that I know they will, but I never can hit the right posture for it. I don't know how to relax into being half-alone but not alone. . . . Mightn't do for you."

"Jees, no, you know *me*. No posture at all. No, it has to be something *real*."

"Like what?" he said.

"Claustrophobia, maybe." Quent was feeling better. "Or what's that thing on heights?"

"Acrophobia." It was hard to stay angry with them — if they had to make catastrophe of some small emphatic of life, in the end they always entertained you with their elaboration of it. "But the house is on the riverbank — I know that much. And she's asking you for the weekend, not burying you." A second cat was nosing at his door. "Why not 'Ailurophobe'?" he said. "They must have half a dozen of them. Cats."

"Cats give *William* asthma," Quentin said dreamily. "Gee, whad you do, swallow the manual? I wish *I* could read. I wish I had your sense of detachment."

Burn your house down then. Burn *William*. It was the one thing for which he couldn't bear to be marveled at — why should they want his priceless capital of non-suffering? He didn't answer.

"Anyway, thanks, Guy, maybe I'll do that. Thanks a million. It's just — I don't want it to sound phony. You know? And with certain people, outside your own close circle of friends, howya going to know you not giving offense?" Quent's voice squeaked — a mouse transfixed in terror of its own moves.

"You don't give it, Quent," he said. "You never do."

"Ah, Guy . . . Anyway. Good to talk to you. Marriage broker is nothing; you could open a whole accommodation agency. But not till you help us finish on the house, hah?"

That house would never be finished — how could they afford to finish this construct that formally provided them with everyone else's troubles — and pleasures of course — from maid trouble to gourmet shopping, to spats over the discipline of the curly-headed dog-child? He didn't say this either.

"Anyway, good-by now," said Quent. "And William always asks for you. I'll give your love to William."

"Yes, do that."

"And good to talk to you. I'll be honest with you, that's why I called." Quent's repetitions were more for his own ear than for others — it was the way he knew he meant something. "Thanks again," he said. "You don't know what it means to me, to be able to talk to another normal person."

He put down the phone. Phone calls often made him think of lantern slides, the kind even the high schools probably didn't use anymore, and views of life, not Borneo. Any housewife might go through a box of them heavy enough to make her hand tremble, any morning. He took up the lamp again.

In the past seven years, he had fulfilled all the fine dreams the hospital had had for him, meanwhile never hiding from himself that these might be limited dreams. It was only now and then that the old fire lit in his head — or the dream of a new one to which he would get there on time. Life, though so much more gently, had still come to him by accident. It had been on his first fishing trip alone, driving back on the Vermont side, that his attention had been caught by a farmhouse flying two flags, British and American, and idly inquiring down the road where he'd stopped to refuel at a gas pump in front of a china-stuffed façade and further sheds receding, had been given the whole of that rumrunning story. He had knelt to look at, not buy, an old lamp of a kind he hadn't seen since and now knew to be as rare as pemmican — and had been given the history of such lamps. History, he found, could be picked like daisies all along the roadside, if one were willing to take it a little squeegee — what had fascinated him from the first was the squeegee — the narrators themselves. And in the end, just like them, he'd acquired a business, and one just like theirs, "on the side."

For not a man jack of them (or a woman in that gallery of whittled women) who hadn't been beached up on his wrack of metal and porcelain from somewhere other. Or if not, then whatever in them had settled early or late for this flotsam had done so in lieu of something else. It hadn't been until much later, of course, that he saw this clearly, and much more: how even in winter or bad times the hunt had to go on, if need be, with each other; how in the end the rooker had to be rooked. How each, drily scanning "the trade," saw this as well as anybody, but denied it for himself. And how each, like himself, had arrived at the specialty which made his game worthy and the others' silly — and which he would not exchange. Sometimes, one came upon an antiquer whose wares, invading his house, had coiled into closet and bed and pushed out the humans entirely, leaving him wedged in its clockwork like a single, bright, movable eye. In his own case, the reverse having happened, he'd been helpfully pushed out of the house altogether, where he was kept tethered like a buoy in a tide, perhaps, but still in the world's tide.

His own specialty was necessarily invisible. But if he could have stood people up in rows — like Romanies with their hands out, who were in turn his soothsayers — the shop would have been filled with them, and his best customer was always himself. He supposed they were his substitute for history — whose? — as history itself had always seemed to him in a way a substitute. In the hospital, in his last phase but one, which he had taken to be religious, he had done a great deal of such reading, only to find out that, like so many of his era, he had merely been lonely to hear about other eras, especially of that pure time when people made their own constructs of God. And in the final months of his cure, he came to understand what the dead were — at least, his dead. The dead did not own history, as he had once supposed; they only could not move forward into it, being fixed in what they had. In the worst of his sickness, he had wilfully refused to move on without them — he would stand with them. He was mad with jealousy for them and against himself — for all they would never know. He hated himself for having to grow forward into it. In the end he had been able to, to leave the hospital — and them. Sheer luck had then nudged him into a modus vivendi whose limits were so exactly modulated to his own — one exactly useful to a man able to move on, unable to forgive himself for it.

He had come to this place not long after, on a day's trip to the impeccably kind lawyer who had all that time held in trust for him his now more modest good fortune. Even the barn, a mile or so uproad, had been so forbearing with him, so high and mild, with autumn riverwind coming in at its windows just a cast too weedy — so willing to wait. Even the real estate agent might have known of his mishap, unless he spoke to all clients as if only his properties could heal. In geography, of manners as well as hills, this was still that formal countryside of the hospital he had just come from, where wealth, and perhaps goodness, too, were sometimes still ecclesiast. To the north of him, one great estate had humbled itself to Capuchin, hard by another, to be sure, that had gone more militantly, to golf course. Down below him, rectors in board-and-batten snuggeries presided over the lesser manses, alongside here and there the heart-piercing needle of a still New England church. Sports cars knitted amicably as petunias between all of them. A safe visual goodness still ringed him. Everything was in repair. And — as he had the perspective to say laughingly — the opportunities for picking up church candlesticks were endless.

He had good perspective. Down still lower in the town, in certain side streets that had once been "native," or more often now in the supermarket for new cottagers of the class just below commuter, he sometimes saw a Saturday family he recognized. They had come from the north. The young man, one infant on shoulder, was beset by two other jumpers demanding to be taken to the Mi-Dream Ice-cream. The woman, the Ellen, was still pretty in her postpartum fat and had been to Marnie's Beauty Den; she would not comb the curls out until morning. She was a girl who would name her eldest "Chester," against all lost eighteenth-century New England, because it "went with" — who would name her infant daughter Coral. She was a stranger, an utter stranger. The young man, given the privilege of naming his second child, had called it Constance, but only out of a simpler maleness, or perhaps, though he was unaware of it, because fidelity was going to be so important to him. They both were blind to him, Guy Callendar, as he was now. She was ensconced in her family, never to look at another man, never at one like him. Perhaps the young man, not necessarily smarter than she, only properly keener by way of army, business college, and business, had paid him a look, as to an example of what he himself might someday aspire to: this lean, older man who so resembled him, who still had his hair, his own long, pleasant enough Connecticut face, inside a style of dress and haircut already noted down at conventions — this older man who, in ten years and with a little of the right kind of luck, might be him. Both the couple were oblivious to his own — snobbery. The children were smartest of all; children always sense fear. For though in the book of phobia he had a clean slate, even to fire, he could not sit through any movie or story in which a child was mistreated or in peril — and this was not in the book. The children knew he preferred not to look at them at all but could not help looking. Like animals they sensed their mastery over him and often acknowledged it in some gawky mince or persistent turning back that bewildered their parents. It was in his face perhaps, what he feared for them

— even the infant often gave him a patient, peach-cheeked smile.

He never saw them, that family, as any older; they stayed where they were. He was the one who had moved on. To the degree that he had, he could bear it now. Perspective was what any man carried on his back, not a cross, but an easel to which pictures were supplied slowly, always from an unknown hand. He merely knew better than most what had happened to him. The hospital had taught him not to expect that the world would continue to recall his extremity and pity it, had warned him that he must not either, and they had been right. What more had come, they couldn't have anticipated. The heart educates, and unlike the State, is no leveler. Some men tragedy flattens farther back in their grooves. Others it pushes altogether out of their sphere.

The lamp was finished. His hand went to the phone, then withdrew. Instead, he chose a shade of plain old white glass from his stock of them, set it upside down in a carton, placed it and the brass lamp, electrified and polished now, on the floor of his station wagon, and drove off. On Mondays, the inn's bar and restaurant, like his shop, was closed, the chef and assistant barman off; the rare guest in one of the rooms upstairs must take his chances elsewhere. Sligo and Marion always spent the day at home in retirement; any business that took them away was performed midweek. No doubt they could only feel private on the one day the place wasn't convivial. Publicans had little time or will for private friends. If they welcomed him there, as they did now and then on that day, it was more or less because it was his Monday also, and he understood the special coziness taken and given when the shopkeeper entertains others, particularly others of the same, on the day the door is closed. He went there, he supposed, because they were in the same pocket as himself. If he never thought of those two as enjoying their place in nerve and spirit, as he did his, of ever really doing more than accepting it, it was perhaps because to think of them, or of knowing them, in terms of nerve and spirit, was in itself an oddity; they were not that sort.

Good barkeeps, or "your host" as the menus said nowadays, generally kept themselves unknowable. Sligo was a good one. A big, very pale man, both tall and wide, shown ambiguously only to the waist as he stood between the dark mirrors and mahogany of a bar dating from the Spanish-American War, he might have been a mercenary seen through the spyglass of a much earlier war, or perhaps a footman of the size and impassivity then so prized. He had a blacksmith's arm girth, ending in the bartender's pouchily delicate hands. In his silence, he might have been the smith's spreading tree. From his wide gaze, customers assumed that he listened. Rumor said that he drank, or (because he accepted no offers to) once had — but this was always said of men in his profession. Some said that the horse brasses on the wall behind him came from Sligos, who for centuries had been innkeepers in Britain. Others pooh-poohed this because of the name and favored the Abbey Theatre, the wives particularly. His black hair curled low and caddish — or Roman — at the neck; both were thick. Such a figure, so aristocratically pale, must have come from somewhere; the odds were that it had come down.

When the restaurant itself was full, it was Sligo's habit to leave the bar and make a circuit of the tables, inclining his head to each with a query so regally inaudible that only weeks of custom confirmed what he had said to be no more than " 'S everything all right?" Seen at a distance, above the tables, Sligo's profile was suddenly neat, set in his jowled head like one of those cameos purposely carved only half emerged from the matrix, not cut free of it. Weight was the one sign that this great trunk might indeed be hollow enough to have a once much smaller man inside it. At the moment he stepped down from the bar, wholly in the clear, one saw with surprise, beneath the white coat which hid width but no belly, that his legs, long as they were, were bowed. As for Marion, who sometimes tended bar in these interims, at first glance she was merely the good host's wife.

At a break in the hedgerow to the left of the highway, Callendar turned in — there was no sign — drove river-wards for perhaps a quarter of a mile, parked in the big courtyard behind the house, empty now except for the owners' car, and waited tactfully for one or the other to come out, as per custom, at the sound of his tires on the gravel. On Mondays, to get their quiet, they disconnected the phone. He wasn't one to drop in on a couple on their equivalent of Sunday — he remembered how it could be. Once in a great while, Marion called him the same day to ask him over; more usually the invitation was an offhand "Drop in" or "We'll expect you" that same week. Today he was expected, with the lamp. Sometimes it took her quite a while to come from some upstairs region from which Sligo would come down later — it was almost always she. And once or twice, when expected, no one had come out to greet him. He'd the sense not to knock or go in, and he'd been right. Neither of them had ever referred to it after.

Unlike his own place, this one had a straight view. The Canal Zone Inn, as it still was known, was set in the crotch of a promontory that fingered the river, really only a slice of made land just strong enough to hold a concrete pier, no trees. Behind the sandstone house, of the squat Dutch sort that never looks its size, there was backdrop enough of them. The courtyard was good for fifty cars. Nobody except the occasional tourist who bumbled here ever walked out on the little *plage* of false land, either to sit at its umbrellaed tables, or bathe from its fringe of beach. From it, it was said, one could see clear down to the Point — West Point. The inn's late owner, not from the Academy, though military enough to have seen war service in "ninety-eight," had probably acquired most of his rank and all of his legend when well out of the war, and in his last years also, a character. The legend (of cadets sneaking across river and so forth) the Sligos had kept or let stay, even to the large, gold-pronged diamond solitaire in its glass showcase on the bar-top, according to its shaky Spenserian label: "Ring worn by Colonel George when he helped carry the message to Garcia." Customers who had known the old "Colonel" reported that even in his nonage he had been nimble enough in mind to have carried the news from Ghent to Aix, had he ever heard of that circumstance. Nowadays, and not merely because of time passing, there were almost no such customers. In place of the former character of the inn — speakeasy in the Twenties, dirty ladies upstairs in the Thirties, dirty old men downstairs in the Forties — the Sligos had

painstakingly substituted their own. This was no longer
new enough to be shadowy, or shouldn't have been — like
Callendar, they too had been here seven years. Or perhaps
the inn's intended character was to make them seem
shadows of it.

He himself wouldn't have painted the mellow old stone
with white, cleanly as it now looked, pleasingly cleft at
precise intervals, even on the overhanging second story,
with boxes of geranium, all of the same superior pink. The
place now looked reassuringly as much as possible like
others of its kind, with their same suggestion that setting
was only for status, that the real shelter one got here
provided the customary satisfactions — and above all, was
inside. But the Sligos must know their business, for they
had got plenty of it — still uncompromisingly local, if not
the same. "Before we came," he'd heard Marion say, "the bar
had one television, one spider hanging down in front of it —
and often only one customer." If she knew that this might
well have been one or another of the older residents, people
like the Benjamins or their attendant cronies, who now never
came here, she made no mention of it. Now, with no
television or spiders, the trade came from the former
trade's expensively subdivided land, from people well above
cottager, often new country club, who needed to love the
local tradition, and were prepared to do so in a hurry.
Inside, in the games room on the lower level, darts could
be played, or — as a visiting Englishman had once ex-
claimed at — shove ha'penny, played with half-dollars.
(Drinks brought from above were likely to cost twice
that, and to be martinis.) Nobody except that visitor — and
Guy — was likely to wonder from which of the Sligos'

backgrounds this idea had come, or whether it went with anybody else's here. Like the decor, some of it from Guy's shop, the idea was "Colonial." A specialty, like seventy kinds of ice cream, or pizza, had been provided. The rooms above were purposely empty, overnight trade discouraged. Patronage came mostly in pairs here, but not that kind. Even the hosts, shadowy as they kept themselves, were seen to be a pair.

Inside, since Marion was the talker of the two, it took time to notice how noncommittal she remained. Tending bar, when not busy she usually sat on a stool behind the glass case with the Colonel's ring in it, down at one end. The case was small and low enough for her to lean chin on hand and look down into it, if she chose. Guy, in his mild bouts of company, often sat on the last stool at that end; company at one elbow was enough. From the first, he'd seen how useful the case and its contents were. New customers always asked about it; old ones invariably made some reference to it of an evening. The big diamond, high on its gold prongs, couldn't be touched, but its gleam could always be rubbed up into a conversation. "My God, that's a convincing fake!" a man would say. "Have to look at it twice to know it isn't real." Marion would nod, not looking down on it. "Real, they couldn't leave it *here*," said another. This time she might look down on it, or smile, or raise an eyebrow — oh, there were all sorts of variants, on both sides.

"Screw the diamond!" he'd heard a woman say to her husband on one particular evening. "It's a cinch the old guy was a fake. Chrissake, when *was* the message to Garcia."

Whenever the talk turned to the Colonel's card, and thence outward from the bar to the world and history, Marion usually deserted it. She was there, however, when the woman's husband, standing behind her chair next to Guy's, introduced himself as the manager of the new jewelry store downtown, and suddenly took out an eyepiece. "Still think of musself as a practicing jeweler," he said, looking round him. "And proud of it. Want that stone appraised, do it gladly. Gladly. Looks to me from here that's no zircon." He popped in the loupe. "Can't see for sure through that glass. Lemme see now, howzis case open." For the first time, Marion's nod was more negative than — not. Her hand even stayed him. "Don't let those black spots fool you," he said genially. "Just carbon. A mine diamond that many carats could still be —" Marion was called away to the other end of the bar, and stayed there for some time. He shrugged, put the loupe back in a pocket, and said to Guy, undertone, "Be surprised how many people have an old-fashioned piece like that, don't really want to know if it has value." When Marion came back, he addressed her. "Any time your husband want to buy a modern stone for that pretty little hand, you two come down and see me personally. We merchants stand together, hmm?"

Sligo, tray in hand, was just behind them, up to fill a bar order for one of the tables. "Oh Elwood!" the jeweler's wife said quickly, smiling at Marion. Women liked Marion, who always took care of them with a kind of bar delicacy reserved for them. "I think old things are fascinating. That box doesn't look as if it's been opened since the day he put it there — no wonder she wouldn't want it opened. Why even the air in it would be the same as that day!"

Marion looked down at her own hand, at her thin, pewter-colored wedding band.

"Women," said the jeweler. "She must have seen every gee dee holy relic in Italy, kissed 'em too if I'd let her, dirt and all. Yop, we just back from the tour." He appraised Sligo. "You folks . . . you . . . in the faith, aren't you?" Again he spoke in an undertone. Sligo, taking the drinks Marion handed him across the bar, bent his grandee stare on him, but left without answering. "No offense, I'm sure," said the jeweler to anybody handy.

"Cawnvert," the woman whispered to Marion. "Turned for *me*. We're both each other's second. And you know, sometimes —" Marion served them sympathetically, but never took confidences from them. She was a good bartender though. The house quickly stood everybody a drink.

There was nothing of the barmaid about Marion; in her blouse and skirt, with a sweater for nippy evenings, she might have been anybody from around here. On weekends, when the trade slid in on their way to or from dressier places, she sometimes wore one of those matched cardigan and skirt sets which the estate people had once set the fashion for but now meant nothing — even the maids here, copying their mistresses, wore cashmere. He had a theory about that, about Marion. With her short-featured face, trim bones and easily cropped hair, she probably wore clothes of any kind well, giving no sense of touting them. Not tall, because of good proportion, she looked sometimes taller than she was, or smaller. It took a second glance to see that she was middle-sized and slender, well compacted by use — she worked hard — and had looks above the

average, though past their prime. In any woman's face
there came a turning point after which, once passed, there
was no going back, and Marion's, in its mid-thirties, had
passed it. Under the eyes it had two scimitars of flesh, or
in a softer light, of shadow, which put a curious mask
there. One could almost see a young, unformed girlish
face there, and, superimposed on it the blunter scope of
the features as they were now, but never the face as it
must have been in its prime. Her voice always surprised
him, half because he recognized it, though no one else
here seemed to notice. It was that high, rather small voice,
babyish but not whiny, not lisping but almost r-less, sing-
song without being really melodious, which was sometimes
"finished" at certain schools but really began earlier — in
the never having to speak too loud, from nanny-time on, for
service. If the estate people had ever come here, surely
they would have been startled by it — one of theirs. And
here was his theory — that Marion had once been in service of that kind. It was in the way she tended the women,
one of them but still not one of them, in the almost hungry
way, as they left the place, her glance looked after them,
from her distance. At first he had thought it merely the
natural enough envy of the publican's wife, jealous of their
freer household time. But it was in the way also in which
she and Sligo were joined (rarely speaking to each other
in public or private — if the Mondays he saw were private),
not even in sympathy perhaps, but in some one of the
wretcheder forms of closeness often to be found in marriage-
cellars. For, if they shared something no one was to know
and neither spoke of it, the two of them in their way would
be as close as many couples who spoke. There were things

that joined people far more often than love; one saw or talked to such every day — as he had not an hour ago — people in cahoots over something far less dramatic than hate or murder, some burden that together they had climbed out of, or with. Yes, he was almost sure of it. Sligo had come down in the world; Marion had come up in it. This could well have made them the pair they were.

It was even in the way he himself had gravitated to them, not knowing precisely at the invitation of which of them, but knowing that he was in some way welcome to both. For him this was relaxing in its turn. They never examined his life in the way of his other friends, and they never asked questions, having instead an air of assuming that any person with any sort of life to him had ghosts also. Or even that all three of them had the kind of life where there were no questions anymore. They included him there, he felt, though perhaps not on their scale. No questions any more — this was what the two of them had in common really, whether it was in some monstrous central arrangement, or only in the collection of bits and pieces and talismans that come from running an inn — like their glass case.

It must have been shortly after that night, almost four years ago, that he'd begun coming here now and then like today — not as a customer. That night, the jeweler's wife, after insisting on another round of drinks, had become maudlin and her husband had taken her home. Since then, the wife was sometimes seen in the Canal Zone with a woman crony, but not the husband. As the pair left that evening, Marion, watching them go, had looked speculative, as if she already knew this outcome. The hour was later than Guy usually stayed. He had never before been alone at the bar. As the door closed on the couple, Marion's chin declined on her hand. Her black hair cast a further shadow on the bowfront of the box that held the Colonel. She looked up at Guy and smiled slightly, as if her speculations had included him. "Mr. Callendar." It wasn't a question. "How come you never talk about the diamond."

Today, it seemed they weren't going to be at home to him. He started up the engine. It wasn't until he had done so that he became aware of the other sound, jumped into relief against it — a faint "plock," then an interval, then another "plock." Somebody was playing at darts on the large board that covered one wall of the downstairs games room and hadn't heard the car approach, even with the room's door ajar, as he now saw it was. Even with the large darts that Sligo had had custom-made, it was remarkable how the sound of the play carried — "plock," and yet another "plock." But anyone who lived on the great maw of the river grew used to its tricks of voices fanning or swallowed, small reports of insects an inch from the eardrum mistaken for backfire on the opposite shore. He turned off the ignition again, slammed the car door, and, smiling to himself, carried the carton with the lamp across the gravel and up the two old grinding stones that served as steps. More likely, Sligo, who had a passion for the games-of-skill he was so good at, and had stocked the room with every known apparatus for them, had found yet another one at which Guy could be trounced.

Just inside the door he set the carton down on a polished floor painted with guidelines like a gymnasium's, and stood up, a smile on his face for the player standing motionless in the afternoon shadow, on the mat at the farther end of the room. It was Sligo, poised one foot forward, silent and huge as a plaster cast met at a corridor's end in a museum, pupils as blind, one arm extended, bent at elbow, as if to shake hands with him down the length of the room. On the upturned palm there was a sliver of silver. He had time only to see that Sligo wore a kind of lederhosen whose leathern front came up high, like a scissor-grinder's apron, or was slung about him like a multiple holster, then the arm trembled, only trembled as the sliver left it — *plock* — and the hand retracted slowly, two fingers aloft, thumb across palm. His own head, following the flight, swiveled left, toward the nearer dartboard wall. At first he could not take in what he saw there. A painted bull's-eye normally there had been blanked out by a wooden target-frame just high and narrow enough to receive the shining knives that outlined a figure tensed within them.

It was Marion, flattened to silhouette but still untouched, the crown of her head held high, her eyes and mouth open, her arms raised from her sides like a prim Joan. In the wooden space between each hand and thigh a knife was imbedded. Her eyes tremored, holding him. "'On't move," said the rigid hole of her mouth, "'on't move. He only has two more." There were still two vacant spaces in the outline of hafts that enclosed her, one each to the left and right of her neck, between shoulder top and ear. He felt he dared not move his own head; even his eyes must hold their allegiance. *Plock.* On the left side — safe. Come again, quickly. He prayed for it. He should have lunged for her in the interval. But her eyes held him, saying *No.* Unbearable, not to know what those eyes saw coming behind him. Make it in these shoulder blades, mine, he said to it. Not in those eyes. He saw them close, slump — in the second before. *Plock.* On the right. Safe. He reached her.

When he gripped her arms, she had already raised herself and stepped away from the target, already able to stand alone. She spoke over his shoulder, in a dead voice that told him much. "Better help me with him now, will you. He's about to fall."

Sligo was standing as before, his empty right hand raised *in hoc signo,* motionless except for the sweat stealing down him everywhere. Only the sweat, patched under his armpit, banded across his forehead, held him up; the hand glistened with it. When he began to topple, his body seemed to lean from the forehead, eyes closed. His boots held him to the floor until they got to him. Once, in their gasping struggle to ease him into a chair, he several times muttered what Callendar heard as "Forty low. Forty low." Holding him around the waist, they maneuvered his hips into the heavy captain's chair. Sligo's hand, braced on the low table in front of it, slid forward on the slick maple, his head cracked upon it, and he rested there jackbent, head on arm. As they stood over him, getting their wind back, their arms hanging, they heard his deep intake, steady as a man in a coma, reassuring as the breath of the dying, calmer than their own.

"I never thought of it," said Guy. "I didn't know. Because there was never anything to — But that dead-white color.

I should have known." It was a slapstick notion, that one of the veined cheek, the carbuncled nose. Those were the genial ones, the harmless ones.

"No one does. How should you?" she said. "He doesn't do it like anyone else. He never even smells of it."

They were both backing away from him with sneaking step, as from a sickbed.

"The worst ones don't." He knew them from the hospital, not the red ones, here and gone tomorrow, but the white-faced ones, with self-murder like a thirsty knifehole between the eyes.

"I never knew any but him," she said. Her voice was prim but echoing, the voice of a woman who says, "I have lived all my life in this town."

"Periodic . . . is he?" He couldn't help the phrase, like a doctor's. There were only so many to use.

"Yes." Her teeth began to chatter. "Once a week."

He got her a chair, leapt about looking for a wrap for her, expostulating with himself. "Let me get you a —" He looked down at her. They both grimaced at the absurdity of it. She nodded. "I'll get us both one," he said.

When he came downstairs from the bar with the whiskies, she had found a sweater for herself and had cowled a thick raincoat over Sligo. He lingered on the stairs for a minute, staring down with a grinding distaste. Upstairs, the late sun was buttering all that cheap brass with a commercial cheer. No, it was impossible; they couldn't leave him here.

They sat sipping the whisky. He was sure she felt the same uneasy sense of conniving. Because they had always been three, and still were, they spoke in sickroom voices.

"What was he saying there?" He glanced at Sligo, including him. "Forty something. Forty throw?" He glanced at the target-frame, and away.

She leaned on her clasped hands, her glass put aside. "His weight. He's been ashamed of it ever since —" She cleared her throat. "In recent years." The little cough made the phrase sound like an obit. "Actually — actually, he must be fifty pounds more than that by now. But when he's this way, he always says it. 'Fourteen stone.'"

He nodded, as if this was always the way men reckoned weight in America. Then there was silence. Some people's diffidence was helped by it, not hers. She was helpless against the years of her own silence. He felt that she was not to be left with it.

"Nobody else knows?" It struck him that he wouldn't be much help to her if he kept to questions to which he already had the answers.

She shook her head. After a while, she said: "Maybe both of us were —" She grimaced at him, lowering her face in the coyness of agony. "Hoping you knew."

"Audience?" he said.

Now the silence was his.

"Can you — speak for both?" he said. "Are you that much a pair?"

"Yes, why not?" she said. Then her face slipped into her hands; she must be exhausted, might want to lie down. He no longer knew anything about the energy of women. Though outside it was August, it was already autumn in this basement, in this summer-kitchen of yore. In that light, dappled from above, the polished racks and mallets and wickets, sets of balls, nets and checkerboards, hung as in an armor room, above the yellow, black, and green stripings on the modern, balsa-colored floor. Games looked ghostly when left to themselves, whether for an hour or a century. When she took her hands from her face, there were no tears on it in the place for them, only those crescents of flesh. "Why not? We suffer the same."

He saw into that tiny, stifling pit. Must he envy it?

She got up from her chair then, and strode away from him. "One gets on better without talking. Pity is fatal." At the target-frame, she knelt to a long, slender box at its base. "You won't be coming back now. Better that you stop coming." Box in hand, she stood up, her back to him, musing over it as people do who recover a memory, good or bad. "I didn't even know he had these around any more. He tricked me into standing here. After all these years with it, I'm still not very bright."

"Where did he ever get things like that, learn them? A circus?"

"Sligo?" She was staring at the wooden backboard. "By inheritance, you might say. He had a ve-ry rich . . . sporting inheritance, I'm told — at one time. Polo, fencing — though I never saw him at those. Guns." For the first time, she switched about to look at the man hunched there. Then she turned back to the target and began drawing the knives from it, one by one.

He came up and watched, over her shoulder. All haft or all blade, the knives had the elegance of any such balance. The chest she was fitting them into was lined with purple velvet. "Marion? Talk, then. Since I'm not coming back."

"What do you want to know?" She was intent on the shaft in her hand.

"I'm not sure. How can I be?"

"Ask." Her whisper went into the box, with the knife. "I don't know where to — how to. Ask!"

Another knife went into the box before either of them spoke.

"Why does he drink?"

"He always has."

"Why do you stay?"

"He has no one — no, that's not true. I left once. I even worked in — it doesn't matter. Twelve years ago. We'd been married five. Then his landlady called — he had the dt's. He had no one." She held a blade over the box. "Neither did I."

He watched the blade go in. "Is he often like this?"

"Comes and goes. Sometimes — more than a month goes by." Her voice lightened to that.

All the knives were housed now except the six that had ringed her head, a zodiac sign filled with darkness.

"He will kill you."

"Never has yet."

He was silenced.

"Sorry. I meant — he doesn't really want to. Or somewhere in between."

He shivered. "Maybe you like it."

"Maybe, once."

"Not now?"

It came slowly. "Not now."

She turned. "Once I wanted him to kill me, but that was

only at first — Odd, isn't it. Ought to be the other way round." Quickly she dropped her eyes, and knelt to set the box, heavy now, on the floor, straightening its double row of hafts. "Twenty-four," she said, and closed it. "You see —" she said, before she stood up again. There was something secretive about her face again, if not sullen — the cast of a struggle that could be as much against honesty as toward it. "I — used to be fond."

He bent and lifted the box. "They're heavy. Heavy as silver. Maybe Damascene."

"Could be."

"Better let me take them along with me."

"Why?"

"*Why!*"

She answered him with a half-shrugged wave of the hand. He saw why, of course. The sun, now sinking outside, had reached even here, dappling on mallet and rope, on quoit and bow and all other implements for game, as outside it must be touching, one by one for tomorrow's life, the trees.

"I don't like to take away any of it. He hasn't very much of his — of those years. Before he knew me. I don't like to — seem against him."

He stared at her.

"Don't you see? He did me an injury. Long ago. And he can't forget it. Forgive."

"So you have to let him keep on — trying."

"No. It was nothing physical. Not really. Not with *those*. He —" Her hand went to her mouth. "Oh — what does it matter? He married me under a false name." She made an odd, stretching grimace with her lips, like a child released from medicine. "No worse than what I did to him."

She swayed then, and he would have shut up — but she held her hand out, for the box.

"But don't you want anything else!" he cried. He heard it echo. "You could leave. Again." All the unaskable questions — to her, to anyone, tumbled out at once. "Can't you pity your*self!*"

"I can, I do," she said. "But not without Sligo."

They exchanged a glance conjoined but unseeing, the mutual hold of two people in their separate ways looking back.

"Don't come again." Her voice was harsh. "I can't afford the perspective."

For help, he turned to the man sleeping there. It was said that sleepers remembered what was said while they slept, poison or balm in the ear. He wondered. In the hospital he had seen nurses speaking for hours on end to catatonics, who it was said registered everything, and if their lips ever broke open again, would recall. No one could lie there as Sligo was, except in stupor, the head sideways on the arm now, position otherwise unchanged. He could think of nothing to tell that ear. "Hadn't I better help you get him to bed?"

"He gets up himself. After a while."

"Will he remember?"

"Not always. Not — for a while."

"Not until Mondays?" He slapped the box.

She held out her arms, hands cupped. Quite suddenly, he laid the box along them, and strode to the door. At his name, he stopped.

"You're welcome," he said, without turning.

"Guy —"

She was holding the box clasped to her as if it were an infant, or two dozen long-stemmed American Beauty roses. "Is it sick of me? That I stay."

Hair prickled on his nape. Questions on leaving were so often for the leaver as well. He heard an answer, long ago inserted in his own ear. "Without help —" He choked on it. "Surely — ? But why do you ask me?"

She bent her head.

The door behind him was stuck with dampness. He kicked it open. No sun came with it. "Without help," he said again, half to himself, hand on knob. "I'll come Mondays."

When he got home, he began rustling up his usual meal for these nights, a cold evening supper anybody might have on his day of rest. During the week he was a fair enough straight cook, though he had never been able to become one of those over-interested bachelors. There were a number of other things he hadn't been able to become, again or newly, but these did not intrude on him now. His mind was the merciful blank that warded off the black infections of others. Later on, when properly immunized, he might safely ponder those, but not now. As he banged the refrigerator door open and closed, crackled butcher's paper and clinked dishes on a tray, taking comfort in all this domestic voodoo, he kept hearing a cat mewing at the small window which gave directly from bathroom shelf to high grass bank outside. He went to open it. The cat stepped in daintily among his toilet things, then drew itself up with the wariness of all cats that are helped. It was one he'd never seen before, a Siamese with the brown and buff markings called "points," and the clenched head of its breed — like a child's fist holding up eyes. At the sight of it, he could hear his mother, all her life a yearner for more than Hartford calicoes, sigh in her grave. This one would not be fed, but circled the house, calling, and after a minute he put it out again, through the same window. He himself preferred dogs.

When he had brought his tray to the screened porch — "terrace" the builder had called it — where he had all his meals summers, he heard the cat again, nosing at the screen and retreating somewhere into the dusk outside. He got up with a sigh of his own, fetched a dish of milk and set it outside, then sat down to his meal, on a low settle he'd placed to face the grove of trees that hid the river, holding the tray on his knees. Above the grove, the sky was still full of western light. After a moment, a cat came to feed, but not the first one — a black tom he'd fed once or twice before. Shortly, a high, silvery voice, young girl or young woman, wended here and there through the grove. "*Here,* kitty-kitty, here, Max. *Ma*-ax." The tom lifted its head, then bounded off, in the opposite direction. This drama too had occurred before. The voice, still calling, after a while always blended away. He'd never decided whether or not the cat was Max.

He was still eating when a girl in a bathing suit stepped into the clearing and came toward him, head bent. Halfway, she stopped, facing the trees, put both hands to her mouth as if she were blowing on a conch and said faintly, "Max?" Circling the barn, not calling again, she came round to the screen door, hands locked behind her, head still bent, saw the dish and gave a start of surprise, saw him, and palms at her chest, gave another. He smiled tentatively at her, not sure whether she could see this through the screen at this hour, but did not rise. The heavy tray held him indolent now. The thin figure, dim in its faded robin's-egg suit, barefoot, was close to a child's. And it was his porch, his clearing, hidden without sign or path, where even in daytime he was almost never surprised.

"Excuse me," the girl said, "but you don't *have* a cat, do you."

"Well, no, I don't. But I've been feeding somebody's."

"Oh." She seemed to peer in at him. "A black one? Oh, that's ours," she said, before he had a chance to nod.

"Oh, is he. I wondered. He always seems to run the other way."

She giggled. About fourteen, he'd say, with those pointed little breasts that couldn't be counterfeited, nor the way her hands latticed at them. "Oh, he's just one I found. He's been giving the others the worst habits. But the rest are really ours."

"Are they." He couldn't help his stiffness toward those who were too casual to the young of any breed, even when they were themselves the young of another. "There did seem to be several, and there didn't seem to be anybody —"

"My p — my people are away, you see." The manner was suddenly elegant, the voice theirs from five to fifty, kin to the one he'd left only an hour ago. "Which ones have you seen?"

The tray felt heavy on his knees, too awkward somehow

to rise. He judged her after all about twenty. "There was a Siamese here, just a few minutes ago."

"*Itty*-Katty!" She clutched her brow. "Oh God and criminy, that's my mother's, she'll be frantic."

"And a striped one, yesterday."

"Fatty-Kitty! I haven't seen her for *two* days. Oh dear, will I catch it. They're not allowed in the house, you see. Because we've been staying at Gran's."

More likely twelve. She was small in size, and he hadn't been around children. Possibly even ten. "We could go hunt up Itty, er, Kitty," he said. "I don't think the other one's been around today. That is, Fatty, er, *Katty*. The striped."

"Got you!" she said, clapping her hands.

"I beg your —"

"Itty-*Kat*. Fatty-*Kit*. Oh it drives everyone wild. Scatrhythm, to coin a pun — as my father says. Makes you say it on the downbeat, you see. The other would just be Dixieland." She peered in on him, as if at another world she expected to see there. "Jazz. We all pretend to be fanatic on the subject. To annoy Gran." Her voice was suddenly shy.

"Tell me something," he said. "Is any one of those creatures named Max?"

"Why, that's the one you've been feeding!" she said. "The *lost* one."

"Oh, the lost one." He looked down at the dish. "Good old Max."

She giggled. "That's what my kid cousin said. Bill, he's a senior at Stanford. He was here till today, but he had to go back early."

Good old Bill. Eighteen? He gave up. It was the gloaming hour, just before all cats became gray.

"Oh, don't get *up,*" she said. "You finish your meal, fevvens sake. And don't think of helping hunt — that's my responsibility. I was going to ask you a favor, but not that one. If it wouldn't be too much of a drag. Oh gee — well, *thanks.*" As she came through the door, she looked up at him. All he could be sure of was that she wasn't ten. "I guess I ought to introduce myself, hadn't I, I'm Alden Benjamin, we live just down the road." She recited this rapidly.

"Oh, how do you do, I'm G —"

"Oh I know who you are, of course." She refused a chair and sat on the floor, clasping her knees. "You're Mr. Callendar. *Gwee* Callendar." This last came very softly, as if it were being tried out for the first time. "The tenant," she said.

"Ten — ? Oh." He glanced up at his own eaves, the fine old triangulated ones, deep enough for swallows to nest in, on whose rescue he had rubbed his knuckles bare.

She giggled. "Oh, I *know*. Not really, any more. But it's always been called that, kind of, ever since the land grant — it was one, you know. Some revolutionary jerk, way back. And it's marked that way on the map that went with it — 'tenant's land.'" She gave a small, convulsive smile. "They still like to think . . . you know how p —" She coughed. "— people are."

"Oh." He drew out a cigarette. "Your — people."

She nodded. "Parker and Buzzie."

"Cigarette?"

She lit the filter end. He gave her another. She addressed

the trembling end of it, deeply. "It's just, you know, I smoke these plain fags."

He stood up again. "Just about to get myself another beer. Would you — ?"

"Oh, no *thanks*. I mean, I *do*, but no thanks."

He brought back a Coke and a plate of store cookies, the filled kind.

She ate one. "Peanut butter! God. Haven't tasted it since I was six."

"Your — people," he said. "They're — your parents?"

"Oh dear." She sat back to survey herself, unclasping her knees. Sparks flew from her, and the cigarette. She retrieved it. "I catch everything, don't I know it. There was this boy at the Proot, he used to say it."

"The — Proot?"

"Prewitt Country Day."

"Oh." He remembered the term, from Hartford. "A school."

She stared. "It's just down the road from here." She waved a hand, inland. "I used to go there."

He often had a sense of how much in this landscape was just down the road from him, from childless people living in inns and barns. This was one of the times. "Which is which?" he said.

"Hmm?"

"Your people."

"Mummy is Parker." Suddenly she took another cookie. She gulped it. "Oh, you mustn't think — Buzzie is very dignified. He can't perform an instrument or anything, but he has this very serious interest. He even wanted to go to the Newport Festival, the jazz one. But Parker dragged him off to the Casals. Spain, or somewhere. She recruits for Gran, you see." She hefted a sigh. "That's why I'm here."

"To see me?"

"Oh, no. Well, partly. But I meant here in this god-forsaken end of nowhere. *Home.*"

It was almost dark now. "You must have a huge view from there."

"Oh no, our part's all overgrown, been that way since I was a child, not that I mind. And Gran won't give us the money to —" She broke off. "Anyway, the only place you can see out is up-river. From Gran's tower."

"Oh yes, I think I've seen it," he said. "An old American Gothic. Way, way on south there, there's one open spot. Through those trees. But I should think my trees would block — the tenant's, that is."

In the dark, her eyes shone. "No. You're our view."

"Oh." It had never struck him that anyone could look in on his solitude. "Dull for you."

She was silent for a time. "Summer!" she said then. "Summer around here is sure a real dark nervous green."

"Nervous?"

"Oh God," she said. "Me again. I'm an absolute *ensemble.* We had a guest last week — Hollywood. That's what they say out there. For anything awful."

He repeated it. "It does have a lilt."

"Mmm." Her voice was shrewd. "So did he."

He turned on the porch light. "You mind telling me something? Exactly how many years ago was it you tasted peanut butter. Since you were six?"

She lowered her chin, then raised it. It was a more than nice face, not quite lovely, but sympathetically planed, already shaped both to give and to receive. She tilted it higher. "Ten. Ten and a *half.*"

He was less relieved than he should have been. "I judged you older, somehow," he murmured.

Her look said that his judgment was profound.

"All I ask is to be old enough to be natural," she said gruffly. "I just pray for it."

"Other way round, I thought. When you're young is when you are, I thought."

"Not when you're me. I'm just only bits and pieces of whosever's around. *Simply* hilarious." She gave a doleful shrug. "It can last on and on too, Buzzie says, the way it has with himsel —" She coughed. "Unless you have a serious interest." She flung her head back, and her hands — flung the world off. "I don't mind Gran, though. Funny thing, when a person is themselves, no matter what, they're not so catching. To me, that is."

"She's old enough, I gather? To be nat —"

"Boy!" She giggled. "I'm supposed to be looking after *her* — and the cats, of course. And she's supposed to be taking care of me. But that's Parker for you." She rested her chin on her knees, eyes up. "Anyway . . . summer around here is sure a . . . grim. I don't see how you stand it. I should think it'd drive you absolutely nuts." Then, with a horrified glance at him, she sat up very straight, open-mouthed, arms at her sides. He had a feeling that only manners, or perhaps the delicacy which already showed so plain on her, kept her from clapping a hand to that mouth.

He was used to this of course. One couldn't expect them to be as used to his history as he was. "Tell me," he said. "The favor you wanted to ask me."

From what he could see of her cheeks they were red, but she answered in his own tone. "I was wondering. If by any chance you were going to be around next weekend. Labor Day weekend."

"Why, yes." The past afternoon rose up in him, dark pool so alien from this light refreshment its own dusk offered him. "As a matter of fact — I was planning to."

"And you don't seem to mind cats. At least, you've been feeding them."

"We-ell, that's about it, I don't mind them. I prefer dogs, of course."

"Of course," she said. "But then — you don't have a dog."

He stared at her, at their image of this clearing, minuscule in their distance, across which a toy man, toy solitary, never walked a toy dog.

"Apparently Gran isn't too old for twenty-twenty vision," he said.

Her face was still pink. She kept it lowered. "Oh — she never goes up there. It's hot as blazes, and full of dead flies. Lucky for me. You see — they're supposed to be off the place altogether. The cats. And I've been keeping them up there, or trying to." She looked up at him. "Cats need a *place!*" Her lip trembled.

"And yours is closed up?"

"Rented. So *they* could go, you know. And we couldn't ask the renter to keep *four*. And for four, there just wasn't enough — well, a kennel was just — out. So it was up to —" She cast him a faint smile. "Gran never thinks about money. Far as she knows, that's where they are."

"So it was up to you," he said.

"Oh, I'm quite dependable."

"Yes." He watched that movie. "I can see that you are."

"And it would all work out," she said. "Only dammit, just for this weekend I'm being sent away."

"Ah yes," he said. "From your tower." When his powerful garage light was on, as it often was if he worked evenings, then his clearing must hang in the trees like a fair. Still, it was cruel of him. "Like Rapunzel," he said. "Or, no. Rapunzel was *kept*."

"Oh, I'm not *de trop*, or anything," she said. "Gran wouldn't give a hang. It was Buzzie who insisted. She's having a very sophisticated bunch up for the weekend, some of her screamers — you wouldn't know about that — and . . . and I'm not supposed to be that sophisticated. So Parker had to arrange for me. Buzzie was really very strong about it." She looked proud.

"Good for Buzzie." A sudden thought struck him. "Cats give some people asthma," he said absently.

Her face fell.

"Oh, not me," he said hastily. "I thought perhaps that was why —"

"Gran? No, far as I know she just ha-ates them. Really she's just one of those people who's mortally afraid of them. There's a name for it."

"Mmm."

"If one comes in a room where she is, she jumps up on a table. They do rather go for her extra. They *know*." She chewed a finger. "Could be her color too, of course. She's got some vein disease that doesn't bother *her* otherwise. But she *is* blue. I expect you've heard."

"N-no, I — " He leaned back, arms folded. "Your gran. Mrs. Aldrich. She jumps on tables. And she is *bl* — ?"

"Really, rather turquoise."

"N-no," he said. "I h-hadn't." Hiccups engulfed him. "Heard."

She waited until he'd finished, to stand up. "I didn't think you'd laugh. At other people's misfortunes. I didn't really think you would."

"I didn't think so either." But he felt as if he had been for a swim in laughter.

"Or you don't believe me."

"I believe you," he said.

"I guess it was me then, you were — People do."

"No, it was a coincidence," he said. "I was laughing at the smallness of the world. Or the enormity. Anyway, please believe *me*. I can't possibly explain."

"Oh, I believe you," she said. "I certainly do. And I appreciate your language."

He stood up. "Cats need a place," he said looking down at her. "But I'm afraid you'll have to do the rounding up. Or else rename them."

"Oh!" she said. "Oh-h. I could come tomorrow morning and start feeding them here. I could come here every day, so that by Friday — I don't have to go, you know, for four whole days."

She was going to be a bore, the kind that could be painful. He hadn't come near one of her for years. He already wanted to get rid of her. She was the young. "Where are they sending you?"

She made a face. "Friends of Parker's. They have a girl my age, and they keep wanting us to be. We haven't a thing in common really. Bianca O'Brian. She's French."

"She doesn't sound very French."

"Oh, she had an ancestor — some marshal. To have an Irish surname in France is the utter. And her live grandmother is a princess in Rome."

"Oh? And what color is *she?*"

She giggled. Then she stood on one leg.

He sighed. "And is Bianca at the — Country Day?"

"Oh no," she gasped, "she's already been at Le Rosey. And at Brillaumont. They couldn't do a thing with her." The other leg twined. He watched, in fascinated recall of how it had once felt, to be literally beside oneself.

She began to speak very rapidly. "She has this little face that pooches out, and she wears her hair scissored all around it, the way they do. Y'know? As if some sex-maniac had been chewing it. And all she has to do is scatter this talk of hers, like birdseed, and the boys come hop, hop. And wherever we others are wearing our belts, she isn't."

"I hope it isn't catching," he said. "It's certainly utter."

"Oh, it's very poisemaking, to have a line," she said. "If you haven't yet got — the other." And finally, the leg came down. Standing there, all of her implored him to see that she would give anything to rid them both of her company.

He would have liked to pat her, in sympathy. Instead, he looked at his watch.

"Oh, I must go!" she said at once. "Gran will be wi-ild." Her hands crossed on her bathing suit. "I hope I haven't given you a — a false impression of us. We're really a very devoted family." It gave him a glimpse of how she might be, once she had achieved what she aspired to — and a wish to give her something toward it. He hadn't been able to give anyone else anything, all the long day.

"I knew a girl once," he said. "Only a very little older

than you are." It came as a shock that Ellen had been only three years older than this girl when he married her. "She wasn't any prettier than you. And probably not as — smart." His voice ground. To think blasphemy was different from speaking it. "But she had a way with her, if it's any use to you — I suppose one could call it a line. Whenever anyone paid her a compliment, or she was at a loss, she used to look at him sideways — you'll know how — and say, *Oh, you're just saying that!*" Once, at Niagara Falls, Ellen and he had donned the oilskins they gave one, and had walked through a passageway under and back of the Falls. Strange images, octahedrons of glass were at the other side of them. Ellen stood with these now. "It was very fetching," he said. "It made the boys come hop, hop."

"Thanks," she said. "Thank-*you*. I'll study it up in a mirror sometime." Then she bounded away from him. He gathered that he had somehow offended her, but at least it had made her free as a gazelle. Across the glen, he watched her bound backward over a hedge.

His own youth had been awkward. "Pleased to meetcha!" he called from it. "Pleased to meetcha, Alden."

She paused, then she came running fleetly. Halfway across the clearing, her hands clasped at her breast exactly as before. She rediscovered the barn, the screen door, him standing there. A moon had risen since, and was coldly shining. Walking as if her bathing suit were a skirt, she included the moon. It was like watching a tic of the imagination — hers — acted out on his obviously dream-forested land. "You're just the way I thought you would be," she said softly. "Good night — Gwee."

She was there the next morning, and more of each day

thereafter, sharing his lunches and once, in the company of a dealer-friend up from Pennsylvania, his supper, even offering him a muted assistance in the shop — and all with a manner so altered that he could find her unimportant presence lightly welcome. The dizzy reel of her confidences had altogether stopped, like a carnival ride shared by strangers. She made no more references to her family, and in his own mind they no longer struck the monster, papier-mâché attitudes she had so carefully pointed out to him along the ride. It was probable that they were quite ordinary, in their own way. Her subdued manner now almost called upon him to notice that so was she. Even the soapbubble chain of her giggling had vanished over-night, as if somewhere quieted at the fount. Overnight — it amused him to think — she might have consulted one of those Carmencitas who squatted over such matters behind windows crayoned with the zodiac, to which the words *Readings, Advisor* also adhered. Somewhere, in the depths of herself, she was being advised. In his own, he knew he was being worshiped, and felt himself too humble to question it. It was pleasant to find himself amiably concise with her in a way he was seldom able with his sharper-tongued New York friends — in the way perhaps, if things had been otherwise, that fatherhood sharpened the tongue. As a proprietor, he was used to lingerers, hangers-on, even apprentices such as, in the late, Urbino light of those August afternoons, pottering after him in her shirt and shorts, or shorn tan head seen bent across an intervening field of objects and tasks, she increasingly appeared to be.

In that light, age was their duenna — and her hair wasn't gold; she was merely in the absolute russet of health. He recalled better now how the flesh at that age was aureoled in its own fuzz. But, as she lounged, sun-struck in the doorway, he had no visual terror of her; she wasn't Ellen, but what might have been Ellen's child. A dealer had just left them. The shop's business was always by appointment; few itinerants came here.

"I admire you," she said. "For the way you do nothing and people just come to you." For the rest of the afternoon she was silent. It occurred to him, absent in mind as he'd been all week — or elsewhere in mind — that her prayer might be being answered; she was certainly more natural.

Early Friday morning, before leaving, she came by for an uncalled-for visit to the cats, who were by now accustomed to his feeding them. He was mildly surprised at her appearance as she bent daintily over their dishes — travel suit, hat and bag, hair brushed to a burnish, from what he could see of it, and a new, sooty dimension to her unremarkable eyes. When he heard she was walking to the station, he of course drove her there, and waited with her for the dusty, division local that would take her on to Grand Central, where she would be met by a chauffeur, she said, and driven on. The station, merely a junction beneath the once Indian highland, was bare of persons on this national weekend away. Beyond the sheds and other ramshackles, deserted outbuildings of another century, that quietly rotted here and at other up-Hudson junctions, the flat valley of water took the sun. As always, the wide expanse made him uneasy; he turned his back to it. The girl beside him, taking the compliment to herself, smiled gratefully. Now that she was leaving, he was suddenly great with a four-day-repressed need to be by himself again. When he put her bag up for her in the train, he was already irritated with her for making herself out a waif to him, as she could apparently do without moving an eyelash. There were others on the train dressed exactly like her, most with friends or parents it was true, but her own were returning in a few days. Still, her hat, though so regulation, reared back from her forehead like the pure feather of flight. He felt he ought to make it up to her, for not being able to keep his mind on her, somehow to explain to her that she was simply at that interim in her life when no one was around to do it. "Good-by," he said. "And good luck on the weekend, don't you worry now. You have no idea how different you look in shoes."

He hurried home to his house, to be alone with being alone there. It was good, infinitely good to mosey and loll, a man in no way bereft of the small things of life, one whose phone was contrarily atap with friends, waifs and peti-tioners — merely a man who preferred dogs, but had no dog. Toward dusk, he set his meal on a tray, and once more brought it out to the porch. No one, entowered somewhere in the tree-murmurs, was there to watch him. At last he was at peace enough, if it could be called peace, to dwell on what all week he'd been powerless to keep his mind from — to let it ring its changes inside him.

On Tuesday, he had called the Canal Zone. During the day, there'd been no reason to fear she might be bereft; Tuesday, when the place reopened at four, was always a big day domestically, with cleaning to be done, suppliers' salesmen to be dealt with, and the full staff in attendance, two waitresses, Carlos the cook, and sometimes Roy, the assistant barman. He had restrained himself from calling until six, the busy hour at the bar, when Sligo was always in attendance there. Roy had answered the phone. He had asked to speak to Marion.

"The missus, she's in the kitchen," said Roy. "Talkin' to Carlos."

Everyone knew of course that Carlos did drink; his temperament, often to be heard from the kitchen, was cherished as much as his cooking by those patrons who liked to think that they haunted a bar for its colorfulness. No one would have known of it otherwise. The staff, loyal to each other and apparently to the owners, never gossiped.

"You want to talk to the mister?" said Roy. "He's awful busy, Mr. Callendar, we got a rush on that IBM Country Club crowd."

"No thanks. Just ask her —" He hesitated. "I just called to find out if the lamp I left was okay. Just ask her if everything's all right. About the lamp."

"Okay, sir."

"Maybe I'll stop by myself to check on it tomorrow," he added half to himself, as Roy hung up.

He did that. During the period when he had helped furnish the upstairs, the staff had grown used to his checking. Wednesday afternoons, as he knew well enough, Sligo and Marion were usually in town with the station wagon, doing all the weekly errands from meat inspection to talking improvement loans with the bank manager. He pretended to have forgotten this.

"Wednesday their town day," said Roy. It was the usual midweek afternoon, trade dull. Everything appeared normal. Of course, everything always had. Why was he here?

"One day gets to be like another, out where I am," he

said. He knew how to talk to Roy, not that it took anything special; anyone did.

"Out where anybody is, around here!" Roy said at once. "I tell you, Mr. Callendar, we can't wait for winter." Winters, Roy did the Miami run. "We" meant his wife and mother, as devoted as he to the crowd, the tables, the money, the sun and the sea, in that order — to all the big-time externals of life. It was hard to imagine any of the three ever suffering from one of the inner varieties of love-death, certainly not from love of death, or even perhaps from the death of love. They were happy. But knowing how to talk to Roy meant knowing that even he, they, were in their own way extreme.

"When you going?" Guy said.

"December twenty-sixth, leave here six-thirty A.M.," Roy said promptly. "I drive the buggy down, U.S. 1 all the way. Ma and Vee fly National. Next night we'll all three be in our suits at the beach, dinner at the Alcazar. And three nights after. I don't start work till the first."

"Sounds wonderful." He was having trouble keeping his mind on Roy. He stared at the diamond ring in its glass case. Roy's blunt, shaven head didn't shadow it.

"I tell you. Whyn't you pick up and go down. Even for good, you could make a living. They got antique shops galore." Roy was capable of assuring a banker that Miami had banks.

"Maybe I will."

"I tell you." Roy leaned forward. Now came the climax of this refrain. "If we could stay down there —" The pre-amble was always the same, the conclusion too. Only the metaphor varied. "If we could stay down there — !" Each of Roy's eyes shone as if it were the only one he had. "Nee one of us ever ask nothing more in this life. Nee one of us ask for two more tail feathers from a duck."

He almost forgot to make the drink-offer which was the ritual end of this conversation.

It was answered with the ritual headshake. "Thanks, Mr. Callendar. But I'll have a cigar."

He put his elbows on the bar, trying to recall how it felt to lean outward into life from some heavy focus, glowing or dark — instead of cordially, temperately, holding the phone. "Roy?" he'd said, as if Roy could tell him. "Roy — what's your last name?"

Roy, just nipping the cigar, looked up. He spat the tip. "Grotz. Roy *Valerian* Grotz. Must be why I became a bartender, huh, whoever asks a barkeep his full name?" He doffed the cigar. "You ever ready for info ree down there, you just write me. Care of the Alcazar."

"Thanks," he said, "I just came to wonder. Don't know why in particular." Looking round the calm, empty bar, with its faint smell of bitter from old limbos, he'd shivered his shoulders. "Certainly not waiting for winter."

"You're telling me!" said Roy.

When he came home, he found a note from Marion in his mailbox; she must have driven by to put it there. "Please don't call. And don't come. My thanks." With the proper chance, he might have met them there at the end of his driveway, she bending to thrust the note far back in the box, Sligo sitting immobile in the car as one sometimes saw him, hunched forward in the posture of men in World War I statuary groups — a member of the Battle of the

Marne temporarily hacked from his stone brothers. Marion always drove.

Thursday — last night — his dealer friend, Sprague, had stayed for supper, and the girl. Though he addressed her by name, in his mind she was "the girl." He'd been grateful for both their presences. In the summer dimness after the hot glade of the day, as they sipped the wine Sprague had brought, the rise and fall of their own voices had had a pre-fall, alfresco charm. The girl had sipped too, with an over-distinguished air.

"Nice kid," Sprague had commented, in a moment when the girl had gone in for a bit.

"Lonely summer," said Guy.

Sprague nodded. "I get 'em from the summer theaters. Apprentices. Sent round to borrow." A former painter, he now dealt mostly in authentic American primitives, had a shop in the Poconos, and knew Joe and Milly Pink. "Terrible stuff they have," he said.

"Terrible." He listened to the echo. "Their boy is getting married."

"Oh, I know that boy. Different from them." Sprague, pouring himself another, had gestured with the bottle in the direction where Alden had gone. "Like her, they're luckier. Kids like her, you can see their whole background behind them, ahead of them, too. Meet a boy of the same, and with a little luck they'll live their whole lives that way. Lost in the background. The best way."

Sprague's history was unknown to him, or whether Sprague knew his — but that each had an unlikely one was one of the comforting assumptions of their trade.

"She looks a little like that print you have inside there," said Sprague. "The girl in profile — who's it by, Polliaiulo? Just a pretty girl of the day, but you can see the whole Renaissance behind her. I've got a little Federalist one at home now. A stiff little girl of the period, all her life, probably. Only the painter happened to single her out. She isn't the subject anymore. The subject is 1810." He gestured again at Alden, who had just reappeared, and was now circling the porch, fiddling with the cats' dishes. She bent there with the bursting shyness of one who knew herself the question. "Girls like that are like stencils," he said. "For what's around them. Boys too, of course. Hmm. Used to wish I could paint that way. You know? I wanted to do it for now."

Alden came in and sat again at the table.

"What's the name of this county?" Sprague asked her.

"Dutchess."

"There you are!" said Sprague. "Girl of Dutchess County, with the light behind her. American primitive, *circa* 1970, artist unknown. All I need is a hundred years."

"A hundred years and I'll be dead!" said Alden gaily. She flung it out like a garland.

"They'll be nice ones, honey," said Sprague. "Just marry some neighborhood boy."

"*This* neighborhood?" she said.

Both he and Sprague had roared, of course. "Alden's family is musical," he had said, in reparation.

"How about that!" Sprague had answered, with the trade's tone-deafness. "I took in a harpsichord once. Inlaid with Wedgwood medallions. Not the blue jasperware either. The gray."

He thought now of the girl riding to her destination, for today, somewhere on Long Island — of whether she would ride all her life jogging in the "background" expected of her, through the minor hazards to the final, profound ones — all of her happily submerged life. Right now, as Sprague had said, she was only a mild darkness at whose edges one could see the whole bright pattern of her segment of life, from costume plates of the period to chapbooks of the road-and-home-life of the times. It was in her very voice and no doubt in the fillings of her excellent teeth — all the successive decades of the woman she would almost certainly be, already counterparted by the versions of such women to be seen, in their own decades from blond hair to mauve, in the streets and shops of towns near places like Garrison. And it didn't have to be that stratum, of course. A same unconscious innocence of itself could work in any — he remembered Hartford. As Sprague had said, innocence of its own import was what was required, of the life that was the subject, as well as of the painter's hand. And even for those who knew themselves to be the extreme, there might be degrees of innocence. All that was needed was a hundred years.

As for Alden, the girl — He looked up at the trees, behind and behind whose layers there was somewhere a tower from which she had spied on him. He thought of the feather in her hat. Probably the next ten years would show. It might be touch and go — as to whether or not she would be singled out.

Toward dark, the Siamese returned to the edge of the clearing. All that week she had been away — since Monday. Her flanks were fallen in. As she drank greedily from one of the other cats' saucers, he remembered with a contraction of sadness how, last time, she had proudly refused to be fed. When she had cleaned herself, she stood off and regarded him, eyes opening and closing, head tucked in. He had no trouble identifying of whom she reminded him — that snub head, those mask-clenched eyes. Nor had he any intention of taking her return as an omen — this random, itty-kat vagrant between silk pillow and forest. Just because he was now aware of what must have been being enacted for years at the Canal Zone, didn't mean he could interpose there. Marion's note had made him see his place — he was audience. All the watching in the world couldn't force their stagelight closer to his own quiet demi-brown. After a while, as the moonless night closed in, he could no longer see for sure whether or not the eyes were still regarding him. Only a stencil remained, a head-shaped importance of darkness with the light behind it — ringed round with knives.

On Saturday, as he did the week's shopping in town, he found himself looking with a purpose, in the store queues and the parking lots, down the market streets and at crossings. He was looking for a family, never the same one of course but one always constituted the same, that over the years had now and then presented itself to him without warning. He didn't see them. But the quality of the change came home with him, like the edge slid into one at the change of seasons. He had never before looked.

On Sunday, he began the turnout of the barn, long self-promised, and never yet done. The weather was glorious, as people were no doubt saying all over the nation. Out on that highway from which he was a quarter-mile in, the smart ones were already bearing back to the city, to be safe there on the murderous third day of the holiday. There and elsewhere, cars must already be smashing and piling up, duty bound to fill in that annual Tuesday headline for which the funeral presses were waiting. Tuesday seemed to him distant as a new life, or an old one that had to be resumed. It was Monday, day of the smash, that had to be got through, here where the great stasis of land, water, and tree would uphold him in the silent conjunction of all their valleys. As he dragged object after object out on the lawn, none, however curious, lovely or valuable, seized him with that griping in the bowels of possession which afflicted others of his trade. He was neat of habit; there was really no need for this housecleaning. But he had an urge to see the barn as empty as it had been when he came. Meanwhile, there were corners of his eyrie he had forgotten. He turned up the first table he had refinished but had never sold, of itself an honest maple, but in the last rays of daylight too auburn by far. In its drawer, he found the one relic he had saved from the burned rubble, only because it predated it — a small vase of cloudy glass with a cheap scene scratched on it, from its position in his mother's window, in his childhood always called the "sunset" vase. By nightfall, the place was emptied, except for his huge rolltop desk, weighted with business, that had been the first thing in here anyway, and hanging above it, that archaic reminder to "Resource." He left those two inside, all the rest of the array turned out to the starlight. The night was as clear and soft as the inside of a grape; no rain would fall. Even if it did, all he stood to lose was some of the money which helped to keep him suspended in life, immovable to the waves of need. And he had all Monday to put everything back. He brought his bedroll to the center of the lawn, and lay for a long time looking up at the barn's dark ogives, that now seemed to breathe with him, in their earlier communion. The barn was what he loved; he had rescued it.

By late afternoon Monday, he had everything back inside and in order again except for the lamps and the pictures, touches of comfort with which he would fill out the evening. He walked down to the mailbox on the highway: though there wouldn't be any mail, there was always a chance that someone had left a note there. And it was his usual walk. Less than halfway back, having found nothing, he heard the clear bell of the telephone, brought to him by the river, a nagging rhythm of a phone that went on for a long time. It had stopped well before his desperate run brought him up short in front of it. The call had been a friend's of course, faithful Poll perhaps, homing from her three-day weekend, or Quent reporting in, or any other of his phone regulars, like him suspended in a network of friends, not relations — horses running abreast in their own National, and today, like the rest of the world, galloping home. Still he stood there, and at last he dialed the Canal Zone.

On the instant, he heard the buh-beep, buh-beep of the busy signal, a quietus he might listen to now for as long as he wanted. They had taken the receiver off, as usual. They were in the eyrie couples made for themselves. That settled it. He listened to it telling him so — just then, it stopped. On the other end, someone had replaced the receiver. He redialed, heard the ring and the connect. No one spoke, but the wire was live; he could hear heavy, animal breathing. "Sligo?" he said. "It's Guy." In the pause, he could still hear that strangely reassuring pulse of brute calm. Then the line went dead. "Sorree," said the operator, when he made his plea. "Sorree," she repeated — a flute stuck at the stop of eternal patience. "That line is out of order now." He hung there, in the queer dejection, less paralyzed than timeless, of those accustomed to lives ordered and rebuffed by the phone. When he wheeled about, the girl was standing in the archway of the barn.

"Well . . . hi!" he said. It was hard to focus on her, but he was grateful for it. "Welcome back."

She was dressed just as he had last seen her, in what must be her "best" and now showed up as rather badly worn, and perhaps not even hers to begin with. Only the angle of the hat was still freshly her own, as if just before he turned she had reached up and knocked it back like a forelock. At his blinking smile, her hands clasped at her breast. It didn't go with the hat.

"Well," he said, "and how was Bianca La Borgia?"

She shook her head ruefully. "Don't. We were horrid."

"Oh, were we?"

She took a step forward. "Why didn't you tell me?" she said deeply. "That your name wasn't Gwee."

He couldn't think of an answer.

"Bianca says you would pronounce it the English way. *Guy.* And that even if you didn't, the French don't say Gwee, but G-gee."

"They do? I don't know French."

A perfect aureole spread on her face, in time with a long intake of breath. "If that isn't just like you."

"Not to know French."

"No," she said, on another breath like a chord. "To be the way you are."

"Tell me about Bianca," he said.

She spun halfway on a heel, came inside, touched a table, intimately tap-tapped a lamp. "Oh, you've changed things around. You've tidied." She gave him a gay smile, turned away again, and spoke nonchalantly over a shoulder. "There were some boys there too. Putrid. We both agreed on that. Simply putrid. Anyway, Bianca had to wear her retainer the whole weekend."

"Her —" Impossible medievalisms came to mind.

She gave him one of her shrewd, flat looks. "Teeth. She's having them straightened. And she cheated all last year in Switzerland, and didn't wear it. Now she's getting to look all chipmunky again, so she has to." She almost giggled. "When she has it in, her mouth looks just like Penn Station. Which reminds me." The giggle was born as a shrug. She whirled again, infinitely Gallic. "Anyway, the boys had to hang around somewhere, and — I was there."

He grinned. "All in your own teeth."

She hung her head. "Of course," she said in a low voice — "I didn't let them make out, though."

"Oh?" The phrase was new to him. "Of course." He felt like a father. "Er — Penn Station, what were you going to say that it reminded you of?"

"Oh that. Bianca's dream. We sat up all night, exchanging them. She has this dream she's walking around inside something's mouth, a great big pink cave. She has it all the time."

He laughed out loud. "Common enough to all races. Jonah and the whale."

She stared meaningfully, making their eyes meet. "Don't be sil-*ly!*" Then she blushed. And suddenly she began to speak very rapidly. "Bianca says, you should never let a boy your own age make out. She says in France it's the same for girls as for men now; you have your first *aff-aire du coeur* with a much older person. Like in *Bonjour Tristesse.*"

"You forget I don't know French. He took out a cigarette but didn't offer her one. "Is that why she cheated — in Switzerland?"

She nodded, head bent.

He lit the cigarette. "Well, I can see you certainly stayed up all night."

"We talked a lot about you. Bianca thinks —" She whispered it. "Bianca thinks you're wonderful."

"Oh, she does, does she. Why, what could that little — what could she possibly —" He broke off, to look at her.

"Your . . . your *life,*" she said. She was close enough for him to see that her eyes had filled with tears but that she was holding on to them, not letting them spill. It was too lovely a sight to turn from. He could see what she was going to be.

"Aren't you going to ask me about the cats?" he said.

"Oh, the cats — they can manage." The new planes about her mouth quivered, in time with her shrug. This time, she carried it off.

"You know . . . Alden," he said. "I believe you've made it. You're natural."

"Oh? And meanwhile I've changed, I'd rather be a mystery." She said it lightly, and carried this off too.

"You are," he said. "I suppose you're both." She was near enough for him to identify her smell. He was stupid enough to touch her on the shoulder.

"Oh —" She made the most awkward of gestures, a cygnet breaking its glassy dream of itself — and yet saving it. She touched her throat, jerking her hand away from it toward him, as if, if she could, she would give him its apple. "Oh," she said. "You're just *saying* that."

The kiss tasted of all she wanted to give him. He held on to her, merged in what for her was only a whole summer's ache. Behind them, the barn waited, a bed among the trees, prepared. He well remembered that summer of himself. But even while he held her, in this silence a quarter-mile from the highway, he could hear within himself the sound of lives, regular as rockets, riding to their Monday smash. He had his perspective. He was the one who was unnatural here.

He was able to force her away from him. She was smiling, not in retrospect. He couldn't see the landscape she was looking at, but he could remember how it had felt to be there. "I'd like —"

He stopped, for honesty. That his wife had been just this age when he'd had her, that his own child would have been the same age by now, was merely one of these peculiar marvels of time from which people made almanacs, hoping to tether within reasonable, man-made bonds the life that kept escaping onward. If this girl once stayed the night, she'd want to stay on always — he knew that much about her. She was no Bianca. And a week ago — he knew himself as well. A week ago, he would have singled her out.

"But I've got to go," he said. It was true, the minute he said it. "I've got to run off this minute to somebody, somewhere." He put his hand on her cheek. "It's the only thing I can say to you worth a dime."

He could see its worth, from her face — even at her age. He was the one who was running. She was the audience.

She knelt to the line of feeding dishes and hunched there, playing hand-over-hand with them.

"It's important, where I'm going," he said. "That much you can believe."

She stood up; she nodded — both with her new grace. More than this was beyond her. "See you around."

"Oh, Alden," he said. "Luck." He said it as if he could give it to her. "Luck!"

She must have looked at him this way from her tower, small but dependable, up among the dead flies, and the dark nervous greens of summer. She was able to toss her head. "No sweat!" she said. A talisman floated down to her from somewhere, a bit of Hollywood or Stanford, or even Spain. The corners of her mouth turned down, or in. "Don't sweat the small stuff!" she said.

When she was well enough away, he reminded himself how seventeen loved promises. "And Alden —"

She turned, as if to a teacher, or a parent, without hope.

"No more binoculars. Promise me?"

Whatever her age was, it judged him. "Opera glasses," she said. "Parker's."

She was well into the trees, almost lost to view, before he called after her. "The Siamese! The Siamese came back."

Out on the highway in his car, it couldn't be said that he had forgotten her, an after-image still resident in his body, in his now conscious flesh — the catalyst — sunk like a performer through a trapdoor. Around him, real cars whizzed loud as imaginary ones, but with the coarser hopes of people who were on the move. He wanted to put it to them, call out to them — I'm with you again. I'm part of this violence.

The road to the Canal Zone was solitary in the dusk, but halfway there, he thought he saw lights — were there people? It was the hour on the riverland when brilliance came and went in patches of gilt, the mauve mingling with the sun. His step crunched on the gravel. The courtyard was empty. In it, the Canal Zone squatted with the prescience of an old building, at dusk aware of all its history, tawdry and benign. The lower level of the games room was black under its overhung eaves. The top story, where the bedrooms were, was dim. Light was pouring like music from all the windows of the main floor bar. He could see the chandeliers at every second-story window, at battle with the retreating sun. Who could have entered the close-coupled dream that went on here, that only the personae themselves made real? Yet there wasn't a sound, not a sound of trade.

Then in the bedroom story, a window was flung up. A figure appeared between its shutters and looked down at him. Beneath her wrists, the dim, pompom row of geraniums were a row of footlights that hadn't sprung on. "How did you know?" she said. "I rang and rang, but no answer, and then he . . . how did you know to come?"

Now that he saw she was safe, he understood better his own errand — he knew for whose rescue he was here.

"Your phone's out of order now." This was reality; he remembered it — a blow, good or bad, that slowed the mind.

"He's cut the wires. Oh, hurry. I haven't heard him for the last hour. I'm afraid . . . that he —"

"Where is he? Down there?"

"Go there first," she said. "I can wait." She saw his bewilderment. "I'm —" Her shame told him that he was still a stranger. "I'm locked in."

He ran up the service stairs, and released her. They crept down them, interlaced like skaters. "What's that you have in your hand?" he said, but she was already ahead of him, across the passage into the main barroom.

"Yes," he heard her whisper to herself. "Yes."

Sligo stood in the damage like a man in a prism, angled at from all sides. His posture, bent at the knees, head in the vise of the shoulders, arms close to his sides, was like that also, a double image of a big man superimposed on a smaller one, a man enclosed in the bottle of himself. Around him, chairs were kindling, tables crumbs of zinc, their chromium legs junked skyward. A tidal hand had swept the glasses and decanters to a thousand refractions, through which waters were still seeping. The mahogany pillars of the bar had been scored, and behind them, the dark pride of the room, the etched mirror that ran its width, was irised open from end to end.

His eyes were what was moving. By these, they too could see his hallucination. It traveled wall over wall, haunted corners, or was sometimes beneath him, a small thing that teased. He tremored to it. Sometimes he screamed to it, though no one could hear. Clearly, he himself knew he was *seeing* it. In the hospital, these had been the most desperate.

Behind him, Marion crept closer, in her hand a syringe. His eyes whitened in their sockets; he saw her. Now that he saw her, she walked steadily toward him, at a bridesmaid's pace. He trembled under her advance, but differently. He saw her, and knew she was real — this was her role. Above their heads, one saw the thousand refractions of it, of who might have forced the role on whom.

She stood beside him now, waiting. It was like a wooing.

And quite suddenly, he was able to move. He moved with caution, outward through the parallelograms. He even pantomimed to her that he wasn't dangerous. See, I'm only grasping for the bar, steadying myself against it. So that I can stand, and bear what you have for me. His lips turned in. The sound that came from behind them wasn't fear, but the catholic moan of all animals, forgiving someone for the general pain. Then he held out his left arm. Cool as a lay sister, she took care of him. Then she stepped aside. But her eyes flickered a signal, at Guy.

Sligo surveyed them, amiably. Sleep was already arriving in him; he was sane with it. The shakes caressed him once, then he stood pridefully straight. He extended his right arm, palm stiff, as one did for doctors; he could have balanced a tray. Slowly he clenched the hand to a fist, drew the fist in toward his own chest and outward, shoulder high, his eye following it as if magnetized. Head in bas-relief, he stood that way, a gladiator measuring the strength in his mortal glove. He spoke to it, clearer than Guy had ever heard him, but his eye did not turn. It wasn't possible to say whom he addressed — a plaster cast perhaps addressing its own inhabitant, its small Greek soul.

"I saw you coming," he said. "All the time."

He raised the fist, triumphant. Too late, they saw, shining beneath it on the counter, the glass case, still intact with its ring. He plunged the fist in through the case and down. As the glass trap darkened with his blood, he smiled.

It was Guy who broke the box apart and got it off with his own quickly bleeding hands, his shoe, and some implement Marion brought him, that dropped back into the rubble again, unidentified. By a miracle, the artery wasn't severed;

with all the glass splinters in the flesh, they couldn't have tourniqueted it in time. By some miracle so often granted to the Williams of this world, to the Sligos.

And now, Sligo's hand lay upturned in the sedated sleep that had finally overcome it, its owner, once more deserting his bystanders, stretched on the floor to which this time he had slipped so easily. It had been so lucky that the sedation was already in him; his bystanders could never have overcome him in time. By the usual luck. On the hand, the many surface cuts and slices had flooded with red on the instant, filling the box like an ewer. But the wound on the wrist, that should have been the worst, was nothing, already puckering and congealed — not a fine seam, but a seam. Beneath it, whatever directed this man still pulsed, an anatomist's secret.

And she was finished crying now, or retching — the sound, dreadful as it was, a relief to him, a sign that her life had not rendered her inhumanly able to bear anything. Still, her competence was what he had to fear. He held her, each contracted toward one another, inward and away from the blood that was sticky and dried on them both.

Finally she was able to speak. "It's the — repetition of it. The repetition. I can take each separate time. But the other finally gets to you. Like a rhythm. Like killing with drums — don't they do that somewhere?" She slid apart from him, from where they sat, on the floor too. "And now you're part of it," she said. "Of our Mondays."

He stood up at that. "Oh, no. No, Marion. *No.*"

Her eyes were the first to lower. "Of course not. How could I think — ?"

"Because it's your habit, to —" To defend, he'd been going to say, but saw that it wasn't just. "Because it's gone on so long, whatever it is. A kind of double dream." He brushed himself off, plaster dust and other crumbs, wooden splinters, and here and there, a sparkle. He bent to take her hands, and didn't take them. "He's got to go to a hospital, you must know that. Not a local one. Not for local wounds. A place where he can be — for a long time."

When she spoke, it seemed she hadn't heard this. "I lied to you," she said. "Last time. When I said 'I *used* to be fond' . . . I don't know really, what I *used* to be." She looked up. "So I don't know — what I am now."

"As it happens," he said. "As it happens, I — I know of such a place. Usually it takes longer to get in, much longer. But if I ask —" He swallowed. "I think they'll come on my say-so. I think they would come, in an hour or so. Today. Now."

Her glance wandered, vague over a shoulder. "The phone's . . . *cut*." The voice might have come over just such a line.

"That stuff you gave him," he said. "Can I leave you here with him? How long does it last?"

"For hours," she said. "You can leave him. I often do."

"I'll go in the car, then."

The scar marks under her eyes stood out sharply. The resemblance bled him, but instructed.

Finally she spoke, an inch nearer. "The public phone booth, in the games room. It's separate. I forgot that."

She got up and followed him to the door, picking her way through the breakage. "While you . . . I'll — pack a bag for him. And I'll —" She looked down at her stained hands and dress, almost thoughtfully. He nodded. Both of them cast a backward glance at the room's ruin. From hers, he couldn't tell what she thought of it.

When he had phoned and had cleaned himself up in the little washroom under the stairs, he looked in again at the main bar. The figure there lay just as they had left it. There was no one with it. No answering call came from the upstairs bedrooms. He went down to the games room, in its heavy-browed way a beautiful room when bare of people and left to its armorial shadow. He had no panic at not finding her here. She would have a place of her own, where she could hide. It was intended that he find it. Through the open door, he saw a bright sweater, down on the pier.

He walked down to the little pier, past the over-cute tables and umbrellas toying against the river, the paper scurf of tourists, the beach unused, lapped and lonely, the water healing dark through its pebbles. She was there, on a last bench. He sat down beside her.

The long evening, projected by the river, was still alight. Less than an hour had passed since he had arrived here. There was still a disc of sun, the part that always sank within minutes.

"Will they come?" she said.

"In a couple of hours."

They were well out from shore here, naked to the whole expanse, whose orange magnificence would for some time hold off the arriving blue.

"Open views make me uneasy," he said after a while. "They didn't used to. Before. Or when I was a child. But maybe that's because in those days, we didn't have a view."

"I couldn't do without this place. I grew up on the river, but it's not only that. Nobody comes here much, and it's always —" She stood up, spread her arms.

Behind him, he felt her turn to look back at the house. He didn't turn with her. In front of him, the long casement of water extended, infinitely extended, on and on. In that wide, stealing amber, the little beach in front of them lay suspended, as small in that infinity as his mother's sunset vase, with its paintscratch of beach and one palmetto.

"There's not enough ruin there!" he heard her say. "There's not enough ruin to *show*."

His lips were stiff. "There never is."

When she sat down again at her end of the bench, she was as he'd always known her, the old Marion, remote, cold with an experience whose poles he was only beginning to see. He waited. This time there was no other way to help.

She spoke, an inch nearer. "Do you — want to know about it?"

He looked back at the Canal Zone, at a house which, for all its ruin, was still standing. "The original injury?"

"In comparison with what we made of it, you mean." He felt her grimace.

"I've no such secrets to tell you," he said, turning. "Everybody already knows my —" His life was on the roster for all to see, an open book. He was used to the humility of it.

Her head was lowered. "I once heard you say — you come from Hartford."

"Yes. . . . Why?"

"I went to school in a little town not far from there."

"You did? Which one? I know all the schools up there —

and all the towns." He paused. "But you grew up here, you said. On the river."

She nodded. "Then you'll have heard of it, maybe. It had rather a — gardens. And a fence. Miss Trent's? In Netherton?"

Once more. Reality slowed the mind — a profound deduction, especially twice. Once more, out of his sphere. "Yes," he said, "I've heard of it."

"Mmm." She was facing away from him. The sun edged down — gone. The world was flowing; let humans never forget it. "Well, you know that old story, the girls who marry their riding masters? You ever wonder what happened to them?" The sunless air showed him every line of her face. "To her."

"I had a theory about you," he said. "But it went the other way round." On one of the hands in her lap there was still a faint smear of brown. He touched it. "This happened, then? Sligo."

"No!" she said, rubbing at the smear. "Not Sligo. Not yet. Ferenc Von Dombaretski, Captain. Son of Captain the same, of his something Majesty's umpteenth Hussars. Polish on the one side, Magyar on the other. Miss Brown, who was the Miss Trent of our day, told us how to pronounce it — Magyar. He rode like a prince, she said, too well for us really, but his mother wasn't noble. He had a bale of uniforms, swords, saddles, medals and brasses, that filled the chauffeur's cottage. Hereditary candlesticks — knives. And always the stories, stories about horses." She folded her hands. "And at the foot of his bed, a pair of black velveteen house slippers with silver crests on them, much worn."

He made the sound one made to children detailing their nightmare.

"Oh, yes, very long ago," she said. "I was seventeen."

"Ferenc Von Dombaretski," he said. "Sounds — he was a fake, then?"

"You know —" She was silent a space. "I don't know for sure. I've never been sure. And later on, of course . . . it didn't much matter."

On the river it was later on, too, but still tartar yellow and bronze. Even the world at times thought slowly.

"There's such a lot I don't know," she said. "You wouldn't believe how much. There's so much I missed."

"And a lot you know," he said. "A hard exchange. Never belittle it."

After a while he said, "Don't look back at the house. When they come, we'll hear them. Go on."

"On? Why, that's all there was, really. The rest, you know enough to imagine. In a straight line."

A straight line would be horses, men of that same bow-legged world. "Then, Sligo?" he said. "Then you married *him?*"

She looked at him for so long that he could see the *plage* darken behind her, at the pace of the seal-colored cloud traveling west like a barge. "The original injury. Have you forgotten it?"

"A false name!" he said, then. "It *was* Sligo, under a false name."

"Yes. Yes. There wasn't a Von Dombaretski, anymore. Oh, there had been. All his papers and medals, Miss Brown saw them — they were always very careful at Trent. And all his gear, that Sligo, traveling with him for so many years after all — had inherited." She gave a short laugh. "That's what happened to her, that girl. It was even more romantic than one had imagined. She didn't marry the riding master. She married his Irish — ostler — they once used to call it. It has its own lineage. Groom."

"I see," he said.

"Are you sure you do? Do you see that this wasn't what I minded? Do you see that after all of it, in spite of it — and in spite of the fact that I couldn't half talk to him, and he couldn't or wouldn't — what I minded was that I . . . *still?*" She sat back. "Oh, there were the social things too of course, my family cutting me, and my friends too, and no money — but I was young, resilient enough. That was only the part of the story you'd expect. But it was the other, that did us in. That he could never get used to what he'd done, or to me he'd done it to. And that I —" She choked on it. "That I — *still*—" She touched Guy's arm. "You know something? After all these years, I don't know him well enough to say whether it's that he can't talk to me, or he won't. After all these years."

He thought of the diamond, thankfully lost somewhere in the shards back there, and of all she must know about fakes that became real.

"And then —" Her voice was hard. "Then *I* began to do *him* injury. I was built for it, of course. Speech, taste, needs, a million discriminations people like me, girls like me, didn't even know we were born with. Oh I was primed for it." Again she put her hand on his arm. "Do you know?" she said, her voice so charged, so tender that he caught an unbearable glimpse. "He just couldn't think what else to do when Von Dombaretski died. Since he was fourteen, he'd spent his life with him."

"So you've never stopped pitying him," he said.

The cloud passed on, stately.

"When I said I didn't want or hope for anything —" she said. "I lied. The inn was my idea — an aunt died and left me money. We were on our uppers, we hadn't known anything else but uppers, and it looked like heaven. The years we worked on it — those weren't so . . ." She got up and strode away to the edge. Standing there she looked back, inland. "But now — how I hate it, how I hate it. I see all I don't know, here. Everything passes by here. All the possible. It's like perfume. All the possible passes by."

In his mind's eye, in his muscles, he got up from the bench, seized her by the shoulders and shook her, not for herself alone.

As she strolled back to him, he watched her absently pause to turn over a crushed paper cup with the toe of her shoe. She stooped to tear it up and bury the fragments. He saw how the beach — merely a prospect to the inn — was tended.

"So now you know. What we made of it — between us." Crouched over, not a foot from him, she prodded the sand again. This time, only a natural object was revealed, a worn stone. "What *I* made." Stone in palm, she looked up at him. "Too much."

He bent and drew a finger along each of those permanent shadows on the bone, her cheek marks, tracing what almost could be seen there beneath them. "No — you couldn't have helped it. You — were singled out."

At that moment, a gun reported, clearly — even with the ricochet of the river, not a gnat in the ear. She stood up. He stood up with her. The Canal Zone watched them grasp one another. All the possible passes by.

Color returned to her face slowly. "From the Point — West Point. A sunset gun, I guess. You can always hear it on hazy days here, when sound travels north."

Across her shoulder the night was arriving — volumes of blue through whose drift, down all the darkening inlets of the shoreline she must know so well, there were being lighted, one by one, the small, persistent fires of habitation. It was said of people native to this place that even if brought up from a cellar blindfolded, they could tell which way they were turned to the current of the river — by the play of the air on their faces, in the felt promise of the harbor.

"Can you see my place from here?" he said.

She took his hand and guided it. "There. Between there and there. That's your place. Between the dark stretch, and that one high light that's just gone on. There you are — in that great fan of trees, some of the biggest on the river. They hide the barn though, even when the leaves are off, in winter."

He thought of her standing here in the ice-gray winter days of people who live in inns, looking past his trees and forward, watched by whom? It was always the other people who had the view.

"I suppose . . . they'll send an ambulance?"

He nodded. Arms still around her, he understood the strain words must put upon those blind who remember or dream of another communication. The inn watched them, as if only it had sufficient history not to judge.

"Do I go along in it? With him?" She bowed her head. "I suppose."

In each window of the Canal Zone, a chandelier stood out strong against the night, beside each, its double. They had conquered the day.

He seized her by the shoulders and shook her. "Pity *yourself*. For God's sake. So you can leave here." He dropped his hands, in tribute to the brute lack of honor in the processes of life. "So we can go."

He couldn't imagine her answer. When it came, it did so on her own terms. Brutal too, she touched his cheek. "He saw you coming," she said.

Lights of cars trickled through the hedge that bordered the highway. The Canal Zone's powerful guide light, not visible from here, was there to welcome the one car that would be for them. Walking back, they had time for the swift catechism that comes when absolution is near.

"Singled out?" she said.

"It happens."

"And no one — is to blame?"

"Not — forever."

"And the ones who are left?" Even in the dark he could see her movement toward the figure lying somewhere inside there. Asleep or dead, the ones with whom one could no longer mesh nerves or spirit, were the same.

"We're the ones who've been left," he said.

"He was romantic to me once. Maybe he still is. It wasn't all bad."

"There's no need to — throw that away. One's history."

Car lights passed, not for them.

"Yours," she said. "I think Sligo knew it."

"Mine? Everyone does."

They reached the dark-browned eaves of the games room. "But he never said. He didn't talk."

And Sligo would have been her only gossip. He recalled now how her glance had followed the women going back into the world from the world of the bar, a glance too proud to take confidences from them, across that bar.

"I thought you must have a special one, from all those Mondays — the quiet ones." She gave him the thoughtful smile of the isolated. "I thought you must have been married once, that always shows. I couldn't tell about children; unless people talk about them you can't tell how they feel about them, in a place like this. But it seemed to me — somehow . . . that you were dead to . . . family."

It moved him beyond reason, that she should have been creeping painfully, a slow but conscientious student, toward this knowledge of him that was so brashly open to the rest of the world.

"That's why I —" She flung back her head. "— ought to tell you. Children. We never tried not to. There was nothing separately wrong with either of us. I think we must have been like two acids, that could only corrode." Again her head reared. "But the things I don't know, I don't belittle them. And I'm only thirty-four."

"Mine are dead." A pale light filtered on her cheeks, those starved flanks. He traced them again, moved toward what he had thought himself never again to be moved. "But I — I can see how you would look in your prime."

"Ah, you don't know me," she said in her tough, blunt way.

It seemed to him that all the brief, successive pictures he

had of her were being filled in with a tough central dark criss-crossed with broad black strokes of knowledge that might shift but never fade. "Hard to know. *We'll* be." He peered into the games room, in which a floating will-o'-the-wisp of light fancied a surface now and there to stencils of darkness, circles of knives. He turned back to her. "We'll be strange enough for each other. We're the extreme." From which the single-legged, each to each, may still take heart.

"I thought —" She put out a hand. "The quick way you got on to the hospital. You — have friends there, perhaps?"

"Yes, I have friends there," he said. "Many friends."

She took his hand at once. Standing backed against the old house, they stared into the blind current of the river, and beyond it, into a current wider than it or any harbor, into that vast multiplicity where there might be no sure order of good or evil, but surely a movement, too wide even for unease, too irrational, of which both of them knew. He knew it was there, this force that had flung him out, and drawn or flung him in again, this movement which, like some god of unbelievers, which did not bear thinking of or speaking to, both took away, took away — and gave. This was nothing to make either a religion or an unfaith of; it was merely the doctrine, not to be palmed onward, which lived somewhere in the tough, central dark of those to whom it had happened. For extreme cases there was some-times — an extreme magic. It could be merely a falter, a pause in that vast territory which humans could never persuade themselves was not human, one of those illumi-nated moments when unseen kinships brushed one like lepidoptera passing, when birds flew south from a north they did not see as misery, and in a clearing, his own clearing, a man came upon rabbits, paws lifted to the quiet of evening, staring at Mecca.

"So we can go," she said. "Where?"

He pointed, to that spot on the dark where a barn which was not to be seen behind its fan of trees, not even when the leaves were down in winter, now lighted up the dark for him like the bush in the Bible. In the conflagration he'd never dared hope for, his house was burning, though no one else could see it, and because he'd got here on time, it was not consumed.

When the long car that was for them turned in and bore down upon them, it came down the lane with normal slowness, not nemesis, nor yet a miracle. Its revolving dome-light bypassed the night skies, stood the trees at stage-green attention, swept white the gravel and swiveled to rest on the Canal Zone. The old inn returned the light like a stockade from another century, indifferent to either. Pointed at it, the long hood of the car seemed to him a hold in which he could see the stored lives of all those in hospitals, each life regularized round its one small hole of the possible, like those prints in which if one looked hard enough one could always see somewhere the upside down V of Fujiyama. It even crossed his mind to wonder where they might be sending Sligo, into or out of what sphere.

They walked straight into that treacherous glare.

There came back to him again how it felt to be only half-alone — in all its separate lights and darks. Once inside the double dream, one no longer tallied these, or no longer dared.

"But I don't know you," she said. "You don't need me."

"No," he said. "You don't know me."

"You're sure? You're not — you're not just —"

"No," he said. "I'm not just saying it."